I0537161

# SEA FOG

# SEA FOG

## J. S. FLETCHER

BROWNSTONE BOOKS

Copyright © 1926 by J.S. Fletcher.

# INTRODUCTION

Joseph Smith Fletcher (1863–1935) was an English journalist and author. He wrote more than 230 books on a wide variety of subjects, both fiction and non-fiction, and was one of the most prolific English writers of detective fiction—the work for which he is chiefly remembered today.

Fletcher was born in Halifax, West Yorkshire, the son of a clergyman. His father died when he was eight months old, and his grandmother took him in and raised him on a farm in Darrington, near Pontefract, in Yorkshire. He was educated at Silcoates School in Wakefield, and after some study of law, became a journalist at age 20.

He started work as a sub-editor in London, but soon returned to Yorkshire, where he worked first on the Leeds *Mercury* using the pseudonym "A Son of the Soil," and then as a special correspondent for the *Yorkshire Post*. Among other things, he covered Edward VII's coronation in 1902.

Fletcher's first books published were poetry. He then wrote numerous, and now largely forgotten, works of historical fiction and history, many dealing with Yorkshire. His regional work led to his selection as a fellow of the Royal Historical Society.

Michael Sadleir stated that Fletcher's historical novel, *When Charles I Was King* (1892), was his best work. Fletcher wrote several novels of rural life in imitation of Richard Jefferies, beginning with *The Wonderful Wapentake* (1894), but it wasn't until 1914, when Fletcher wrote his first detective novel, that he truly found his calling.

Over the last two decates of his life, he went on to write over a hundred more mysteries, many featuring the private investigator Ronald Camberwell.

Fletcher is sometimes incorrectly described as a "Golden Age of Detective Fiction" author, but he is in fact an almost exact contemporary of Arthur Conan Doyle, the creator of Sherlock Holmes. The bulk of his detective fiction works considerably pre-date the period considered the Golden Age, and even those few published within it do not conform to the closed form and strict rules professed, if not unfailingly observed, by Golden Age writers.

His work is still enjoyable today. Although some volumes have mildly racist elements, as were common in fiction of the era, the modern reader should keep in mind the period in which they were originally published.

—Karl Wurf
Rockville, Maryland

# CHAPTER ONE

## THE MAN WHO ASKED HIS WAY

I'll say at once that Mr. Andrew Macpherson, the Scotch grocer of Horsham, from whose shop I walked out to a glorious and unexpected wildness of liberty and adventure the morning on which this story properly begins, was a man in a thousand, for it was he who, at his own suggestion, threw wide the door of what I had come to consider a prison-house, and cheered me on my way with a word and a smile, instead of helping me across its threshold with a hearty kick.

Most other men would have considered me deserving of that kick; five out of six might have given it. For Mr. Macpherson had been a fine friend to me; he took me to his hearth when I was left a defenceless orphan lad of ten years old; he gave me a good schooling; he tried to teach me his own business. I picked up the schooling readily enough, but not the grocery trade; the buying and selling of that stuff made no appeal to my nature. And on the particular morning I speak of, Mr. Macpherson himself reluctantly arrived at the same conclusion. I forget what I had been doing; maybe I had mixed green with black in undue proportions, or sent the parcels to the wrong places; but anyway, the good man looked at me with a sorrowful shake of his head, and let out a heavy sigh.

"Man Tom," said he, "I'm thinking ye'll never do any good at the grocery! It's a peety, but ye've no intellectual inclination to it!"

"I've been thinking that a long time myself, Mr. Macpherson," I answered him. "It's not my line; I don't like it. And I'd have said so before, but for the fear of hurting your feelings."

"Aweel!" he said, with another sigh. "Ye're eighteen years of age, my lad, and I'm not the sort to stand in any young fellow's way. What is it ye want to do, Tom?"

"Mr. Macpherson," said I boldly, "I don't want to be fastened up in a shop! There's times when I can't breathe! I want space!"

"Ye'll be for going out and seeing the world?" he suggested. "Aye!— it's in yer blood, my man! And where would you be for setting your face, now?"

"Anywhere there's ships and sailors, and the sight and smell of the sea, Mr. Macpherson," I told him. "Portsmouth—Southampton—Plymouth—any place the like of them! I want adventure!"

There was more said between us, much more; all kindly and sympathetic on his part. And the end of it was that within an hour I was in my best clothes, a bag in my hand, and ten pounds in my pockets, standing in the street—free! There was Macpherson's blessing in my ear, and the grip of his big hand was warm on mine, but I never as much as looked back at the shop. That life was over.

It was a beautiful May morning. There was the sharp zest of the new springtide in the air and the smell of flowers in the streets; above the old roofs and chimneys there was a wondrous blue sky, and for one who had just emerged from the gloom of an ill-lighted shop the blaze of the sun was like an illumination from heaven. It was the sunlight more than anything that made me suddenly change my direction. I had taken my first steps of liberty towards the railway, intending to travel in that fashion to Portsmouth. But the sun, and the spring air, and the smell of growing things, reminded me that I owned an unusually strong pair of legs—why ride in a stinking railway carriage when I could foot it, at my own pace, across the hills and downs of Sussex?

I turned sharp in Carfax, and instead of going north, went away across the stream by the old church, and, choosing footpaths rather than highways, made boldly for the open country to the south.

Already I had a very definite notion of what I was going to do. I would strike for Portsmouth, by way of the South Downs, taking my time and looking about me. If I found nothing that appealed to me at Portsmouth, I would go on to Southampton by way of the coast. I was well prepared for a journey of that sort. Eight of the sovereigns with which Mr. Macpherson had presented me (for this was in the days when we were as familiar with gold as we now are with paper) were safely stowed away in a leather belt worn under my shirt; another was hidden in a waistcoat pocket; the tenth, changed into silver in the shop as I left it, lay in my trousers. And I had not lived with and been brought up by Mr. Andrew Macpherson all these years for nothing!—it was my intention to look well at and think long over every sixpence of my silver before parting with it. I had no fear of travelling expenses; Macpherson himself had shoved into my bag enough eatables to last me all that day and most of the next, and I was one of those lads who have no taste for cheap cigarettes or for drink. I reckoned as I walked along that I should have made small inroad on my silver by the time I reached Portsmouth; as for breaking into the gold in my belt, I took that to be a necessity which I meant never to acknowledge. It was my ambition, or, rather, my firm resolve, to present myself in a year or two to Mr. Macpherson once more, in the proud position of being able to show him that his one-time mouse had been metamorphosed into a man.

I went along all that day, my bag slung over my shoulders, through the Sussex villages, taking my time, rejoicing in my liberty, breathing the good air that increased in savour and quality the nearer I drew to the downs and to what I knew lay beyond their swelling outlines—the bright waters of the English Channel. But I was not to see those waters that day. By the end of the afternoon I had come to Petworth, at a distance of fifteen miles from Horsham, and, stout as my legs were, I was beginning, as they say, to know that I had feet at the end of them. That place, Petworth, had its charm, and, chancing on a little shop kept by a widow-woman whereat you could get a cup of tea, I turned in, and, finding the owner a motherly and come-at-able person, bargained with her for my supper and my bed and my breakfast next morning, all for two shillings.

It was still but the middle of the evening when I had eaten my supper, and the light being good, I went out to see the place, and it was while I hung around the old church, wondering at its queerness, and, as I thought, its ugliness, all the stranger because of the picturesqueness and charm of its surroundings, that a man came up and asked me, without preface, if I was well acquainted with that quarter of the country.

Having acquired a good deal of caution during my tutelage under Andrew Macpherson, I took a precise observation of this man before replying to him. He was a middle-aged man by appearance; a good fifty, no doubt, and already grizzled in hair and beard; a man, I fancied, who had lived much under strong winds and fierce suns. What with his brown skin and his blue cloth, and a rolling gait that he showed as he made up to me, I set him down as a seafarer. That inclined me to him, and I spoke, though, to be sure, it was but one word.

"No!"

"Stranger, then—like me?" he asked.

I nodded. Mr. Macpherson had taught me never to waste tongue-power when a gesture would serve the purpose. But the man persisted.

"Just so!" said he. "And which way are you from, now—did you come in here from north or south or east or west, young fellow?" Then, seeing my distaste, he went on hurriedly: "No offence, my lad, and no foolish curiosity!—I've a reason for asking. The fact is, I'm searching for something, and, d'ye see, you may ha' seen it, in which case——"

"What are you looking for?" I asked abruptly.

Before answering, he drew out a brass tobacco-box, on the lid of which I noticed a curious design, and, taking a plug of tobacco from it, cut himself a quid with a clasp-knife, and stowed it away in his left cheek. It was not until he had put box and knife away again that he answered my question.

"To be sure!" said he. "That's nat'ral! You couldn't tell me anything if I didn't tell you something. Very well!"—here he paused and looked about him, suspiciously, as if there might be listeners amongst the old tombs and yew-trees around us—"very well, I'll tell you! A mill!"

I dare say I looked at him as if I suspected his sanity, for he shook his head.

"Queer, no doubt, young fellow," he said hastily. "Queer you think it, and maybe queer it is! But—a mill! Not one of these here new-fangled mills, all steam and machinery; nor yet a water-mill. A windmill, d'ye see?—that's my object!"

"There are a good many windmills in Sussex," I remarked. "I've seen a fair lot myself, here and there."

"That's the devil of it!" said he eagerly. "It's which of 'em is which! However, this here is like that game the children play, when one hides some little thing, a thimble or what not, and t'others seek for it, and him what's hid it tells 'em if they're hot or cold, according as they get nearer or farther. I reckon I'm getting hotter, for you say you've seen many mills hereabouts—windmills! Now, have you ever seen, do you know of, a windmill, very old, unused, what stands, all by itself, on top of a lonely down?"

"No!" said I.

He let out a heavy sigh, as if very seriously disappointed; but in the next moment his face became brighter again, and the old, eager look came back.

"Just so—exactly—you haven't!" he said. "But, to be sure, you admit you're a stranger, and what you mean is that you know such mills in your parts, and there ain't such a mill as that I'm a-describing of. Now, without offence, what might your part be?"

"Horsham!" I answered.

He shook his head with a gesture of satisfaction.

"Ah!" he remarked. "Horsham? That's all right!—wherever else it was, it wasn't Horsham! Horsham isn't in the down country—no! I'm thankful, truly, to hear you say you come from Horsham. I was afraid you was from the southward."

"What do you want to find this mill for?" I made bold to ask.

He had very small eyes, this man, and they seemed to grow smaller when I asked him this question. Once more he shook his head, but this time in different fashion.

"Ah!" he replied. "And you may ask! But for a good reason, young fellow. 'Tis a sort o' landmark, d'ye see? A—well, a thing to steer by!" He took off his cap and scratched the top of his head with his stubbly fingers. "Ah!" he went on, "I ha' used the sea a deal in my time, and I ha' known hours when I'd ha' given much to see a sail, or a light, or a star in the night-sky; but I'd give as much now to see that there mill as we've talked about, and I'm getting uncertain as to where it lies, for blame me if I can hear tell of it!"

"Are you sure it's in Sussex?" I asked.

But even as I spoke the man was off, and, whether he heard me or not, he never looked round. I watched him curiously as he made his way out of the churchyard, and I fancied that he talked to himself. At that I came to the conclusion that he was probably a little mad, and had got his deserted windmill on the brain, and the affair being none of my business, I put it out of mind and attended to my own, which was to go back to the little shop and to bed, where I slept so soundly that it was nearly eight o'clock next morning before I woke, and by that time I had forgotten windmill and man.

But I had the man brought up again before noon; to be exact, I saw him again. By noon, wandering across-country in the same fashion as before, but, the day being very hot, not making such progress as at first, I had come to the very foot of the downs, which now rose up in front like a great green rampart. My precise location at this hour was the village called Graffham, right beneath the vast woods that stretch from Heyshott to Lavington. There I sat down on the roadside in the middle of the village, under the shade of a tree, to eat my lunch of bread-and-cheese, and while I was eating I saw, coming along the road which I had already traversed, the man of Petworth churchyard. He had his hands in his pockets and his head down, and once more he was talking to himself.

There was an inn nearly opposite to where I sat; the man caught sight of it, and straight-way turned into its open door. He was in there half an hour; when he came out again, a couple of rustics came with him, evidently to direct him. They pointed him to the south-west, and when he left them he went in that direction, taking a narrow lane, and presently I saw him no more. I had no doubt that he had now heard of his windmill, or of a wind-mill, and was making for it. He passed within twenty yards of me as he left the village, but he never saw me, and I had no mind to hail him, and when he turned his corner the only thought I had of him, if I had one at all, was that he and I had now definitely parted. For while he was making for the south-west, and so keeping to the land, I was intent on a due south course, that being a straight one for the sea.

I made up through the overhanging woods after my rest, and over the crest of Graffham Down, and again into the woods on the other side of the tableland. These woods were thick, deep, far-stretching. I got lost in them, and I spent most of the afternoon in endeavouring to right myself. When at last I got out of them, it was only to entangle myself in others still farther ahead. Evening had come on, and twilight was gathering, when, after much casting about (for I had somehow lost any real path), I emerged on an open space of moorland. And the first thing I then saw was the open sea, shining faintly far ahead of me, miles away, but clearly discernible in the glimmering light. The second, outlined against the shimmer of sea and sky, was a black, gaunt shape, suggestive of vague mystery, perched in strange isolation on the bowlike surface of an arching down.

This, whatever it was, was still a long way from where I stood. But as it was in my direct line to the sea, I made for it. I dipped down into a valley and lost sight of it. I climbed the other side of the valley and saw it again. But then came more deep woodland, and by the time I had traversed that the twilight was rapidly merging into darkness. I got out of the wood at last; there was the thing right above me, clearly outlined against the sky. I thought as I climbed the hill-side towards it that it was a tower, but as I drew nearer and nearer I knew it for what it was—an ancient windmill. And I knew, too, that I had found what the stranger-man was looking for; this was his mill, the thing he wanted. But he wasn't there; nobody was there. It seemed to me just then that beyond the mill and myself there was nothing in the world.

# CHAPTER TWO

## THE SECOND MAN

It would have been strange if this impression of utter solitude had not forced itself upon me, for—at that time of advanced evening and under those circumstances—my situation was one of entire loneliness. There were the deep and silent woods through which I had passed; here was the bleak plateau on which I stood. At first I saw nothing near by, nor in the distance, to indicate life, and the silence was profound. But as I gazed about me this way and that I became aware of two or three twinkling lights at perhaps a mile's distance, deep down in the low country which lay between me and the coast; they, of course, suggested the presence of some village or solitary farmstead. And after a while, as I stood looking seaward, I saw a trail of flame coming along rapidly from west to east, not far away from where I judged the coast to be; that I knew for a railway train, speeding along the line that ran parallel with the coast itself. So there was life near at hand. Yet, none there; that place was the loneliest, and most curiously suggestive of loneliness, that I had ever been in. But even then, as I realised this, there came companionship; a nightjar went by, uttering its strange note, and as that died away amongst the neighbouring woods a nightingale suddenly burst into song in some coppice down the hill-side.

While I had stood near the mill, staring about me, a full moon had been steadily rising, and had now got to a fair height in the south-east sky. I went closer and looked at the mill. It was a great, massive structure, and so high that I saw at once that it must form a landmark for miles around, and probably far out to sea; I saw, too, that it had evidently not been in use for many a long year. There were gaps in its masonry, the doorway gaped wider than it should have done; the remnants of the long, raking sails hung desolate. A shaft of moonlight lay within the wide gap of the door, and I went inside and looked about me in the gloom, and saw then that the interior was still pretty much as it had been in working days; there was machinery there, rusty and useless, no doubt, but still in place, and there was a wooden stairway that led to upper regions. I saw, too, that somebody had turned the place to account as a shelter; there was a quantity of dried bracken stored on the ground floor, together with other things which I knew to be used by shepherds in charge of flocks. Here, perhaps, the shepherds kept house while their charges browsed the hill-sides; it was a convenient place for that. And it suddenly struck me that it would make quite a good lodging for me for that night, and save me the necessity of exploring the village or hamlet in which I had seen the lights. I might not find anything there, and the next likely place might be a long way off. Here, at any rate, I was certain of shelter, and I had still enough food in my bag to serve for supper.

It was just as I had made up my mind to stay where I was that I heard footsteps. They were still some little distance away—perhaps fifty yards— but the turf was hard and dry and crisp on the top of that hill, and I heard their slow, regular fall quite plainly, and I sprang to the door and cautiously looked out. There, plainly seen in the moonlight, was the figure of a man coming towards the mill. He came from something of the direction in which I myself had come, but rather more, a point or two, from the north-west, and that fact immediately suggested to me that this was the stranger-man of Petworth churchyard, who, after I had seen him at Graffham, had wandered round until he hit on what he was seeking. Certainly the figure resembled his. . . .

I had to think with uncommon rapidity during the next few seconds. Did I want to meet this man again, and especially in that old mill? I knew nothing of him; I was not sure that I liked what I had seen of him. He had said that he would give much to find that mill; perhaps he would resent finding me in occupancy of it. Again, I had formed the idea that he was, or might be, somewhat cracked; if so, and he happened to carry a revolver or pistol on him, which was quite likely, he might take it into his head to rid me of his presence in unpleasant fashion.

The end of that brief spell of thinking was that while the man was still twenty or thirty yards away from the door, I sped up the stair, as noiselessly as possible. There was an open trap-door at the top; I passed through it into a wooden-floored chamber the interior of which I could make out quite well, there being a great gap in the outer wall there on the side from which the moon shone. And, standing well back in the shadow, I kept as quiet as a mouse and looked down through the trap, watching for the man to enter. There was some delay in that; evidently, having reached the place he wanted, he paused a few minutes to take a look at it and its surroundings; indeed, I heard him pacing about outside for awhile. But at last he came in through the ruinous doorway, and the moonlight falling full on his face, I saw at once that he was not the man with whom I had exchanged talk at Petworth.

Within another minute, whatever ground I might have had for uncertainty on this point was swept clean away. The man had no sooner entered the ground floor of the mill than he lighted a small but powerful lantern, and in turning it about here and there as if to examine his surroundings, he twice gave me a full view of his face; his figure I could see well enough in the moonlight. That was somewhat similar to the figure of the first man; both were solid, thick-set, shortish of height. But while the man of Petworth churchyard was bearded, the man of the mill was clean-shaven, save for a goatee beard which I took to be violently red in colour. He had the face of a rat, or a weasel, or a fox, or perhaps a mixture of all three; anyhow, he was an evil-looking customer, and I wished myself anywhere else than where I was, and cursed my own stupid foolishness for running up that stair.

Another moment and I cursed myself more than ever. For it became, nay, at once was evident that, like me, the man had made up his mind to make the old mill his quarters for the night. He set down his lantern on a ledge of the machinery that stood in the centre of the floor, and, unstringing a sort of knapsack from his shoulders, produced from it a parcel of food and a big bottle filled to the neck with some colourless liquid which looked like water, and was, of course, gin, with perhaps an admixture of water. Very fortunately for me, who stood in a somewhat cramped position at the trap-door, some idea occurred to him before he began his supper, and he hurried outside—I suppose to assure himself that there was nobody about. The instant he had vanished I sprang to some sacking, a pile of which I had noticed on coming into the loft, and hastily made a couch for myself, close to an opening in the floor through which a couple of great chains passed from above to below; thenceforward I was able to look down on my undesirable fellow-tenant from immediately above his head. And at the same time I made up my mind that if he put his head through the trap-door I would give it a crack with my oak staff—a present from Andrew Macpherson—which would make him see even more stars than the thousands which were already challenging the moonlight.

He came back after prowling around outside for awhile, and, settling himself comfortably on the piled-up bracken, he proceeded to eat and drink. He had cold meat and buttered bread, in generous slices, in his parcel, and he made great play with both by means of as ugly a knife as ever I saw, and one which he used with great dexterity. Also, he every now and then took a generous draught from his innocent-looking bottle; altogether, he struck me as being a man of good appetite. Not a wolfing man, though; he ate and drank leisurely enough, and left meat and bread in his parcel, carefully wrapping it up again and restoring it to his knapsack. Then followed exactly what I expected to see: he produced pipe, tobacco, and matches, and proceeded to smoke. I gathered from this that he anticipated complete freedom from any interruption of his tenancy, and that he considered himself as much alone as Robinson Crusoe on his island before he chanced on the footsteps.

I was by that time anxious about two things, and two things only—the first, that this goatee-bearded fellow wouldn't take it into his ugly head to climb the stair with his lantern; the second, that he would finish his pipe and bottle and go to sleep, so that I also might. But he showed no sign of falling in with my wishes. For awhile he sat with folded arms, smoking, and— I presumed—thinking. Now that he had eaten his fill, the bottle did not seem to have any great attraction for him. But after some time, his roving eye chancing to fall on it, he drew it to him, took out the cork, and treated himself to a hearty swig, afterwards measuring the remaining quantity with an appraising glance, as if he were either reflecting on the amount he had drunk, or were thinking that it would be well to leave the rest for his next morning's refreshment. I hoped he would knock the ashes out of his pipe then, and compose himself to sleep; instead, after putting the bottle away from him, he turned his lantern so that its full flare fell on the level surface of the machinery which he had used as a table, and, putting his hand into some inner pocket of his clothes, drew out a square packet of whity-brown paper.

I had been inquisitive about this man from the first moment of his appearance, but the sight of that packet roused feelings of curiosity to which my first speculations became as nothing. There was mystery in that, and I watched for all I was worth while its owner proceeded to unwrap it. There were many wrappings: first, the whity-brown paper aforesaid, with the appearance of which I was familiar enough, having wrapped up some thousands of small parcels in its like; then, a sheet of a better sort of paper; then, a piece of what undoubtedly was canvas; finally, a square of oiled silk. Out of the oiled silk he carefully took a folded paper, and, spreading it out very gingerly, laid it on the flat surface at his side, immediately in the glare of his lantern. I saw then that what he had before him was undoubtedly a map.

But it was not a map of the sort with which I had been familiar at school—an affair of careful engraving and colouring. It was what I then called a map; what it really was, I suppose, was a rough plan, or chart. From my overhead perch, I could not, of course, make it out; all I could see was a certain very conspicuous black dot in the very middle of the paper (which was about eight or nine inches square), some lines and marks, and, in one place, a cross, as conspicuous as the dot. These I saw, but there was more that I could not see, or, rather, could not make out—lettering, I felt certain.

The man remained poring over this chart for some little time; eventually he restored it to its wrappings as carefully as he had taken it from them, and put the packet back in its secret receptacle, which, I think, was in the lining of his waistcoat. That done, he knocked out the ashes of his tobacco, taking heed to see that no spark remained alive on the floor of the mill, and, having taken another pull at his bottle, he extinguished his light and curled himself up in the dry bracken. I could see him in the moonlight, all bundled together, his head on his arm, and before five minutes had gone I heard him snoring contentedly.

I did not go to sleep just then, but I went to sleep after a time. Until I dropped off, my brain was actively busy in wondering about what I had just seen, and in speculating on various matters connected with the man of Petworth churchyard and the man who now slept in the basement of the mill. Was there any connection between the two? What did the man of Petworth churchyard want with the mill? Why had this goatee-bearded, hatchet-faced chap come there? What was his much-treasured map about? What would he do if he found me there? Should I wake him if I stole down the stair and fled? I thought of fleeing for a time, but I was curious, and more than curious—I wanted to know what it was all about. The morning would bring light in more ways than one; I would wait till morning. And I went to sleep on my sacks and slept like a top—until I sprang into instant, keen-witted wakefulness at the sound of a scream.

\* \* \* \*

I think my first notion was that this was the cry of some animal, trapped close by, or seized by another. But on the instant it came again, and I knew it then for the cry, desperate, terrorised, of a man in deadly fear and peril. I had sprung to my elbow at the first sound: at the second I looked sharply through the opening of the chains into the ground floor beneath me. The man of the map had gone; there, plainly outlined in the bracken, was the place where he had slept, but he and his bottle and his knapsack had vanished. And at that I jumped for the gap in the outer wall and looked out on a morning thick with milk-white mist. A great sea fog had rolled up from the coast and enveloped the plain and the hills, and from where I stood all the land was wrapped in its curling vapours. At first I saw nothing; then, a stifled cry coming again, I looked to my right, and there, some twenty yards away on the plateau, their figures strangely magnified and distorted in the mist, I saw two men struggling.

Two men!—but it was impossible for me to tell which of the two was my man, though I knew he was there. It seemed to me that one of the two had the other by the throat, and was endeavouring to force him to the ground. I could hear their pantings and groanings as they swayed this way and that. They were like two wrestlers, straining every muscle and sinew to throw each other, and for a time neither seemed to gain any advantage. They drew farther and farther away from me in their struggles; sometimes a curling of the mist wrapped them altogether; sometimes, as a strong shaft of sunlight hit their bending and twisting bodies, I saw them more plainly. It was in one of these sharp gleams of the sun that one suddenly mastered the other and forced him groaning to the ground, and in the same gleam that I saw the flash of something that shone and brightened as it caught the sun. There was a deep, horrible sound after that, and the next instant the man who had fallen was lying still, and the other was vanishing in the morning mist.

I suppose I stood there at the gap in the wall for several minutes, staring—just staring. But my brain was busy. Who was the second man? Was he the man whom I had seen at Petworth and again at Graffham? Had he come to the mill in the night, or in the early morning, found the other man there, and quarrelled with or attacked him? And which of the two men was it that was lying there, so awfully motionless? And would the man who had run away come back? Was he, perhaps, only a few yards away, hidden in the sea fog?

I waited awhile in the profound silence—then, unable to bear it any longer, and grasping my oak staff firmly in my right hand, I crept down the stair and out of the mill, and across the dew-besprinkled turf to the fallen man. It was he of the goatee beard, and he lay there with his arms thrown wide and his eyes glazed, and red blood was still running from the gash in his throat.

# CHAPTER 3

## THE CAPTAIN AND THE SERGEANT

I took to my heels on making this discovery, running down the hill-side, through the mist, in the direction of where, from my remembrance of the lights of the previous evening, I supposed the village, hamlet, or farmstead to lie. I don't think I stayed a second by the dead man; certainly—a matter that became of serious moment to me before long—I never made any examination of him or his clothing. He was dead!—dead as man can be—and my instinct was to run, possibly to get away from the sight of him, a truly horrible object, possibly to find somebody to whom I could tell what I had seen. The thing is that I ran harder than I had ever run before in my life. And as I ran, going in great bounds down the slopes, I heard, not very far below me, a clock strike six.

I ran, suddenly, out of the mist, upon level ground to find, in front of me, the house and outbuildings of an old farmstead, ringed about with tall trees. It was a fine old place, and at any other moment I should have paused to admire its quaint architecture, and the effect of the morning sun, now dispersing the sea fog, on its red-brick walls mellowed in tint by age, and here and there half covered by a wealth of ivy. But I was looking for human life—and in another moment, rounding a corner of the outbuildings, I saw it. There was an orchard there, at the foot of an old-world garden, and over its low wall a man and woman were talking; she on one side, he on the other. I took a hurried glance at both as I made for them. They were not young people. She, who had a basket balanced on top of the wall, from which she was throwing corn to the fowls on the stretch of grass beneath, was a tall, buxom, handsome woman of something near forty; the man, a big, loose-limbed, athletic-looking fellow, with the unmistakable air and bearing of the soldier about his bronzed face, keen eyes, and grizzled moustache, was still older. But even if these two were of middle age, or approaching it, I remember that I saw, in that quick inspection of them, that they were lovers.

The man was on my side of the orchard wall, and I hurried straight to him, and he heard me coming, and turned sharply, and I saw his eyes widen at the sight of me.

"Hullo!" he exclaimed. "What's this? What's the matter, my lad?——"

I realised then that my breath was spent by that headlong rush down the hill. But I managed to choke out a few words.

"There's a man been murdered!" I gasped. "Up there—the hill-top. Knifed! I saw it! The—the other man's run away."

The woman made an inarticulate sound of surprise and horror; the man gave me a good searching look.

"When was this, my lad?" he asked. "How did you come to see it?"

I told them as briefly as I could; they listened intently, staring at me. The man turned to the woman.

"Send one of your men down to the Sergeant," he said. "Tell him to come up to the old mill at once and bring help with him." He turned to me as she hurried away towards the house. "I'll go back there with you," he went on. "What's your name, my lad, and how did you come to be on the hill-top?"

"My name's Crowe," said I. "Tom Crowe. I've been in the employ of Mr. Andrew Macpherson, grocer, of Horsham——"

"Aye!" he interrupted. "I know Andrew Macpherson—I've served on a jury with him once or twice at Quarter Sessions. Well?"

"The grocery trade didn't suit me," I continued. "Mr. Macpherson and I agreed it would be more in my line to try a sea-life. So I set off for Portsmouth or Southampton, day before yesterday. The first night I lodged at Petworth; last night I came to this old mill, above here, at dusk, and I decided to sleep in it. Then this man came. I've told you the rest."

"You didn't hear the second man come?" he enquired.

"I heard nothing after I went to sleep until I heard the scream," said I. "When I looked out, they were fighting—struggling together."

"And you didn't get any clear view of the second man?" he asked.

"I didn't—the mist was too thick," I replied. "And he was off, clean lost in it, as soon as he'd struck the other man down. He seemed to be a man of about the same size; a thick-set man."

He made no further remark just then, and we went steadily up the hillside until we came to where the dead man lay. The fog had cleared a great deal by that time; the plateau around the old mill was quite free of it, though it still lingered amongst the fringes of the woods on the northern side. And beyond the dead man there was nothing to be seen; he lay still enough, and, as far as I could see, just as I had left him. The man I had fetched stood gazing thoughtfully at him for awhile, but he made no offer to lay hands on the body.

"A seafaring man, this, by the looks of him," he said at last. "And in a new rig-out, eh? New clothes, new boots, fresh linen—I suppose there'll be some clue on him, but we'll wait till the policeman comes up. Show me where you saw him sleeping."

I took him inside the mill, and pointed out everything relative to the doings of last night. He looked curiously at the place where the man had slept in the bracken, and presently picked up a crumpled newspaper which lay near, whereon there were grease-marks. I remembered then that this had been thrown away by the dead man when he unpacked the meat and bread from his knapsack.

"*Evening News* of last night," said my companion, pointing to the date. "That looks as if he'd come to these parts by train. Some strange mystery in it, my lad——"

Just then we heard voices, and, hurrying out of the mill, saw men coming up the hill-side. Two, obviously, were farm-labourers, agog with excitement; the third was a burly, round-faced man, half dressed, but with the unmistakable cut of the drilled and trained policeman about him. He was already stooping over the body when we joined him and his wondering companions.

"Strange affair this, Captain!" he remarked, with a salute to the man who had come up with me. "Pretty savage thrust that's been!" Then he turned and gave me a look that seemed to take me all in. "This the lad who gave the information? Just so!—Um!" He bent down again to the body and began examining the clothing. His fingers, deft enough, went from pocket to pocket. "There's nothing on him!" he announced, glancing up at us. "That is—this is all!"

He threw out on the turf a handful of loose silver and copper, a handkerchief, and the knife with which I had seen the dead man cut up his bread and meat. And at that I let out a sharp exclamation.

"Then he's been robbed!" I said. "He'd more than that! He'd a packet, inside that waistcoat—an inner pocket. Look!"

He unbuttoned the waistcoat still more; he had already had his fingers inside it at his first examination, and he found the pocket I spoke of, but there was nothing in it. Gingerly, he drew off the man's knapsack, which lay crushed half under his shoulders and side; there was nothing in it but some remaining bread and meat and the bottle, of which one-third the contents still remained. And at that the sergeant got up, brushed his knees, and gave me another searching look.

"A packet, eh, young fellow?" he said. "And how do you know that?"

"Because I saw it, last night," said I. "He took a map out of it!"

"A map, eh? And of what?" he asked. "This part?"

I had realised for some minutes that my best plan was to tell this representative of the law the whole story of my adventures since my walking out of Andrew Macpherson's doorway. For I saw that he was regarding me with a sort of suspicion, and being conscious of my own innocence, and of the fact that I had ten pounds on my person, I resented it. "I'd better tell you everything that I know," said I. "I've already told this gentleman a good deal, and he knows a man who'll answer for me—I'm no tramp, if that's what you're thinking, and I could have afforded to stay at the best hotel in Portsmouth last night if I'd liked!—I only slept in that mill because——"

"It's just because you did sleep there that you're a valuable witness!" interrupted the sergeant, with a smile at my companion. "And you'll have to tell what you know at the inquest, my lad! If you like to tell us now, by way of rehearsal——"

"I'll tell you everything from the start," I broke in. "And gladly, for it's my belief I know the man who did this! If you'll follow me——"

I begun at the beginning—not omitting to mention my possession of the ten pounds—and told them every detail of my adventures since leaving Horsham to the moment in which I saw the murderer run away. Once, at an early stage of my story, the sergeant interrupted me to send off the two labourers for a horse and cart; thenceforward he listened with keen attention, especially when I arrived at the episode of the packet. And in the end he once more examined the dead man's clothing, more thoroughly than before, eventually rising to his feet with a decisive shake of his head.

"There's no packet on him now!" said he. "You're sure he put it back in his pocket after looking it over last night?"

"Dead sure!" I answered. "He wrapped the whole thing up carefully, and put it inside his waistcoat."

The man whom I had brought up the hill looked at the sergeant.

"The fellow who knifed him must have stolen it," he suggested. "Probably that was what he was after."

The sergeant jerked his thumb at me.

"But he says that the murderer made off in the mist, the very instant he'd knifed this chap!" he remarked. "The very instant!"

"He did!" I asserted. "That very instant! He'd no sooner knifed him—I saw the flash of the knife!—than he was off and clean gone—down there. I'll swear that he never even touched him after he'd used his knife on him."

The sergeant stood with his hands clasped in front of him, calmly regarding the dead man, for some minutes, evidently musing.

"You ran off as soon as this happened, you say, and came across this gentleman, Captain Trace, at the foot of the hill?" he asked. "How long was it before you got back up here?"

But I was not competent to answer that; my brain was still confused with the events of that first awakening.

"I heard the clock strike six just before I reached the house down there——" I began. Then I stopped, and Captain Trace finished for me.

"We were up here within twenty minutes, Preece," he said. "And, of course, within twenty minutes——"

"You're thinking just what I'm thinking, Captain," said Preece. "Time for the murderer to come back and rob his victim, eh? Maybe! But if the murderer had no reason to think that there was anybody about, why didn't he seize the packet at once?"

"Well, I wasn't thinking that," replied Captain Trace. "What I am thinking, now that I've heard more, is that within twenty minutes there was plenty of time for a third person to rob this dead man. Eh?"

Sergeant Preece started, rubbing his chin.

"Third person?" he said. "I don't follow you, Captain!"

"No?" replied Trace. "Look at this man, now! That's a very good, rather expensive suit of the best blue cloth; his boots are good; everything about him shows that he wasn't wanting money. What's the exact amount you found there in his trousers pockets?—nine shillings and fivepence-halfpenny, in silver and copper. I think he'd have more than that on him, Sergeant! And I think he'd have a good watch and chain."

"He had a watch and chain!" I exclaimed, suddenly remembering. "I saw them on him last night."

"Gone, now!" continued Trace significantly. "I think this man was robbed after his death, during the twenty minutes in which his body was left alone. Probably he'd money—notes, perhaps—in that inside waistcoat pocket, as well as his map."

Preece made no remark about this theory, though I could see he was thinking about it. He pulled out a note-book and pencil and turned to me.

"That man you met at Petworth, and saw again at Graffham?" he said. "Just give me an accurate description of him. Make it close, now!—don't forget anything."

I gave him a faithful, even circumstantial, description, and by the time he had got it all down the two labourers were coming back with the horse and cart and another man. I watched them winding round the hill-side as I furnished Preece with the final details.

"All right!" he said, putting his note-book away. "Now, you'll be wanted at the inquest. Where were you going—Portsmouth? You'd better stay here, in the village down yonder, until to-morrow—I'll try and get the inquest opened to-morrow afternoon. You've money on you, so——"

"I'll take him home with me," said Trace. He turned to me with a friendly look. "Come along with me, my lad," he went on. "I know Andrew Macpherson, as I told you, and I dare say I can help you to what you want in the seafaring way. Come to my place if you want him, Sergeant—or me, either!"

"I shall want both," remarked Preece dryly. "First and second witnesses!"

We left him superintending the removal of the murdered man's body to the village inn, where, said Trace, it would have to lie in an outhouse until the coroner and his jury could sit on it, and went down the hill by the way we had climbed it. But instead of going forward to the old farmstead where I had found him talking with the handsome woman, my guide turned aside through a path that led through apple-orchards to the centre of the village, stopping at last before a cottage on which, it was evident, a good deal of money and taste had been laid out.

"Half in ruins, this, when I found it!" he remarked, with a smile, as he opened the gate and motioned me to enter. "I did it up. How's it strike you?"

I said that I admired it greatly, especially the garden, which was already beginning to be bright and gay with flowers.

"Aye, it's not half bad!" he answered. "Well, come in, my lad, and we'll have some breakfast. Murder is a beastly thing, and vile to see—but it won't have spoiled your appetite!"

# CHAPTER FOUR

## SUB JUDICE

I was certainly at the age in which it takes a great deal to interfere with a healthy and growing lad's appetite, and though I had been more than a little upset by the events of the morning, I was fully prepared to do justice to the breakfast which was presently set before my host and myself by a motherly-looking woman, his housekeeper, in a bright little parlour overlooking the garden. He was a tactful man, this Captain Trace; he not only made me feel at home with him, but kept off the affair in which I had just so unwillingly figured; instead of talking about that, he talked of Andrew Macpherson and my leaving him, and pretty soon he came to a direct question.

"So you want to go to sea, Tom Crowe?" he asked. "Made up your mind, eh?"

"I don't want an indoor life," said I. "There were times when I felt I'd burst, there in the grocery shop. Mr. Macpherson, he said it was in my blood."

"Very like," he agreed. "You're not the sort to spend your time weighing pounds of sugar. Well, there is the sea. And there's the Army. Ever thought of that, Tom?"

"A soldier!" I exclaimed. "No!"

"That was my line," said he. "I was at a bit of a loose end when I was your age. My father had put me to the engineering—paid a pretty stiff premium, too, with me. But when my time was through—no work! Not a job to hand anywhere. And I wasn't one for waiting, or idling. I took the Queen's shilling—meaning to get on. Well, I did get on. Lance-corporal in nine, full corporal in twelve months; sergeant in two years. Then the Boer War came, and I got my chance—got my commission, you know. And in due time I got my company. Pretty good innings, eh?" he continued, laughing. "Raw recruit at twenty; captain at thirty. I might have been a general, or perhaps a field-marshal—who knows?—if I'd stopped in!"

"Why didn't you?" I made bold to ask him.

He laughed again and made a wry face.

"Why, to tell you the truth, my lad, I got very badly wounded in the last stage of the Boer War, after I'd got my commission," he answered. "And

I've never really got over it. I carried on all right in peace-time, but the effects were there, and are there. And I had a bit of money left me, and so I thought well to give up soldiering and take to a quiet life—here."

He said nothing then, and it was not until some time afterwards that I found out that when he got his wounds he also got the Victoria Cross.

"It's very nice here, too," I remarked, feeling it polite to compliment him on his situation.

"Yes, I took a lot of trouble to make it so," he said. "It was a ramshackle old spot when I bought it. And I've got some fine prize fowls, and I keep bees, and I have a bit of a boat, a small yacht, as some folk would call it, down at Bosham—oh yes, it's very pleasant, Tom, very pleasant!"

But as he said this he sighed, as if there was something behind the pleasantness; also, he became silent, eating his eggs and bacon with his eyes on his plate.

"Mr. Macpherson says my father was a sailor," said I. "He was in the Royal Navy."

"Ah!" he answered, looking up. "That accounts for your wish for the sea, no doubt. But if you want adventure, my lad, I think you'll not get it there—nowadays. Travel, perhaps; but the good old days are gone. A fine, big sailing ship, now, trading to the far-off places——"

He checked himself at the sound of voices and footsteps outside, and both of us turning to the open window, we saw, coming in at the garden gate, two men, at sight of whom Captain Trace made a gesture suggestive of good-tempered annoyance.

"Tom!" he said. "Here are the two biggest gossips and tittle-tattlers in these parts—and that's saying a good deal! They're after you, my lad!— Preece has no doubt told them what's occurred, and they want to see and question the eyewitness. Keep close!—don't tell them anything—I'll settle them. One of them, the big man," he went on in a whisper, "is a sort of retired gentleman, name of Fewster; the other, the little man, Chissick, is a builder and contractor—and they're both the sort who like news, and love to retail it. Say nothing!"

The callers were in the little hall by that time, and presently the housekeeper opened the parlour door and showed them in. I saw at once that they were of the species that scorns ceremony, and as each gave a careless nod to my host and dropped into the easiest chairs they could find, I took a good look at them. Fewster was a big, heavily built man of a solemn cast of countenance, and small, ferrety eyes; the sort of man who carries a stout stick, crosses his fat hands on it, and rests a double chin on his hands. Chissick was a rosy-faced fellow, alert, sly in expression, with a trick of looking quickly about him that reminded me of a perky cock-robin. And both men, after a mere glance of greeting to the man whose privacy they had so summarily invaded, fixed their eyes on me.

"Morning, Captain!" said Chissick cheerily. "Strange doings in the parish this morning! That'll be the young man, I suppose?"

Captain Trace rose from the table as if he knew exactly what to do in these circumstances. Without replying to Chissick's question, he went straight to a sideboard and to a spirit-case that stood in its centre, and, mixing two glasses of whisky-and-soda, silently handed one to each of his guests. Each man made some remark about the hour being early, but each took the glass.

"Best respects, Trace," muttered Fewster. "As Chissick says, that'll be the young man that we've heard of from Preece?"

"That's certainly the young man you've heard of from Preece," agreed Trace. "You seem curious about him!"

"Good ground for curiosity, I think, when there's murder, genuine bloody murder, done at your very doors!" observed Chissick. "Now, what did you really see, young fellow? Haven't you got a single clue?"

I gave Chissick a quiet, steady look; then, just to let Trace see that I was no fool, I spoke before he could.

"I mustn't say!" said I. "The matter's in the hands of the police. It's *sub judice*!"

The man's eyebrows went up as Trace laughed, and he looked from me to my host, and from him to Fewster, and back at me, viewing me from head to foot.

"Latin, eh?" he exclaimed. "Oh—oh! And how does a young fellow that talks Latin as natural as all that come to be sleeping out in an old mill—what?"

"That's *sub judice* too, Chissick," said Trace. "Come!—this boy can't tell you anything. You know there's got to be an inquest to-morrow—he'll have to tell his tale then. You'll hear it, all in good time—you're sure to be on the jury."

I was pretty quick of observation, for a youngster, and I saw that our visitors were somewhat taken aback by this: in each man's face there was an expression that seemed to go deeper than mere curiosity; it appeared to me that both were anxious—with an unusual sort of anxiety, too.

"I don't know about that—about waiting, Captain," remarked Fewster, after a pause. "Here's murder been done—at our doors!—and this young fellow seems, according to what I'm told, to be the only person that can say anything about it. As—as what I may call citizens, and if that isn't the right term, ratepayers——"

"That's the term," interrupted Chissick. "Ratepayers! Two biggest ratepayers in the parish, for that matter!"

"As ratepayers," continued Fewster, with an approving nod at his fellow-caller, "as ratepayers, and the most considerable ratepayers, I contend that we've a right to what I may call immediate information! And what I want to know from that young man is—can he recognise and identify the murderer?"

"Just so!" murmured Chissick. "Good! Couldn't have been better put! Can he?"

Trace drank off his coffee and, pushing the cup aside, rose to his feet.

"He's not going to tell you!" he answered. "That, too, 'll have to wait till the inquest. It's all *sub judice*, gentlemen—good term that! We're precluded from speaking—till the law bids us speak. We'll speak hard enough then!"

The two visitors looked at each other, and then at me and Trace, sourly.

"Not going to say anything, then?" asked Chissick. "Me and Mr. Fewster's the two most important people in the place, Captain!"

"I dare say!" agreed Trace good-humouredly. "But—this lad's mouth is sealed, till the coroner opens it. And his mouth's just now in my charge—and I'll keep it sealed!"

Fewster took his double chin off his hands, and his hands off his stick, and rose slowly.

"In my opinion," he said gruffly, "in my opinion, Captain, that young fellow 'ud do better if he were assisting the police people to find the murderer! There's railway stations at hand—three of 'em—and they ought to be watched! Murder is a very serious thing, and it isn't pleasant for law-abiding people to know that a murderer is at large! And with a knife too!"

Trace picked up his cap and glanced at the door.

"I quite agree with you, gentlemen," he said. "But you've come to the wrong shop! Try Preece. He's the representative of the law! Go and put your views before him. Sorry—but I've got to go out."

Whether the two men took this as polite hint or plain dismissal, I don't know; they went away down the village street, talking in confidential whispers. When they were outside the gate I looked at Trace.

"What did they really want?" I asked him.

"Can't tell you, my lad!" he answered. "Except that they wanted to turn you inside out, to ascertain for themselves how much you knew and didn't know. But why?—ah, that's what I don't know! Deep fellows, both of 'em—crafty. Last men in this village to tell anything to. But come along with me—I'm going to see an old friend of mine before whom you can talk as freely as you like; he's confined to a wheeled chair nowadays, and can't get out, and a bit of talk's a godsend to him—what's more, he's a wise man and keeps counsel."

We went out through the garden and up the street towards the foot of the hill down which I had run that morning. At the gate of the farmstead where I had found him in my hurried rush for help, Trace turned in.

"This is Mr. Hentidge's farm," he said as we crossed the garden. "He's a very, very old man, over eighty years of age, Tom. Lost the use of his legs, and has to be wheeled about; spends his time by the fire in winter and sitting out in the sun in summer. But wonderful in his faculties—clever as ever! Lost nothing but locomotive power, eh? Marvellous old chap! That was his daughter you saw me talking to this morning. Equally marvellous woman! Manages—everything!"

I saw at once that Trace was very much at home in the Hentidge farmstead. Without any ceremony of knocking at the door, he led me into the house and through a great stone-walled hall into a living-room that was half parlour, half kitchen. The woman I had seen that morning was shelling garden peas at a table in the wide window-place; near her, a newspaper in his hands, and in a big wheeled chair, sat an old man, who, I saw at once, had in his time been a man of unusual height and breadth, and still gave one the impression of uncommon vitality. He was reading his paper without spectacles, and the eyes he turned on me as Trace drew me forward were as brilliant as they were black. The woman, too, turned her eyes on me, and I saw that they were like her father's, brilliantly dark and large; I saw, too, that she was even handsomer than I had thought her in the early morning light. She paused in her task as we entered, and, going over to the wheeled chair, whispered something to its occupant. The old man nodded, still looking at me.

"Just so, just so, my girl!" he said. "I understand! So that's the young man, is it, Trace? Sit you down, young fellow."

Trace pulled a couple of chairs close to Mr. Hentidge, and motioned me to take one of them.

"This is the chap, Mr. Hentidge," he answered. "He's told me all about himself, and I'll vouch for him—I know his late master at Horsham. Now, Tom," he went on, "you can tell Mr. Hentidge all about it, without fear— it'll not go outside these walls. And Mr. Hentidge can, maybe, throw a bit of light on things—he knows that old mill and its surroundings better than anybody in the place. Begin at the very start of things, my lad."

I told them the story as I had already told it to Trace and the police-sergeant. I had a good audience. The old man never took his eyes off my face. His daughter, leaning over the back of his chair, watched me from start to finish; she had an unusually mobile face, and it flushed or paled according to the quality of my story. I think, big and fine woman though she was, that she was marvelling how a boy of eighteen should have seen this horror and remain so very matter-of-fact about it. When I came to the actual murder she drew in her breath sharply. But the old man listened unmoved, taking in every point and nodding his head now and then. And when I made an end he immediately asked me a sharp question:

"You never saw the man's face, boy—the man that made off?"

"No, sir," said I. "The mist was too thick."

"And he went off—which way, now?—which way from the mill?"

"Due east, sir—towards where the sun had risen."

He nodded at that as if it was exactly the answer that he had expected to get.

"Aye!" he murmured, as if to himself. "He would—if he knew these parts. The woods are thick on that side. But——"

He relapsed into what was evidently a mood of deep reflection, which continued so long that at last his daughter, with a look at Trace, laid her hand on his shoulder.

"What are you thinking about, father?" she asked.

Mr. Hentidge started and looked up, first at her, then at us.

"I was thinking back, my girl!" he said, with a smile. "Many a long year ago, there was a man came into these parts, a seafaring man——"

What more he was about to tell us I did not learn at that time. My chair faced the window, and just then, chancing to look that way, I saw a man going slowly past on the road outside, and in him recognised my interrogator of Petworth churchyard.

# CHAPTER FIVE

## NAME OF KEST

I broke in upon whatever it was that old Hentidge was going to tell us and startled him and the other two, by leaping to the window with outstretched hand.

"That's him—that's him!" I shouted, forgetful of the grammar lessons I had learnt at Horsham School. "There!"

Trace leapt after me, staring.

"Who—who?" he exclaimed. "What's the lad mean?"

"That man there, just going by!" I said. "That's the man I talked to at Petworth, and saw at Graffham—you know!"

"Come on, then," he responded. "Let's be after him. If he's here——"

He raced out of the house and I followed sharp on his heels. At the edge of the garden we caught sight of the man again. He was going slowly towards the hill-side, his hands in his pockets, his head dropping forward, just as I had seen him twice before. I vaulted the low wall and bawled loudly. He turned on the instant, stared at me for a moment, and then began to retrace his steps slowly. From the very leisureliness of his movements, I knew that this man was innocent of the murder of that morning; no guilty man would have taken his time as he did. He recognised me as we drew near each other, and he grinned in a sort of sheepish fashion. I scarcely knew what to say to him, but he relieved my uncertainty by speaking first.

"You, eh?" he said. "Here, too? Well, I reckon I've found it, at last. Up yonder—unless I'm sore mistaken."

"The mill?" said I.

"What else?" he retorted. "As I say—if not sore mistaken. But"—here he turned, pointing to the mouth of a lane which opened on the village street just beneath Hentidge's farmstead—"I've been taking a view of that mill for the last mile or two as I come along there, and in my opinion yon is the very mill I'm seeking, and that I told you about. Leastways, as far as I could observe the lie of the land where it stands. I was going up there when you called me back."

Trace had come up by that time and was looking curiously at the man. The man returned the look, equally curious.

"You came along that lane—just now?" asked Trace suddenly.

"I did, master—if you want to know. A long cast by it, too—miles!" answered the man. "And—why?"

"From—where?" enquired Trace.

"Seems like this was a catechism class," remarked the man, smiling. "But, Lord!—I don't mind saying. Chichester!"

"You've only just come into this village, then?" continued Trace.

"Five minutes ago, master."

"Spoken to anybody?"

"Ain't seen a soul to speak to, till I see you two!" said the man with a grin. "And once more I says—why? Why this here catechising?"

Trace gave me a look, and I saw that he wanted me to do the next speaking. I gave the man a glance that was meant to be full of significance.

"Look here!" I said. "You know all you told me about your wanting to find that mill? Very well!—there was a man murdered up there this morning!"

We were both watching him narrowly, and we saw at once that this curt announcement hit him full and hard, and that deep in his mind there was something struck him about my news which was secret to himself. His eyes grew wide; his mouth opened; he remained open-mouthed for a full minute, staring at me. When at last he spoke, his speech came haltingly.

"A—man—murdered—this morning?" he said incredulously. "What man?"

"That's what we don't know," remarked Trace. "A strange man—unknown. Look here!" he went on after a pause, during which the man continued to stare at us. "Why did you want to find this old mill?"

The man looked Trace up and down, very slowly.

"My business, master!" he answered.

"Very good—so it is, no doubt," said Trace. "But you told this lad you were very keen about finding it. Do you know of anybody else who was equally keen?"

At this point the man did precisely what I had seen him do in Petworth churchyard: he pulled out his queer tobacco-box and helped himself to a liberal quid of the plug which he kept there.

"There may ha' been," he answered, as he closed his clasp-knife with a snap. "I won't say other than that there may ha' been. But 'tis odd—if so be as this is the mill I want—that another man should chance on it about the same time as I do, and then meet his death there! Murdered, you say?—and unknown?"

We nodded, silent; we were still watching him keenly, and I think Trace had the same wonder in his mind that I had. But the man was now cool as granite under our inspection.

"Who done it?" he enquired suddenly. "Where there's a murder, there's a murderer! Who was it, in this here case?"

"That's unknown too," replied Trace. He turned towards the village. "Look here!" he said. "You'd better come and see the murdered man! His body's at the inn, awaiting the inquest. The policeman lives just down here—he'll show you."

The man showed no particular emotion one way or the other. He immediately turned to go with us.

"No objection," he said. "A dead man or two makes no great difference to me. Seen a fair lot in my time!—under various circumstances. White 'uns and black 'uns!" he added, with a strong emphasis on the conjunction. "And yeller 'uns too, for that matter. This man—I reckon he's white, eh?"

"Of course!" replied Trace.

"Of course, says you?" he remarked. "Aye well!—but in my train of thought I was thinking he might—just might, you observe?—ha' been a nigger. There was a nigger, now I come to think on it—but let's see this policeman and the body!"

I waited outside Preece's cottage with the man while Trace fetched the sergeant out. Trace was some little time inside; when he and Preece emerged from the door, Preece had evidently been primed with the surface facts, and he immediately tackled the man with leading questions.

"You're the man that this young fellow had talk with in Petworth churchyard the other night?" asked Preece. "About the locality of a mill?"

"We had talk—yes," asserted the man. "A mill it was!"

"And you were at Graffham yesterday noon, eh?" continued Preece, "This young fellow saw you there; saw two men evidently pointing the way to you. Where did you go?—from Graffham?"

"Went all wrong!—along of what those men told me," answered the man readily. "I went through Heyshott to Cocking, and then south to Lavant and Chichester. Them two at Graffham, they gave me certain information, but it was all no good."

"Where were you at six o'clock this morning?" demanded Preece.

I saw at once what he was after, and I turned quickly on the man for his answer. It came just as quickly.

"In bed at Chichester!" he replied. "Temperance Hotel, in South Street. Didn't get up till seven. Breakfast eight—then walked out here. And what's all this here further catechism about, may I enquire? You can see what I am!" He paused and made a gesture of his hands, as if to invite Preece to look him well over. "Man o' substance!—retired. Nice place o' my own I have, at Fareham, with a mast in the front garden and a bit o' glass at the back. My name's Trawlerson—Mr. Hosea Trawlerson, Pernambuco Cottage, Fareham: them's my directions. When at home, of course."

I could see that this readily imparted information had its effect on the police-sergeant. His somewhat peremptory manner changed, and I thought he gave a sigh of relief, as if what Trawlerson had just told him shifted some burden off his shoulders. He nodded towards the village inn.

"Come this way, Mr. Trawlerson," he said. "You've heard what's happened here this morning? Well, you're searching for a mill—a windmill—I understand you think it's our mill, up there. Just so! Now, a strange man comes there last night and gets murdered close by, by some person unknown, at six o'clock this morning. Can you think—have you any idea—who the man can be?"

"At the moment, no!" replied Trawlerson. "Knocked me all of a heap to hear what this young fellow told me just now. Without doubt, what they call a coincidence. Queer altogether! Still, if I think back, and see this here dead man—you see," he continued, after breaking off suddenly and then going on again in a burst of confidence, "you see, me having used the sea all my life till I retired, recent, I ha' known a many things! Many things—queer things! Many men—still queerer! All sorts o' things, some of 'em fitting one into another, and a many that wouldn't fit nohow. Lots o' faces too—white, black, brown, yeller. Now, if I see a face and can give it a name——"

We were close to the inn by that, and Preece led us to an outhouse and produced a key from his pocket.

"Let's see if you can give this face a name, then," he said. "If you can——"

He opened the door, and we all took off our caps and walked in, on tiptoe. The place was a saddle-room, tidy and quiet. What we had come to see lay, still enough, on a table in the centre, with a white sheet over it. Preece slowly raised the head of the sheet, and beckoned Trawlerson to approach.

"Now!" he whispered.

Carrying his hat under his arm, and still tiptoeing, Trawlerson went up and looked earnestly at the dead man. The next instant he started back.

"Good Lord!" he whispered. "It's Kest! Kest! Now, what the——"

Suddenly checking himself, he drew away; the next instant he was outside the door, in the sunlight, beckoning us to follow.

"Come out!" he commanded, clawing impatiently at us. "Come out! Well, of all the—here!" he went on as Preece came last, locking the door. "This here is an inn, ain't it? Of course! Now, is there a quiet, peaceful corner in it where——"

Preece was quick to see what he wanted, and motioning Trace and me to follow, he led the way into the inn, and, after a word with the landlord, conducted us into a small room at the back of the bar. We had that place to ourselves, but Trawlerson would not say a word until he had refreshed himself with rum: phlegmatic as he had always been up to that point, it was very evident that his recognition of the dead man had shaken his imperturbability. And there was something approaching very real and serious anxiety in the first question he put to Preece as soon as he set down his tumbler, one-half the contents of which he had tossed off with eagerness as soon as the landlord put it before him.

"This here man?" he asked, jerking his thumb towards the outhouse. "Kest! What had he on him? Who found what he had?"

"I searched the body," replied Preece. "Precious little, Mr. Trawlerson. No letters, no papers. A handkerchief. A knife. Nine shillings and five-pence-halfpenny in silver and copper. That was all. But," he added, eyeing his questioner closely, "he had had more than that on him. This young man saw things on him last night which weren't there when I examined the clothing. There was a watch and chain. And—there was a map."

The effect of that last word on Trawlerson was marked. He jumped in his seat; the veins swelled in his forehead; he glared at Preece, and I saw his fist bunch itself into an ugly knot of twisting muscle.

"A map!" he exclaimed. "What sort of a map? D'ye mean—but here, I'm all at sea! This young man saw—what did he see? Let him tell! I want to be knowing! Kest here!—knifed—a map?—it's—it's——" He swallowed another mouthful of his drink, and waved the glass at me before setting it down. "Let's be hearing!" he commanded. "Tell it plain—plain!"

I looked to the police-sergeant for his approval, and as he nodded, I proceeded to tell my story for the third time that morning. As I went on, Trawlerson's face grew blacker and blacker; it became thunderous when I came to describe the map. But when I corroborated the policeman in his statement that the map had disappeared by the time the body was examined, his temper gave way, and he broke out on me for a damned young fool for leaving the man. I should have stayed by him, he vociferated, till the sea fog cleared and help came.

"Fool yourself, Mr. Trawlerson!" I threw back at him. "Who are you to be calling names? You were——"

"No words, no words!" interrupted Preece hastily. "The lad did his best, Mr. Trawlerson. But this map——"

Trawlerson, who had thrust his hands into his pockets, stretched his legs under the table, and drooped his head forward on his chest in an attitude of sulkiness, turned on the policeman with a scowl.

"What are you and your like doing to find the man as done this?" he demanded. "Kest, he's been followed! For that map, of course. Either the man as scragged him got it before he done it, or he came back when this lad was gone, and got it. In either case——"

"We're doing all we can, in the time," said Preece. "You'll find no slackness on our part, Mr. Trawlerson! But this map——"

Instead of answering, Trawlerson slapped his hand on the bell, and, the landlord appearing, motioned him to replenish his glass.

"I ain't going to say a word more!" he announced, turning sharply on Preece. "Not one syllable! There'll be a crowner's 'quest on this here body, and I shall be there——"

"You'll have to be!" interrupted Preece. "I don't know any other who can identify him."

Trawlerson gave him a dark look. His behaviour had changed, and was becoming mysterious.

"I shall be there for something else than that!" he said grimly. "In this house it'll be, and in this house I stops till the crowner comes! And till then my mouth's shut!"

# CHAPTER SIX

## UNDER EXAMINATION

We left Trawlerson making his arrangements with the landlord and land-lady for a bed that night, and went out into the street. By that time I was beginning to feel the reaction of the recent doings, and I should have been thankful to go back to Trace's cottage and lie hidden away from everybody. But Preece had been busy on telegraph and telephone, and the village was being invaded by police officials from Chichester, and by pressmen from the neighbouring towns. All these people wanted to get hold of me, and Trace had his work set in his self-constituted part of guardian. The press-men we could elude or choke off, but the police were different, and I had to submit to examination and cross-examination until I almost wished that I was back in Andrew Macpherson's shop. And once or twice I felt that there was an element of suspicion in the manner of some of these matter-of-fact, hard-faced men: it seemed to be against me that I had chosen to sleep out all night, and once or twice I felt the blood rush about my ears as one or other of them questioned me strictly about myself and my past. I got sick of that, and grew restive, too.

"If you're having any doubts about me," I suddenly flared up as a man who, they told me, was a very great personage in the police, was turning me inside and out with his questions, "you'd better ask Mr. Andrew Macpher-son, of Horsham, about me! He'll pretty soon tell you that my word's as good as his own! He knows me——"

"You needn't bother yourself, my lad!" said my questioner, with a dry smile "We've sent for Mr. Macpherson already. And don't you get huffy!— this is a case of murder, and a bad one, and we don't leave any stone un-turned in such cases. You tell your tale all right—but we don't know you, you know."

They let me go home with Captain Trace after that, but I think there was a secret understanding between them and him about his having charge of me, and for the rest of that day—or, at any rate, until Mr. Macpherson arrived during the late afternoon—I never looked out of Trace's parlour window without seeing a policeman near at hand; the village seemed to swarm with policemen. But Andrew Macpherson came, and he talked to the bigwigs in his forcible way, and thenceforward the police treated me with the respect due to a credible and trustworthy witness. Still, whenever they returned to their questioning of me, I had to give them keen disappointment—from start to finish I told them flatly that it was an absolute impossibility for me to identify the man I had seen struggling with Kest in the sea fog. I had a vague, general, not-much-to-be-trusted impression of his figure, but not the slightest of his face.

Trace, on the strength of their previous meetings at Quarter Sessions, greeted Macpherson as an old acquaintance, and took him home to his cottage. Andrew favoured me with one of his sly smiles.

"Aweel, Tom!" he said as he sat him down. "Ye were longing for adventure and the like o' that, and, my certie, ye seem to ha' lost no time in falling head and shoulders into one, my man!"

"None of my seeking, Mr. Macpherson!" said I. "I didn't set out to find that sort o' thing—I'd ha' been thankful to escape it. But how can anybody tell what's going to happen to 'em, Mr. Macpherson?"

"And I could dispute that wi' you, my laddie!" said he. "It's a fine point, but whether it belongs to the domain o' logic, or to that o' theology, or yet again to that o' metapheesics, I'm no very sure. There's such a thing as prevention by anticipation, ye ken, and for my part I'd no advise young fellows wi' good siller in their pouches to sleep otherwhere than in a Christian-like bed. If ye'd no had them Robinson Crusoe notions in your head-piece, and had sought other quarters than yon old mill—but losh, man! what's the use o' talking about bygones?—the thing's done! And beyond a bit smattering o' the facts, Tom, I'm no very well acquaint wi' the story—out with it, my man, and I'll maybe form an opeenion."

I had to tell it all over again as we three sat round Trace's tea-table. At the end Andrew began to sniff.

"I'm no liking what I hear o' that man Trawlerson!" he remarked, when I, supplemented in the final chapter by Trace, had come to a conclusion. "The sound of him is no to my taste! What for is a man that's retired from his business, and by his own account has a nice bit of property and a mast in his front garden and a glass-house at his rear, going stravaging about the country, seeking an old windmill? There's more in it than meets the eye!"

"I wish they'd riddle Trawlerson with questions as they've riddled me all day!" I exclaimed. "He's a far more suspicious character than I am!"

They both replied to that pious aspiration that Trawlerson would be questioned, strictly enough, when he got before the coroner and his jurymen. I supposed that would be so, but I was not so confident that they would get much satisfaction from Trawlerson's answers. Trawlerson, in my opinion, was the sort of man who finds small difficulty in twisting himself out of tight places.

Of Trawlerson himself we saw and heard nothing more until the following afternoon, when the inquest on Kest was opened, in the village schoolroom, close by the inn where his body lay. It was a good-sized place, that schoolroom, and it was packed to the very doors by the folk who came crowding in, not only from the village, but from all round about. In the part railed off for those most closely concerned there were, of course, no end of police, some men in plain clothes whom I took to be detectives, and some others who, said Captain Trace, were lawyers. And with one of these Trawlerson was in close conference; he remained, indeed, sitting by him, and was continually whispering with him until he himself was called to the witness-box. Andrew Macpherson said it looked suspicious that the man should be employing legal help, and he sniffed twice or thrice when Captain Trace told him that the lawyer concerned was one of the sharpest limbs in that neighbourhood. As for me, I was more interested in the coroner and his jury, wondering if their combined wisdom would result in solving the presented problem. Certainly the jurymen showed no great evidence of intellect or power of penetration—still Chissick, who, of course, was on it, looked sharper than ever, and Fewster, who was foreman, wore an air of judge-like profundity. And there was a third man, whose name I did not then know, but whom, that night, I discovered to be one Halkin, a jobbing gardener, who showed particular interest and intelligence from start to finish, and more than once broke in on the evidence with questions of his own.

There was nothing in the earlier stages of that inquest that was new to most of the people there, for by that time, the afternoon of the second day, every man, woman, and child in the district was familiar with the surface facts of the case. There was the evidence of a doctor who testified as to the nature of the dead man's wound, and to the bruises on his body, which showed that he had been engaged in a struggle. There was the evidence of Trace as to my fetching him; of Preece as to his joining us on the hill. And then came my own. I had got so used to playing the part of narrator by that time, and did it so readily, that they let me tell my tale in my own way, without the usual formality of question and answer. There was immense interest in it, the folk listened as if spellbound; it was first-hand evidence. And nobody was more interested than the coroner, to whom, consequent on a shrewd bit of advice from Captain Trace, I addressed myself, looking at him all the time, and paying no heed to anyone else. When I had finished he gave me an approving nod.

"Very clearly told!" he said. Then he turned to the high police official who had examined me so strictly the previous afternoon. "I understand you have made enquiry into the antecedents of this witness?" he asked. "Are they satisfactory?"

"Quite satisfactory, sir," replied the official. "He's a lad of exceptionally good character, and to be fully depended upon. His late employer, who is, in fact, his foster-father, is here to answer any questions about him."

"We won't trouble him," said the coroner. "I'm quite satisfied. Now," he went on, turning to me, "I want to ask you some questions, Crowe. About the map which this man took from his pocket when you were watching him in the mill—you're sure it was a map?"

"It was what I call a map, sir," I replied. "A chart—a plan. Perhaps," I added, after a moment's thought, "perhaps it was more like an architect's drawing—I've seen such things."

"What was it like, now—exactly?"

"It was a sheet of paper, sir, about nine inches square. It looked to me as if it had been folded, creased, a good deal. The man handled it very gingerly, as if he were afraid of tearing it. There was a black dot in the middle, about the size of a threepenny-piece, and then lines and crosses, and, as far as I could make out, there was some lettering."

"You say you saw this, and all the rest, through a hole in the floor—through which the old chains passed down. How much space was there between you and this map?"

"I should think about ten feet, sir."

"You could see the marks on it clearly?"

"Some of them, sir. The black dot in the centre quite clearly."

"And you took that black dot to refer to the mill in which the map was being consulted? Now, why?"

"Well, sir, there was the map, and there was the mill!"

"And you'd already been questioned about a mill by the man you've told us about—the man you met at Petworth and saw again at Graffham?"

"Yes, sir."

"Very well!" said the coroner, and nodded to me to stand down. "The man last referred to is present, I think?" he went on, glancing at the official. "Let him be called!"

But before Hosea Trawlerson's name could be pronounced, the man Halkin leaped up from his seat amongst the jurymen, pointing to me.

"I want to ask that young man a question, Mr. Coroner!" he exclaimed. "Let him stand where he is a minute. Now, young man," he went on, "I want you to tell us something. When you looked out of the mill and saw those two men struggling, could you see their faces?"

"No!" I answered readily. "Not at all!"

"Then how did you tell one from the other, young man? Answer that!"

"I don't know that I did tell one from the other while they were actually struggling," I replied. "They were fighting like dogs when I first saw them!—they were sort of tied up in a knot! But I knew which was which when I went out and found one dead."

"You never saw the face of him that ran away?"

"No! That is, not clearly."

"Could you pick him out, young man, from other men?"

"No, I couldn't!" said I. "I've said all along I couldn't."

He looked round at his fellow-jurymen, smiled in an enigmatic fashion, and sat down. And the coroner's officer called Hosea Trawlerson.

Trawlerson took his time. He exchanged a whispered word or two with his lawyer before stepping into the witness-box, and, once in there, he regarded coroner, jurymen, and everybody with something very like sulky defiance. But as soon as the coroner began to question him, he admitted readily that he could positively identify the dead man.

"Jabez Kest," he said. "That's who he is—Jabez Kest. Seafaring man, like me. That is, as I was, being now retired."

"Do you know where Kest lived?" asked the coroner.

"I don't! Never seen nor yet heard tell of him these twelve years. Last time I saw him was when him and me left the same ship. That was at Southampton—and, as I say, it's twelve years since."

"Was he a man of good character when you knew him?"

"Anything but! He was a main bad' un, Kest! Bad lot altogether!"

"In what way?"

"Every way you can think of! But particularly in thieving—born thief!"

"Was Kest his real name?"

"Never knew him by any other."

"How long had you known him at the period you speak of?"

"A few of years. I was with him on two ships. It was a wonder he wasn't flung overboard off both! Always a bad lot, Kest—sure to come to a bad end!"

The coroner glanced at the police officials.

"I dare say enquiry can be made into the dead man's antecedents," he said curtly. "Now, witness, I want to ask some questions about yourself. You have heard the evidence of the last witness—the young man Crowe? There were certain passages relating to you. Is what he told us about his meeting and conversation with you the other night in Petworth churchyard correct?"

Trawlerson folded his hands on the edge of the desk at which he was standing, and nodded his head.

"Quite!" he replied calmly.

"You told him you were very anxious—keen, I think was the word—to find a certain old windmill, here in Sussex?"

"I did! Asked him if he'd seen such a mill."

"Very good," said the coroner. "Now, why did you want to find that mill?"

Trawlerson let his eye rest for a second on his lawyer; then he turned it full on his questioner. There was open defiance in it.

"My business!" he answered.

"You don't wish to tell us?" suggested the coroner.

"I'm not going to tell you!" retorted Trawlerson. "As I said just now—my business!"

The coroner hesitated for a moment; then he leaned nearer his witness.

"Now listen to me, Trawlerson," he said. "This is a case of murder—of a very brutal murder! The man who was murdered was evidently in search of the old windmill that stands on the downs above this village; he came to it, and there is very good presumptive evidence that he was in possession of a map of it and its immediate surroundings. Now, on your own admission, you, too, have been anxious to find a mill—probably this. You ought to answer my question in the interests of justice. I see," he went on, as Trawlerson shook his head, "I see you don't want to answer it. Will you tell me this, then—have you any idea of your own, any theory, as to why Kest, the dead man, came to this mill?"

"Yes!" answered Trawlerson, with sudden vehemence. "Yes!—but I shan't tell you what it is!"

# CHAPTER SEVEN

## THE CLAMPED CHEST

From the very moment in which Trawlerson had heard from Preece of the existence of a map his entire demeanour had changed. At Petworth, talking with me amongst the gravestones, his attitude had been soft, silky, ingratiating. When Trace and I hailed him outside Hentidge's orchard wall, he had been at least polite and friendly. But everything about him altered as we sat in the back-parlour of the inn and he learned that Kest had a paper on him, which I, sole eyewitness, took to be a plan of the old mill and its surroundings. He grew sulky, suspicious, irritable—and now, as he stood facing the coroner, and while all round remained strangely silent in view of this duel of wills, he typified absolute defiance. He and the coroner remained silent, too, for a good minute, gazing at each other. Then the coroner spoke—smoothly.

"Listen to me, Trawlerson," he said. "You tell us that you are a retired man, having means and property of your own, and I take it that you wish to be known as a law-abiding citizen. You surely don't want to go out of this court bearing the character of one who refuses to help the course of justice? Here, as I have said before, is a case of murder—the police want all the help they can get. A word from you—an explanation—a suggestion as to why Kest should have come to this old windmill——"

"No!" interrupted Trawlerson. "I shall say nothing. My business! Let the police do their own work. What ideas I have I'll keep to myself. I say again—my business. Let them chaps"—he waved his hand at the police officials with a gesture that seemed to indicate contempt—"do their own job! I'll attend to mine!"

"You refuse to tell us why you sought out this mill?" said the coroner curtly.

Trawlerson scowled—but the scowl turned into an obvious sneer.

"I've never yet said, never admitted, that I did seek out this mill!" he retorted. "I agreed that I asked that young fellow if he knew anything of an old windmill the like of what I described to him, and that I was keen about finding it—for reasons of my own. But I never said, and don't admit now, that this mill o' yours, up above there, is the mill I want! Understand that!"

"You may go down!" said the coroner peremptorily. He had evidently had enough of Trawlerson, and he turned to the jurymen, who, one and all, were regarding the retired mariner with uneasy looks. "Since these proceedings began," he continued, "and consequent upon the reports in the local newspapers last night and this morning, certain information has been acquired about the dead man, and three persons have come here who can not only identify, but can also tell us a good deal about him—in fact, gentlemen, we could have dispensed very well with the last witness and his evidence! It appears"—here he consulted a slip of paper which a police official had passed to him—"that this man Kest has been living for some little time not very far away from this place; his landlady is here now; there is also here a policeman who visited her house this morning and examined the room which Kest rented in it; further, there is in attendance a clerk from a local bank whereat Kest kept an account, who has been sent on by his manager in consequence of the newspaper reports I have just alluded to. I think we will hear the landlady first—Mrs. Susan Jordan."

Mrs. Jordan was brought out of a class-room—a little, quiet, middle-aged woman, nervous but determined. She told the coroner she was a widow and lived in Emsworth, and to eke out her slender means was in the habit of letting lodgings to respectable men. She had just been shown the dead man's body, and recognised it as that of a man whom she knew as Jabez Kest, who had lodged with her for about twelve months, and who, she had always understood, was a retired sailor, with money of his own.

"When did you see Kest last, Mrs. Jordan?" enquired the coroner.

"Well, sir, this here is Thursday—it would be Monday. Monday morning, sir. He went out before dinner-time, saying he should be away for a few days."

"What sort of man was Kest—as you knew him?"

"A very quiet, steady man, sir. I never had no trouble with him. Very regular in his habits, sir. A sober man. Of course, he took his glass of a night, but I never had no trouble with him at all, sir."

"Regular in his payments, Mrs. Jordan?"

"As clockwork, sir. Every Saturday morning. Never knew him a minute late at that, sir. Gave me his money as soon as he'd finished his breakfast, Saturdays. I couldn't wish for a better lodger than what Mr. Kest was sir!"

"Did he seem to be pretty well off?"

"I think he'd money, sir—never seemed noways short of it. He never denied himself anything, in reason."

"What did he do with himself, Mrs. Jordan—what were his habits?"

"Well sir, as I say, very regular. After breakfast, he'd read the newspaper. Then he'd go for a walk till dinner-time. After dinner he'd have a nap. Then he'd take another walk till tea-time. After that he'd go round to his favourite public for an hour or two. Then he'd come home to supper, and after talking a bit and smoking his pipe, he'd go to bed. He was often away, sir."

"Often away, was he? Where did he go?"

"That I could not say, sir. Every now and then, as on this last occasion, he'd go away for three or four days at a time. He never said a word to me as to where he went. He was what I call a secret man, sir."

Some of the people who were listening with true rustic curiosity to these revelations laughed at that. But their laughter changed to stares of astonishment presently. A police-sergeant followed Mrs. Jordan into the witness-box. He said that as a result of what had been reported in the stop-press editions of last night's evening newspapers, and again in the morning papers, he, acting on instructions, had very early that morning visited Mrs. Jordan's house, where, it was well known locally, Kest lodged. With Mrs. Jordan's permission he had examined the dead man's room and his belongings, and he detailed what he had found there. Nothing remarkable, save one thing, and that was remarkable enough—or, rather, its contents were. That was a certain box or seaman's chest, clamped at the corners, a strong, heavy affair, with a padlock, to which he, the police-sergeant, at his inspector's orders, had fetched a locksmith.

"And you found inside this box—what?" enquired the coroner.

The witness produced a slip of paper and began to read in formal fashion.

"Three silver cups, believed, from information in our possession, to be the property of Sir John Rodgate, of Rodgate Hall. Silver salver and two silver candlesticks—ditto. Small silver clock—ditto. Silver-mounted paper-knife—ditto. Silver——"

"Are you implying that these things were stolen from Rodgate Hall?" interrupted the coroner.

"Yes, sir! A burglary occurred there about six weeks ago, sir. The burglar has not been traced. These articles correspond with those reported to us as missing, sir. There are several other silver articles on this list, sir—found in the box referred to. I also found a number of gold watches, gold rings set with jewels, and a number of other valuables which I believe to have been stolen. Also some apparently valuable furs, and two bundles of silk. Also a quantity of odds and ends, curiosities, of the value of which we cannot at present form an estimate."

"You conclude that this man was a burglar?" asked the coroner.

"Yes, sir. We have no doubt that all these articles were stolen. At the bottom of the box," continued the witness, resuming his formal manner of giving evidence, "in a separate compartment, I found certain things which, acting on instructions, I have brought here with me, and now produce."

Every neck in that place was craned forward as the police-sergeant, deftly unearthing a small bundle from somewhere about him, whipped off its outer covering of cloth, revealed a wrapping of chamois leather, and, unrolling this, laid out on the shelf on the desk a collection of highly polished instruments that shone brightly in the sunlight. The coroner forgot his dignity.

"Good Heavens!" he exclaimed in genuine astonishment. "What on earth are those things?"

"Burglar's tools, sir!" replied the witness. "Steel. Exceptionally well made. The—the very latest thing in that line of goods, sir!"

Amidst a ripple of excited comment, the coroner examined the various pieces of steel which the police-sergeant had unwrapped. He was obviously as interested as he was inquisitive; so were the jurymen to whom he passed each article.

"Have the police at your station ever had any reason to suspect this man Kest?" asked the coroner after a pause.

"No, sir—no reason."

"Never had any complaints about him?"

"None, sir!"

"Was he known to you at all?"

"By sight only, sir. I've seen him about, since he went to live at Mrs. Jordan's. Never knew him as anything but a quiet, inoffensive man—to all appearance."

"You've no doubt about the things you found in this box you speak of?—no doubt that they're stolen goods?"

"No doubt at all, sir, as regards the silver articles. We've identified them—or, I should say, compared them—with a list furnished to us by Sir John Rodgate when his place was broken into. The other matters—watches, rings, and so on—are brand-new. They look like jeweller's stock, sir. We're already making enquiries about them."

The coroner turned to his jury.

"This man, Kest, appears to have lived a double life," he remarked. "Posed as a quiet, respectable man in the neighbourhood where he lodged, and when he went away on those occasions of which Mrs. Jordan told us, transformed himself into a burglar! We have learned a good deal about him!—however, there is still another witness to hear. Let us have the gentleman from the bank."

The gentleman from the bank proved to be almost as youthful a person as myself; a clerk, who informed the coroner that his manager, having read the newspaper accounts of the murder of Kest, and knowing Kest as a customer, had sent him over to tell what they knew of the man, if the coroner thought proper.

"Very proper, indeed, I think," said the coroner. "Any information at all is welcome! What did you know at your bank of this man Kest?"

"He opened an account with us, an ordinary current account, about twelve months ago," replied the clerk. "He described himself as a retired seaman, and gave a satisfactory reference to a Portsmouth tradesman. He paid in a sum of money on opening his account, and from time to time paid in other sums. He drew on his account now and then. On Monday last he called personally at the bank and drew out a hundred pounds. He made some remark to our cashier about buying some property and paying a cash deposit on it."

"Did you, yourself, see him on that occasion?" asked the coroner.

"Yes, I saw him—just glanced at him."

"Have you been shown the dead man?"

"I have!"

"And he is the man you have known as Kest, your customer?"

"Oh yes—I knew him at once."

The coroner had no more questions to ask, but Halkin stretched a finger towards the witness.

"An important question to that young gentleman, Mr. Coroner!" he said. "A highly important question, considering what we've just heard. Now"—he smiled significantly at the witness—"now, you say this Kest drew a hundred pounds on Monday. In what shape did he carry that there money away?"

The clerk held up a slip of paper.

"I have particulars here," he answered. "He had two £10 notes, four £5 notes, and sixty pounds in gold, sovereigns and half-sovereigns. We have the numbers of the notes," he added, turning to the coroner.

"Aye, but you can't take the numbers of sovereigns and half-sovereigns, young gentleman!" exclaimed Halkin. "Sixty pounds in gold! Now we know where we are! Mr. Coroner, this here man Kest was followed—from the bank, sir. He's been knifed for that gold, sir. Such is my opinion!"

There was a murmur of assent amongst certain of Halkin's fellow-jury men, and a still louder expression of agreement in the crowd of spectators. The coroner allowed himself to smile a little.

"I am not disposed at this stage to dispute your expression of opinion," he remarked, glancing indulgently at Halkin. "He may have been followed from the bank, and he may have been murdered for his money. Unfortunately, on the evidence before us, we haven't any clue to the murderer! Our duty is to enquire into the circumstances of this man's death—to find how it came about, and, if he was murdered, to say, if we can, who murdered him. It seems to me," he went on, after a moment's thought, "that he may have been robbed while asleep that morning by some man who found him in the mill, that he woke while he was being robbed, or as the robber left him, that he pursued the thief and struggled with him, and that his assailant drew a knife on him, with the result we know. But up to now, though we know a great deal more than I had anticipated we should discuss this afternoon, there is no evidence as to the identity of Kest's murderer, and in order that the police may have some further chance of obtaining such evidence, I think it advisable to adjourn for, say, a fortnight. In the meantime, gentlemen of the jury . . . ."

We left the coroner giving the jurymen solemn advice as to keeping their minds free and open, and went away to Trace's cottage. Andrew Macpherson was full of talk. He talked all the time we were at the tea-table and long after. Most of this talk was about Trawlerson, to whom he had taken a great dislike. In his opinion Trawlerson was a deep, designing, crafty rogue, who knew a lot—perhaps everything.

"But I'll tell you what he didn't know, Macpherson!" said Trace. "He didn't know of the existence of that map! That hit him right amidships! Everything changed in Trawlerson when he heard of that map! I was watching him closely, and——"

He paused at a sudden click of the garden gate, and we looked out of the window. Halkin was coming up the path, a curious smile around his lips, and his eye cocked inquisitively at our faces.

# CHAPTER EIGHT

## COMPLEX

Since he had taken me to his bosom, so to speak, throwing a protecting arm about me at an awkward episode of my adventures, I was grateful to Trace, and glad to do things for him, and when I saw Halkin approaching the door, I made haste to get there and to ask him his business. But Trace knew what that business was before I could question the man. As I moved to leave the room, he threw me a half-humorous, half-rueful glance.

"Let him in, Tom!" said he. "Another born gossiper, this!—there's no use in keeping him off. I can see from the turn of his eye that he's bursting with news. And we may hear something."

Halkin got one foot across the threshold as soon as I opened the door to him. He looked past me, with a suspicious enquiry in his glance, and his voice sank to a whisper.

"Anybody particular with him?" he questioned. "That is—no police folk?—Preece, or anybody of his sort?"

"You can come in," said I. "There's no Police here!"

He stole in, still looking round, and, being one of those men who, when they want to be confidential, walk on the tips of their toes, he tiptoed across the little hall, and was still tiptoeing when he entered the parlour. At sight of Macpherson he drew himself up, glancing quickly at Trace.

"All friends here, I hope, Captain?" he said with an oily smile. "On occasions like these here——"

"You've seen Mr. Macpherson before, Halkin," replied Trace. "And heard of him too—when you were in the jury-box this afternoon. So—what's it all about?"

He pointed to a chair, and the man sat down, drawing his chair and himself forward with a gesture that suggested secrecy.

"Jury-box, say you, Captain!" he remarked, with something of a sly chuckle. "Aye, well, there's all sorts of juries in this world, eh? There's—for example, gentlemen, just for example, as it might be—there's the jury of public opinion! D'ye take me, gentlemen?"

"Ye're meaning public-house opinion, I'm thinking," said Macpherson dryly. "Aye, there's that! Ye'll no doubt ha' just come away from it?"

Halkin put his hands on his knees and for a moment sat rubbing them up and down, rocking his body in silent laughter.

"I see you've a pretty sense of the humorous, Mr. Macpherson," he answered. "Just so!—public-house opinion! Well, and a man can know a good deal of what other folk are thinking if he sits quiet in a public-house—when others aren't as quiet!"

"What ha' you learnt, yourself?" demanded Macpherson.

Halkin gave us a sly glance, all round, and jerked his thumb in the direction of the inn.

"They will talk, down there, you know, gentlemen!" he replied. "They ain't bound by no coroner's instructions, that lot! Now me, of course, I can't open my mouth. But a man can keep his mouth shut and his ears open. And that lot—village wiseacres, gentlemen!—they ain't slow to express their opinions. Evidence, now!—bless you, they put their own notions before any evidence!"

"And what are their notions?" asked Trace.

Halkin twisted round in his chair and pointed a finger at me.

"They think this here young man knows more than he's let out!" he answered, eyeing me inquisitively. "They say he was ready enough with his tale before the coroner—over-ready, all cut and dried, says one. But, says another, he'd plenty of time to take whatever there was on Kest and hide it before ever he come running down the hill! That's—village talk!"

He continued to watch me all the time he was talking, and as for me, I kept my eyes fixed steadily on his, wondering why he watched me. Nobody spoke when he had finished; there was a full minute's silence. Then Trace spoke, and there was something, some note in his voice that I couldn't quite understand.

"That'll be one set of opinions! What's the next, Halkin?"

"To be sure, Captain! Of course, there's another. There are those who want to know what you and this young man did when you went up the hill—before Preece came? For you see, Captain, you ain't been in the village more than—what is it?—is it two, or three years?—and so you're a stranger. And——"

"So some of 'em think this boy robbed the dead man, and some of 'em think the boy and I, in partnership, robbed him?" interrupted Trace. "Aye, to be sure, we both had the opportunities! Well—it's not a bad thing to know what's being said of us, Halkin! Any more?"

"Not from that lot—public-house gossips, Captain. But me!—gentlemen, what about that man Trawlerson? In bed at Chichester he may ha' been at six, aye, and at seven o'clock that morning, but—accomplices, gentlemen; an accomplice! Eh?—do you take my meaning? For there was a man!—a man as came, and as did it, and as run away when he'd done it.

Young fellow!"—he turned on me with an eye that was almost affection-ately entreating—"you couldn't nowise identify that man you saw making off in the mist?"

"You heard what I said before the coroner—to you!" I replied huffily. "No!"

"To be sure I heard!" he said, "But now, if you was to think a bit, what? Mist, sea fog, though there was, 'twas a man you saw, and there's a differ-ence 'twixt any one man and the next. Wasn't there nothing, now?—a limp in his walk, a peculiarity in his figure——"

"I couldn't recognise him anyhow, anywhere, from anything, Mr. Halkin," said I, wondering at his persistence. "It's a fact!"

He rose from his chair with a sigh, looking me over with a sort of com-miseration.

"Well, it's a pity!" he remarked. "For by identifying the right man, you'd clear yourself of all suspicion, and, as I've been telling you, these country-folk are nat'rally suspicious—it's mother's milk to 'em, is suspi-cion!—and they will talk, and the more they talk—ah! And I'm talking, but all with the best intentions, Captain," he said, suddenly turning on Trace. "My meaning is—all I've said is with the best Christian intentions, as befits a follower, which I trust I am. I bid you good night, gentlemen both."

I went to let him out, and on the threshold he turned on me with a whisper.

"You couldn't tell that man if you was brought right face to face with him?" he asked. "You couldn't?—nohow?"

"Nohow!" said I.

"Wouldn't know him back or front?" he asked, with a queer chuckle.

"Neither front nor back, Mr. Halkin!" I answered. "Have you got it?"

He went away, silently, at that, and I returned to the parlour, where Trace was describing our departed visitor to Macpherson.

"A sly, canting, psalm-singing rogue, that!" he was saying. "Now, what did he come here for? Not out of friendliness, in spite of all his protesta-tions! He'd some idea, some motive—he was after something. What?"

Macpherson, who was smoking his pipe in the chimney corner, puffed his tobacco in silence for awhile. Then he took the pipe from his lips and waved it at me.

"It's my deliberate and considered opeenion——" he began.

But he got no further, for just as I sat down to listen to him there came another knock at the door, a quiet, stealthy knock. And at a nod from Trace I repaired to the porch once again. The dusk was settling in by that time, and the lamp in the passage had not been lighted, but I instantly recognised the man who demanded admittance. That was he, sure enough—Trawlerson!

I had come by that time, though, of course, in only a vague, boyish sense, to consider Trawlerson as a man of varying moods and emotions. I had seen him in confidential moods and in secretive; in gently insinuating and placatory and in utterly defiant, as when before the coroner and his jury that afternoon. And while he stood there, blinking—he had a trick of that, working his eyelids up and down as he talked—I wondered what mood he was in now, and—to be sure—what he had come there for. But he left me in no doubt concerning the last particular.

"Anybody in there?" he asked laconically, nodding at the half-open door of the parlour.

"Captain Trace, Mr. Trawlerson," said I. "And Mr. Macpherson."

He edged himself nearer me, and, as far as I could make out, one of his eyes gave me a wink.

"It's you I'm wanting to see," he said. "Come outside!"

"No!" I answered peremptorily.

"Come on!" he persisted. "No harm intended! Just a bit of private talk—in the road there."

"I'm not coming, Mr. Trawlerson," I answered. "If——"

"What is it, Tom?" called Trace from the parlour. "Who's there?"

Trawlerson made as if to draw back, but I spoke loudly.

"It's Mr. Trawlerson, Captain Trace," I replied. "He wants me to go out into the road to talk to him. I won't!"

I heard an exchange of words between Trace and Macpherson; then Trace called again.

"If Trawlerson wants to talk to you, Tom, take him into the back room," he said. "Nobody'll interrupt you there."

I looked at Trawlerson, and he hesitated a moment, and then, unwillingly, I thought, entered, and followed me down the passage. There was a small room at the back of the parlour; we went into it and shut the door. But there was another door in the room, one that communicated with the parlour, and his first action was to walk over to it and assure himself that it was closed. Then he unbuttoned his overcoat and sat down on the edge of a chair and looked at me; as for me, I leaned against the mantelpiece, watching him intently.

"Between ourselves," he said in a low voice. "Confidential! Me, as it were, having, in a manner o' speaking, been confidential with you from the time we come together in Petworth, amongst the tombs. And since that there inquest this afternoon, most of which, in my opinion, was tomfool business, done to provide the lawyers and police fellers with something to do, I ha' been listening to what's said down there at the public. Do you know what they're saying about you—and him?"

He jerked his head in the direction of the wall behind which he imagined Trace to be sitting, at the same time giving me a queer smile.

"Yes, I do, Mr. Trawlerson!" said I. "They're saying that Captain Trace and myself, separately or together, had plenty of opportunity of robbing Kest's dead body! I think that's about it, Mr. Trawlerson!"

His queer smile changed into something like a searching glance.

"Heard it, eh, have you?" he remarked. "And—how do you take it?"

"Like I'd take the prick of a pin, Mr. Trawlerson," I said. "I'm not caring!"

"And you're in the right," said he. "I shouldn't care myself. Keep a stiff upper lip!—that's my notion. All the same—and it's what I came to see you about, private, like—you'll be knowing a deal more about this matter than what you told, careful to the crowner and his pack o' fools! Of course!"

"You think so, do you, Mr. Trawlerson?" I asked.

"Why, to be sure!" he answered, with a sly leer at me. "You're a clever young feller, with an uncommon good headpiece of your own, and strike me if ever I see one that knew better how to take care of hisself! And nat'rally, such a one knows, too, how to do his best for hisself. Which is what all of us has a right to do—nat'ral is that."

"Is it what you came to say to me, Mr. Trawlerson?" I asked.

At that he edged his chair closer to where I was standing, and after giving me a look that was intended to signify his sense of some fellow-feeling between us, sunk his voice to a whisper.

"What I came to say to you, my lad, is this here", he went on. "You're a young feller as is starting out in life, and, to such, a bit o' good money is a consideration. Good, golden money!—sovereigns, what tinkles nice and musical one again t'other, eh? I dare say you'd do with—shall we say a hundred of 'em?—as well as anybody?"

"I dare say I should, Mr. Trawlerson," I replied readily. "Quite glad of 'em! Are you proposing to give me a hundred sovereigns?"

He suddenly thrust forward a hand and laid it, with a trembling grip, on my nearest wrist, and a strange light shot into his eyes.

"For the map, yes!" he whispered. "Here!—now!"

I let his hand rest on my arm for a moment, staring at him.

"So you think I've got the map, Mr. Trawlerson, do you?" I asked.

"Or know where it is!" he exclaimed eagerly. "One or t'other—yes!"

"And—why?" I enquired, quietly disengaging my arm. "Why, Mr. Trawlerson?"

He shook his head at me.

"Human natur'!" he said. "Human natur'! I'm well acquainted wi' that—studied it, deep. Same thing, all the world over—white, black, red, brown, and coffee-coloured. All alike! And it stands to reason—though you wouldn't, of course, be so foolish as to admit it—that when you were left alone, all alone, with a dead man, why, you'd go through him!"

"Is that what you'd ha' done, Mr. Trawlerson?" I asked.

"I certain sure should, my lad!" he answered. "And what I'd do, another would—unless he was a born fool! And you're not, and——"

"I'm afraid I am, Mr. Trawlerson!" I interrupted. "For I didn't go through Kest, and I haven't got the map, and——"

But he was already on his feet, staring hard at me. I stared back at him, and presently, making a sound the exact meaning of which I failed to comprehend, he turned away and let himself out of room and house, leaving me to go back, wondering, to the parlour.

# CHAPTER NINE

## THE DITTY-BOX

Whether my two seniors wondered at the story I had to tell them I could not at that moment make out clearly. Trace smiled at it, and Macpherson rubbed his chin now and then as I went from one point to another. Neither made any comment on it, nor, indeed, spoke, until Trace eyed Macpherson quizzically.

"You'll be thinking?" he suggested.

"Aye, I'm thinking!" admitted Macpherson. "I'm a good hand at that!"

"Well," returned Trace, "you were about to give us your deliberate and considered opinion, when this second call came at the door. Eh?"

"Aye!" said Macpherson. "I was! But now I've got another, and I'll sleep on it! Maybe I'll have a still more weighty opinion—a third!—in the morning."

If he had, he said nothing about it. He was unusually silent at breakfast, and when that was done he announced that though it was his stern intention to stand by me while this affair was going on, and that whenever his presence was necessary he would be with us on demand, he must for the time being return to his business. But first he wanted us to take him up the hillside to the old mill, and to the scene of the murder; it was well, he observed, if you were concerned in any matter, to be acquainted with all its details.

Trace and I took him up the rising ground behind the village to the spot whereat Kest had received his death-blow. Preece, on the day of the murder, had caused that place to be enclosed with stakes and a rope, and for a day or so after had stationed a man there, to keep the inquisitive sightseers from trampling the turf. But there was no guardian there now, though the rope was still round it, and we were free to examine the actual spot as closely as we pleased. There was little to see there; the turf was of that short-cropped and wiry sort that is too resilient to carry the marks of pressing feet. But still there was one thing to which Macpherson at once pointed his umbrella.

"That'll be the puir creature's blood!" he said. "Aye, he'll ha' lost a deal of that, by the looks of it. A sair thrust, no doubt. And where were ye standing, Tom, my man, when ye saw it given?"

I took him into the old mill, pointing out all the various details relative to my story of the night and morning I had spent there. Up in the loft, at the broken casement from which I had witnessed the fight in the sea fog, he stared inquisitively across-country. There was no sea fog that morning, and from that lofty position we could see the surrounding hills, villages, and sea-plain for many a mile.

"Which way ran the murderer, d'ye say?" he asked suddenly.

I pointed to a dark belt of wood that lay to the east, at the head of a sudden fall in the land.

"Down there!—straight down there," I answered. "Towards that wood, though, of course, I couldn't see any wood then; you couldn't see many yards before you that morning. But that was the way—and he ran fast too!"

"Aye, for reason that he knew where he was going," remarked Macpherson musingly. "Well, let's take a daunder in that direction."

We left the mill and, going back to the roped-off space, went eastward in the direction in which, according to the best of my belief, the murderer had fled. There was a beaten track there, going straight to a hunting-gate on the edge of the wood; once through that gate, we found that the wood itself was dark, thickly planted, heavy with undergrowth. It was a neglected wood; there had been no clearing done in it for many a year; here and there a tree had rotted and fallen; those that stood, many of them dead, were thick with parasitic growth; the path which led into the heart of this wilderness was padded, inches thick, with the accumulated waste of countless visitors. Trace said that he had never been in that wood before; it would, he remarked, form a highly convenient shelter for a man who, having committed a murder close by, needed a retreat for as many minutes as would enable him to formulate a plan of escape. Here, no doubt, he added, Kest's assailant lay quiet until he could clear off. Neither Macpherson nor myself had any inclinations to dispute that theory; indeed, within a few minutes of entering the wood we found evidence that it was a true one. For suddenly, as we walked aimlessly along staring into the dark recesses on either side, I was aware of certain objects lying at the side of the path—objects which it scarcely needed a second glance to recognise. I let out a cry that woke all the echoes of the wood at sight of these things, and, darting forward, I snatched up and held out to my companions the piece of canvas and the square of oiled silk from which I had seen Kest take out his map.

"See these?" I shouted in my excitement. "These are the wrappings that Kest had the map in! The murderer's been here!—here where we're standing!"

They came close and looked at the things I held up. The piece of canvas was saturated with moisture; beads of dew were thickly sprinkled on the oiled silk.

"You can recognise them?" asked Trace.

"Take my oath of it!" said I. "He had the map wrapped first in this oiled silk; the piece of canvas was round that. The murderer must have examined the packet when he got in here, thrown the wrappings away, and pocketed the map."

"Unless he threw that away too, as useless to him," said Trace. "Let's take a look round about."

But we found no map. Macpherson said we shouldn't; in his opinion, Kest was murdered for the map. Still, we found something going back towards the hunting-gate, and that was the whity-brown paper in which canvas and oiled silk had been enclosed. There had been heavy rain since the morning of the murder, and the whity-brown paper was soaked and pulpy. But I carried it off when we presently left the wood and set down the hillside to tell Sergeant Preece of our discoveries.

We encountered Preece in the open space outside the inn. He had two men with him, each in plain clothes. One was obviously a civilian, and just as unmistakably a Jew—a little, hook-nosed, black-eyed man; the other, a big, burly fellow of an official type. They stood listening silently while we told our tale and showed our finds to the sergeant. When Preece handled the canvas and the oiled silk, the Jew made some remark to him in an undertone.

"You recognise 'em, eh?" said Preece. "Well; we seem to be getting at something, bit by bit!" He turned to Trace and Macpherson, indicating his two companions. "These gentlemen have come over about this affair," he said. "This is Warder Sharpwell, from Parkhurst. He's just identified Kest as a man who served five years there, some little time ago, for burglary. That's a help!—we know now that Kest was, as things seemed to indicate at the inquest, a professional burglar. Of late, at any rate, whatever he may have been in the past. And this is Mr. Silvermore, jeweller, of Portsmouth. He's been at Emsworth this morning, inspecting that small stuff, watches, and so on, that the police there found in Kest's box; he's identified it as his property, the proceeds of a burglary committed some little time ago. And he's seen Kest too, and identified him!"

"As a man whom I knew by sight, but whose name I never knew," remarked Silvermore quietly. "An occasional customer!"

"Well, you knew him, and that's something," remarked Preece, who seemed to be in high good-humour as a result of the morning's revelations. "I say—we're really getting at a good deal, bit by bit! Better tell these gentlemen what you told me, Mr. Silvermore—they'll see how things fit in. And especially since you recognise these bits of things," he added, pointing to the canvas and the oiled silk, which he had carefully laid on the wall of his garden, by which we were all standing. "Tell 'em!"

Silvermore smiled deprecatingly, in the fashion of a man who, in his own opinion, has very little to tell.

"I know next to nothing about him," he said, pointing towards the saddle-room of the inn, where Kest's dead body still lay. "I recognised him at once, just now, as a man—a sailor-man, I always thought—who used to come, occasionally, to my shop in Portsmouth, and bought a thing or two— a cheap watch, or ring, or chain, or something of that sort. What I chiefly remember about him is that he was a slow-going man; used to hang about a long time, making up his mind——"

"Taking stock of his surroundings—that's what he was after!" interrupted Preece, with a knowing laugh. "Getting an idea of the lie of the land, eh?"

"He always paid for whatever he bought, cash down, and took it away with him," continued Silvermore. "So, of course, I never had occasion to ask his name. And, as I say, he never bought anything out of the common. Except once"—he paused, and his eyes fixed themselves on the canvas and the silk. "That transaction," he went on, "has certainly something to do with those things—if they're the identical wrappings that he had a map in."

"I don't think there's much doubt about that," remarked Trace. "This boy is prepared to identify them as the wrappings of the map which he saw Kest produce in the mill the night before he was murdered. What do you know about them?"

"Well," replied Silvermore slowly, "I conclude, from all I've heard here, and just now, that Kest got that map from me. In this way. In addition to my jewellery business, I have a pawnbroking business. Unredeemed pledges, of course, occasionally come into my stock for sale. Now, some years ago, a sailor pledged with me a ditty-box—which is, as I suppose you know—a box in which sailors keep all sorts of odds and ends, little personal possessions, curiosities that they pick up, valuables, if they have any—and he never redeemed it. In time it came into stock, amongst a lot of other miscellaneous goods. This man, whom I now know as Kest, bought it. But I'd examined it, before that, more than once, and I know that amongst its various contents was a map, folded in oiled silk, with an outer wrapping of thin canvas. In my opinion that's the silk, and that's the canvas!"

"Getting at things!—getting at things!" chuckled Preece, rubbing his hands. "Narrowing down, things are—get to a fine point, presently!"

But Trace and Macpherson and myself were concentrated on Silvermore. And Trace put the question that was in the minds of all three.

"The map, now? Can you remember anything about it?"

Silvermore seemed trying to clear his memory. He struck me as a punctilious man, anxious not to lead anybody astray.

"Well, something," he answered. "I've seen a good many similar things—drawn by sailors. It was—I've called it a map, but it was a rough chart. There was a round dot in the middle, with the word *mill* written against it, in very faint characters. There were marks here and there on the paper which I couldn't understand. There was a faint line running from the centre dot down the paper—sloping, I fancy, to what you might call the south-east. And there were some figures—several figures."

"Was there anything—words, lettering, that sort of thing—to indicate where the place was?" asked Trace.

"No! But up at the top in the right-hand corner there was figuring that I took to be the longitude and latitude," replied Silvermore. "And I think— I'm not clear or positive about it—but I think that in one place there was a mark in red ink. That's my general impression, as far as I can recollect."

"Did Kest know the map was in the box when he bought it?" asked Trace.

"I suppose so—he'd full liberty to turn over everything that was in the box," replied Silvermore. "It was full of odds and ends—none of any value. Curiosities, all of them, but not worth anything."

"Do you remember anything about the man who originally pawned the box with you?" enquired Trace. "A sailor, you said."

"A sailor, yes. But I don't remember much of him—it's years ago. This last affair, selling the box to Kest," continued Silvermore, "is recent—a few months since. Personally, I've no more doubt that the map you're talking about is the map that was in that ditty-box than I have that Kest was the man who burgled my shop!"

"Just so!" said Preece. "Not a doubt about either! As I say, we're getting on fine! Well, gentlemen, I think that's all this morning. I must ride into town and report—very satisfactory budget of information too, eh?"

He was turning away, with the warder and the jeweller in attendance, when Macpherson, who had been attentively observing him, tapped his uniformed arm.

"Man," he said, in his driest fashion, "ye amaze me!"

Preece drew himself up, staring, amused and good-natured.

"Oh!" he exclaimed. "Aye, and how's that, Mr. Macpherson?"

"Ye're that well content wi' yourself!" answered Macpherson. "Rubbing your hands and laughing to yourself as if ye'd achieved a great feat o' mental strength. Man, ye've done nothing—nothing at all, so far!"

"I was thinking we'd done a great deal, Mr. Macpherson," replied Preece. "Come, now——"

"Man, ye've a twisted mind!" persisted Macpherson. "Ye can't see straight—not even along your line o' duty! Here ye are devoting all your energies to finding out who and what yon puir murdered body was, and none to discovering who murdered and robbed him! Ye're at the wrong game! It's not the character and antecedents of Kest that's important. What is important is a plain solution of the problem—who killed Kest?"

"We have to solve problems in our own way, Mr. Macpherson," said Preece good-humouredly. "We want to know all about Kest, to begin with. We didn't know at first. Now we know that Kest was a burglar, an ex-convict, a bad lot——"

"Aye, but ye don't know and ye haven't got the least idea who stuck that knife in Kest's throat!" interrupted Macpherson. "And ye're not going the right way about to find out. Man, ye want one of those smart London men down here! I'm surprised at your superiors——"

But Preece had had enough of that, and he picked up the canvas and the oilskin.

"I'll tell 'em what you advise, Mr. Macpherson," he said, as he motioned his companions to follow him. "Of course, we country police haven't got the brains of those Scotland Yard chaps; but we do our best, Mr. Macpherson, we do our best, you know!"

This asseveration failed to convince Macpherson. He went away to the nearest railway station grumbling, and I thought Trace was probably right when he said that we should have him back again before long.

# CHAPTER TEN

## THE HILL-SIDE—MIDNIGHT

I don't know whether Sergeant Preece told his superiors of Macpherson's strictures, or whether he didn't. But within the next few days, and after the authorities had buried Kest in a corner of the churchyard (nobody came forward to claim him, or betray any knowledge of him), two or three men appeared in the village whom Trace declared to be from Scotland Yard, and who occupied themselves in going over the ground which, to do him justice, Preece had already gone over with patient thoroughness. They were the sort of men who wrap themselves in mystery, and what they did, and how much they discovered, or whether they discovered anything at all that was not already known, it is beyond me to say. My own opinion at that time was that Macpherson was just about right in saying that the police took an infinite lot of trouble to find out who and what Kest was, and rejoiced greatly in proving him an ex-convict and a burglar, but very little to discover the identity of the man who knifed him. There was a great deal of talk, and much labour in getting sworn statements from people—I myself, summoned into the presence of a great personage, saw a formidable pile of these things on his desk—but when Kest had been a fortnight in his grave there was not a soul thereabouts who was any the wiser as to the direct cause of his having been thrust there. It seemed to me that there was an inclination to let the matter drop; the clever men from London vanished as quietly as they had come; Preece went about his ordinary avocations. He was a reserved man, Preece, and said little; but I gathered from a chance remark of his that his own belief was that Kest had been followed to the old mill by some man who knew that he had money on him, and had there been robbed in his sleep and murdered on his awaking, and that the murderer had got clean away and would never be found. And, after all, Kest was an uncommon bad lot, and the world could well spare him. Certainly the world wasn't going to stand still because Kest had left it; so said Preece.

Preece's attitude, I think, was that of his neighbours'. Whether they continued to regard me, or Trace and me conjointly, with the suspicion of which Halkin had been kind enough to tell us, we could not tell; there was nothing in the outward behaviour of the villagers to show that they did. The general atmosphere made you think that in rustic opinion the job was over. No thoroughbred countryman ever cries over spilt milk—and the spilling of Kest's blood was no great matter: the thing was done. I question—from what we heard—if Kest's murder remained a principal topic of conversation at the inn for more than the usual nine days—something else, some local topic, drove it out. All the same, there, still lodging at the inn, still sitting, for the most part, they said, silent and morose, in its parlour of an evening, drinking rum and sucking at his pipe, and, when he was not thus occupied, wandering about the hill-side with drooping head and hands in pockets, was Trawlerson.

Trawlerson appeared to have forgotten his desirable residence at Fareham, with the mast in the front garden and the bit of glass at the back. Anyway, for the time being, he had taken root at the scene of Kest's murder, and he divided his day equally between the immediate neighbourhood of it and the inn parlour. I think he used to meditate in the inn on what he had seen or learnt on the hill-side. Every morning and afternoon you could see him up there, sometimes motionless against the sky-line, apparently staring at nothing, sometimes walking about, up and down, this way and that, his eyes on the turf at his feet. He became monosyllabic in his conversation too, they said. Trace and I got none of it, for if we met him, he favoured us with no more than a scowling nod. The only man he was ever seen in talk with was Fewster, the retired gentleman, with whom he was sometimes observed in close converse in lonely places. But Fewster was not a frequenter of the inn. He, of course, had his bottle at home, therefore nobody was in a position to know what he and Trawlerson talked about. When you once got to know Trawlerson, the landlord of the inn said, he was the quietest man as ever was, and carried plenty of money in his pocket.

To everybody officially concerned with the Kest case, Trawlerson, of course, was the mystery man. Trace and Macpherson considered it proper that I should tell the authorities about Trawlerson's coming to me and offering me a hundred pounds in gold, there and then, for the map which I hadn't got, and when the adjourned inquest was held, the coroner had Trawlerson before him again and questioned him strictly about that little matter. He got nothing out of him. Trawlerson said he'd a perfect right to buy the map if he liked, and if he could find it; and as to any reason for his wish to require possession of it, that was his affair. Then he flung a question at coroner and jury which made them stare at him—How did they know the map wasn't his, and that if he had given me a hundred pounds for it, if I'd had it, it would only have been as a reward for restoring lost—perhaps stolen—property? Nobody—not even Halkin—said a word to Trawlerson in reply to that. It was evident that they felt him too tough a nut to be cracked—readily, at any rate.

It was just after the jury, on the coroner's direction, had returned a verdict to the effect that Kest was murdered by some person unknown, that Trace had to go away for a few days to see about his little property in another part of the country. He left me and his housekeeper in charge of his cottage, pressing on me to stay there until he came back, because he had some scheme for my future which he wanted to discuss with me at leisure. I had no objection: looking after the garden and the trees was a much more congenial occupation than weighing out pounds of tea and sugar at Macpherson's. But that pastoral life got broken in upon.

Chrissie Hentidge broke in upon it. By that time I knew all about Chrissie Hentidge and Trace. Middle-aged, or nearly middle-aged folk though they were, Chrissie and Trace were in love with each other: always had been, said Trace, from their first acquaintance. But Chrissie was under a vow. Her mother, on her death-bed, had made her swear, on the family Bible, that she would never marry while her father lived, and Chrissie was a religious woman. So—she and Trace were waiting, and in the meantime both of them, as I saw, doing all they could to make old Hentidge live to be a hundred. That was the sort of man and woman they were—good folk.

Chrissie Hentidge sent for me on the fourth afternoon of Trace's absence. She met me at the gate of their garden, and I saw at once that she had some secret.

"Tom," she said, "I want to tell you something that I should tell Captain Trace if he were at home, and that I don't want to tell Sergeant Preece—yet, anyway. You can keep a secret?"

She said this more as if she knew that I could than as if asking whether I could, and I answered her with a nod.

"Come round to the back of the house," she continued. "I want to show as well as tell you something."

I followed her round to the other side of the old farmstead, where the walls rose abruptly at the foot of the hill on the topmost height of which the mill stood. There she pointed to a window in one of the gables.

"That's my father's bedroom, Tom," she said. "You see, it looks out over the hill-side. Now, my father is often very wakeful at night, and I have to sit up with him, and I spend a good deal of time by that window, looking out while he's dropping off to sleep. I've been at that window a lot during the last few nights, Tom, and last night, and the night before, I saw something!"

I knew at once that she had the recent events in her mind, and I jumped eagerly at whatever it was she was going to tell me.

"Yes, yes, Miss Hentidge!" I exclaimed. "What was it?"

"The figure of a man, Tom!" she answered. "Going up and down, and round about, on the hill-side, up there!"

I let out the first name I thought of.

"Trawlerson!"

She was well acquainted with all Trawlerson's doings and characteristics and sinister behaviour, for Trace kept her and her father fully informed, and she nodded at my suggestion.

"Very likely," she said. "I thought of him. But, of course, I couldn't see who he was. A man! As I say, going up and down and round about. Do you see those trees up there—those oak trees, a quarter or so up the hill-side? There! All in and around there. As if he were looking for something."

"What time was it?" I asked.

"Just before twelve o'clock—midnight," she replied. "There's a moon now—I could see him clearly. Last night it was that time—the night before, a bit earlier."

"How long was he there?"

"Perhaps half-an-hour, each time. The first night I saw him, he was there when I looked from the window, going about; last night, I saw him come. He came up through the gorse-bushes across there; he went back the same way."

"Must be Trawlerson!" I said. "He's always haunting that hill-side. He's there every morning and every afternoon; now perhaps he's taken to going there at night too."

"Maybe!" she agreed. "But, Tom!—suppose—suppose it was the man who murdered Kest?—whoever it is! That map, Tom?—suppose it refers to some place, to something, on the hill-side there, below the mill, and the murderer's come back to seek the place out?"

I jumped readily to that, too.

"All right, Miss Hentidge!" I said resolutely. "I'll know more about it to-night, if he comes again. I'll be there!"

"You won't run into any danger?" she asked anxiously. "If it's the murderer——"

"I'll take good care he never sees me at all!" said I. "But I'll see him!—and close enough, too, to know who he is. If he's anybody I know, all right—I shall know where to find him in the morning. If he's a stranger—then I shall track him wherever he goes."

We talked over the matter a little more, and I arranged with her that she was to watch at the window again, and that if I wanted help I was to make a certain signal, on which she was to send her farm-men to my assistance. And leaving her, I went up the hill-side—on which Trawlerson, for a wonder, was not to be seen just then—and took a glance at the part she had indicated. There was a sort of plateau there with a lot of dwarf oak on it, and a great deal of gorse and bramble—a wild bit altogether, but favourable for my purpose as having plenty of cover. And, there being nobody about,

I made my dispositions for the coming night, fixing on a spot whereat I could hide myself in such a fashion that while I could see whoever came prowling around there, it would be an almost impossible thing for any such prowler to see me.

I said nothing to Trace's old housekeeper about my intentions. She went to bed at her usual hour, and I dare say she thought I went to my bed too. Certainly I went to my room, but before midnight I was out of it again, through the window. Nor did I go unaccompanied, for I had one of Trace's two service pistols with me, loaded and ready in the right-hand pocket of my coat. I thought that a wise precaution—who knew what dangerous situation might not lie before me?

I had timed my excursion so as to gain my cover on the hill-side before the moon rose, and everything went very well. I was safely hidden away amongst the gorse-bushes—and anybody who knows Sussex gorse knows what splendid cover it makes—before even the moon showed over the ridge on my left hand. Everything was very still there, and very lonely; there was not a sign of life anywhere about except the very faint gleam of a night-light in old Hentidge's bedroom far beneath the place in which I had ensconced myself. I heard a clock in the stables of the big house strike twelve; some time passed after that, and still nothing happened. And it must have been getting on towards one o'clock, and the moon was rising steadily to a fair height, when I heard footsteps in the scrub, somewhere down the hill. They came nearer and nearer. At last a man emerged from the thick growth immediately in front of me and came out boldly, and with no apparent attempt at secrecy, on the plateau. He turned a little in my direction, and the moon falling full on his face, I recognised him at once.

Chissick!

I don't know whether I was surprised, or whether I wasn't. I believe that I merely wondered—leaving the Kest case clean aside—whatever Chissick, who could have come there whenever he liked in broad daylight, should be doing there at that hour of the night. I don't think I felt any surprise about Chissick; I was merely curious as to what he was after. I even wondered if he was poaching, and had got some snares set for rabbits. And then I settled down to watch him.

Chissick's proceedings were odd, to say the least of it. He began by striding distances between trees. I heard him counting his paces. Then he measured off some of the ground, also by pacing it. He walked round and round some of the trees. Finally, he paced off a parallelogram which took in most of the trees—all dwarf oak—and a good deal of the gorse. When he had done that he went away. And he went away so decisively, his very action showing that his job was done for that night, that after a time I went away too, and straight home to bed.

I told Chrissie Hentidge all about that in the morning. She seemed relieved, and her eyes looked as if she had found the solution of a problem.

"Chissick, was it?" she said. "Well, now, that perhaps explains it. Chissick—you know he's a speculating builder?—builds houses on the chance of selling them. He bought a great piece of that hill-side some time ago—perhaps a year back. To build on, of course. But so far he's never built anything. Perhaps he's going to begin building."

"Why does he do his measuring in the middle of the night?" I asked. "He isn't killed with work, as far as I've seen. He's always lounging about."

"That certainly seems queer," she admitted. "Perhaps he doesn't want anybody to know what's in his mind. But——"

But just then, as if to answer our questions, we saw Chissick himself. He was coming up the lane. He had workmen with him: some carried tools; one led a horse and wagon in which was stacked a quantity of building material. And twenty or thirty yards behind this small procession, and as if dogging it, came the sinister figure of Trawlerson.

# CHAPTER ELEVEN

## THE LOCK-UP SHED

Chissick threw us a cheery good morning as he and his men went by, and Chrissie Hentidge was quick to respond to it.

"Going to do a bit of building, Mr. Chissick?" she asked. "Where, now?"

Chissick halted and turned towards the garden wall, where Chrissie and I were standing. He pointed up the hill-side.

"Nothing very considerable, Miss Hentidge," he answered. "Couple of nice little bungalows on that bit of land I bought some time ago. On the hill-side there."

Chrissie affected concern.

"I hope you won't spoil the look-out from our back windows, Mr. Chissick," she remarked, "Red brick, now! Not much in keeping with the rest of the place, you know!"

"Well, miss, use comes before ornament," replied Chissick. "There's the land, and it's a pity not to make use of it. But there's no need to fear—I shan't spoil the prospect from your back windows. For one thing, I shan't cut down any trees: they'll all be left standing. Some of the gorse'll have to be cleared away, to be sure, but I shall plant shrubs. Oh, they'll be very smart little places, gay and bright, I assure you, when I've done with them. Here's the picture of them, as they will be—when finished."

He unrolled a screed of cartridge-paper which he carried under his arm, and showed us a vividly tinted water-colour sketch of twin bungalows, with the hill and its mill in the background, the dwarf oak trees *in situ*, and—so far imaginary—gardens laid out in the foreground.

"Of course, the gardens aren't there yet," he continued apologetically. "This picture represents the place as it will be when finished. Highly desirable residences they'll be, Miss Hentidge! Splendid views on all sides; south aspect; the sea in front; the hills behind; plenty of sun and shelter. And in the bungalows themselves, all the latest improvements and conveniences—everything up to date."

"Oh, well, if they look like that!" said Chrissie concedingly. "What I don't like is a hideous red-brick cottage, Mr. Chissick, stuck down where it oughtn't to be."

"Oh, nothing of that sort, nothing of that sort!" protested Chissick. "These, you see, are in thorough keeping with the scenery. What with letting all the old trees remain, and planting the right sort of shrubs, and with the shingled roofs and general style of architecture, they'll melt into the atmosphere like sugar into tea, Miss Hentidge. There'll be no difficulty about selling or letting them, I can tell you! Better get your father to buy 'em off me—when finished."

"How much will you want for them?" asked Chrissie in business-like fashion.

"I'll tell you, Miss Hentidge," answered Chissick, equally business-like. "I can do them, all finished and ready to go into, for a thousand pounds apiece—freehold. Each, of course, has its own plot of land—forty feet by two hundred, Miss Hentidge. Yes—say a thousand apiece."

"I'll think about it," said Chrissie. "We should have bought that piece of hill-side as it was if you hadn't stepped in first. And that's one reason why I don't want to see it spoiled—it's right under our eyes."

"No spoiling, Miss Hentidge, no spoiling!—and you think about my offer," said Chissick. "All complete—spick-and-span order—ready for occupancy—two thousand for the pair—and freehold!"

He rolled up his picture and went hurrying off to the hill-side, and after talking a little longer with Chrissie, I followed him. His men were already unloading building materials from the cart close to the place from which I had watched their master after his pacings and reckonings at midnight. Further away up the rise of the hill, seated on a rock, where, of late times, I had often seen him sitting, silent and morose, for hours, was Trawlerson, watching their doings.

Chissick was a chatty and approachable man, and I feared no rebuff from him when I went up and asked him what he and his men were going to do first. I had my own reasons (arising out of what I had seen during the night) for asking that question, but Chissick took it at its surface value.

"Do, my lad?" he replied. "Why, first lay out this stuff we've brought with us, and then fetch some more and lay that out—all in readiness, you understand. And then—well, then we're going to build a bit of a shed."

"What's the shed for, Mr. Chissick?" I enquired innocently.

"The shed, my lad? Why, to keep tools in, and do odd jobs of carpentry, and masonry, and the like," he answered. "First thing to be done, that, my lad, when you start building a house—must have a shed to work in. Men can't carry their tools backwards and forwards, you know—oh, a nice shed's a great convenience, when you've a bit of building work on the go. Now let's see—where shall we put ours?"

He began to walk about, his hands under the tails of his coat, examining the lie of the ground. He made great show of this, inspecting first one place and then another, but I was not surprised when he finally stopped by a tree which I had seen him examining with great care during his nocturnal visit.

"I think this'll be a good place," he remarked musingly. "Under this tree, and nicely clear of the site, and yet close to it. Catch hold of that, my lad, and give a hand," he continued, producing a big measuring-tape from his pocket, and flinging one end of it to me. "We'll just get the dimensions."

Now, as all this became of considerable importance later on, I wish to be exact in describing what Chissick actually did as regards his preparations for building that shed. The tree to which he had just referred was an old oak which stood on an imaginary line that you could have drawn from the mill at the top of the down to the corner of Hentidge's farmstead at the foot, and about equidistant from either. It was a much older and bigger oak than any of the others on the hill-side; I dare say the other oaks were its children or grandchildren. And it stood alone; in its way, it was as much a landmark as the mill itself. I had noticed that Chissick did a lot of pacing about it when I watched, unknown to him, at midnight; now, I holding one end of his measuring-tape and he the other, he proceeded to measure a distance of so many feet from its trunk in a south-easterly direction; the exact distance I could not see, for my end of the tape began at zero and he kept his figures under his thumb, but it seemed to me to be about forty feet. And there he made a mark in the turf, and motioning me to come up to him with my end, instructed me to put it down again on his mark.

"That'll do for a corner," he said. "We'll start from that as from a corner. Now then, let me see—yes, I think a twelve-foot square shed'll do, or maybe we'll make it fifteen by twelve. Plenty of room—yes, we'll make it fifteen by twelve."

We measured the space he wanted, and he called up a man and made him place pegs at the corners. Then he summoned other men and gave them instructions; within five minutes these men were at work on the preliminaries. Chissick rubbed his hands.

"Have that shed all up and finished by to-morrow night, my lad!" he said gleefully. "Not a thing o' beauty, perhaps, but then 'tis only temp'ry. Yes, my lad, by to-morrow night—lock, stock, and barrel, as they say!"

That was a Thursday—a Thursday morning. Chissick was as good as his word by five o'clock on the Friday afternoon the shed was finished—I was there when the men put the finishing touches to it, and Chissick gave me a look of triumph.

"There, my lad!" he exclaimed. "What did I tell you? Here we are!—all complete. A good, serviceable, water-tight performance. Now, if we could run up those bungalows as sharp as that—what?"

I walked into the completed shed and looked round. And a certain fact struck me at once.

"Mr. Chissick," said I, "you haven't got a window in your shed!"

He gave me a sharp glance and shook his head.

"No!" he replied. "No, we've no window, my lad. You see, it's mainly for a tool-house, and to keep odd things in. Cement, now—you couldn't leave cement out in the rain. No, we don't need a window. It's a wide door-way, you see, and when the door's open there'll be light enough."

He himself was busied at the door just then, and I saw that he was fitting a lock to it, and that it was none of your cheap two-and-sixpenny things that any prowler could easily force, but a fine, strong lock, thoroughly secured to the woodwork on either side. And the lock was only a supplement to a bolt, a formidable bolt, that, with its staples, had already been fixed.

I watched him finish his work at the lock, and finally saw him turn the key in it from outside and put the key in his pocket.

"Good two days' work that, my lad!" he remarked, with a grin. "Preliminaries finished, eh?"

"When're you going to start on the bungalows, Mr. Chissick?" I asked. For as yet nothing had been done in that direction, save to stick white pegs in the ground at the places where the bungalows were to be built. "Soon?"

"Monday morning, my lad, Monday morning!" he answered. "Start preparing the ground Monday morning. Then—full steam ahead!" He looked round the site, and his eye travelling up the hill-side, he suddenly frowned. Following his gaze, I saw that he had caught sight of Trawlerson, sitting motionless on his rock.

"What's that fellow sit there all day for?" he exclaimed angrily. "Hanged if he ain't enough to get on a man's nerves!—always watching—watching, watching! And if he isn't watching, he's mooning. Mooning all over the place! Tell you what it is, my lad—in my opinion that man's dotty! Dotty!—that's it! Why doesn't he go home? Go home—instead of hanging around here?"

"I believe he's looking for something, Mr. Chissick," I answered.

"That's all damn silliness!" exclaimed Chissick "He was looking for a mill—well, there's a mill up above him. Brain, my lad, brain!—that's what it is. Brain gone pappy—ought to be in a 'sylum. Well—I'm going home to my tea. Captain come back yet?"

"No, Mr. Chissick," I answered. "He's coming home Sunday."

He nodded and went off, and I turned down the hill to Hentidge's—Chrissie had asked me to tea. I told her and her father all about Chissick and his doings: she and old Hentidge were mainly concerned lest he should spoil the look-out from their windows. But they seemed to have no suspicion of Chissick. It was certainly odd, observed Chrissie, that he should make his measurements by moonlight; but, anyway, there was the fact that he'd started his building operations.

It was dark when I left the Hentidges'. That was about ten o'clock; I had lingered that late listening to the old man, who, over his evening paper and glass, was fond of talking of bygone days. In the darkness, as I went out of the farmstead garden into the road, I looked up the hill-side and saw a sudden flash of light, such as might be caused by the quick opening and closing of a door. It was a bright flash too, as from a strong lamp. And the thought came into my head—Chissick was up there, in that shed, and had a powerful light in it, and had opened the door for a second, perhaps to admit somebody.

I didn't hesitate a moment about going up the hill. But I went cautiously. Instead of going straight up, by a track that led direct to where the bungalows were to be built, I turned back through Hentidge's garden and orchard, climbed the wall, and skirted right round that part of the hill, finally creeping down to the shed through the gorse and bramble above it. I had no fear of being seen; the night was dark for that time of the year, and the moon was not due to rise for another two hours or more. Nor had I any fear of being heard either, for I slipped along circumspectly, as soft as a cat. In this way I got close up to the old oak tree under which Chissick had built his shed, and as soon as I looked round the trunk I saw a spark of light at the keyhole, and just a ribbon of more light at the foot of the door. But I thought little of that; what I did think something of was the fact that inside that shed somebody was digging!

Digging!—there was no doubt about that. Or, I might say, delving, though, not being a scholar, I have no exact knowledge of the meaning of that word. I know what I mean by it, though somebody in that shed was at work with a pick as well as a spade. I could hear the sounds clearly. Hard work too!—for that was hard stuff. But—there it was.

I crept up to the shed after a time, and put an eye to the keyhole. No good!—that is, I couldn't see anything—anything, at any rate, but the new white wood of the blank inner wall opposite the door. There was a brilliant light on that; whoever was in that shed had got a splendid lamp with him. But of him, and his pick, and his spade, and of the stuff he was tearing out of the earth, I couldn't see anything: he was evidently working in a corner.

As I crouched there at the door, I heard somebody coming up the hill, from the village, stealthily. At that I jumped for cover; first to the oak tree, then into and behind the nearest clump of gorse. I made a bad mistake in that second move: I ought to have stuck to the oak. For I was a bit too far off, and when a man emerged into the open, by the shed, and, after standing still for awhile, began to prowl around it, I couldn't tell who he was. A man of a medium height and thick-set figure—that was all I could definitely decide on. But I believed he was Trawlerson.

Whoever he was, the man, after stooping at the keyhole, went away, by the way he had come, and after a time, during which the digging went on more or less continuously, I too went seeing no use in staying. I hoped to have a look into the shed next morning, Saturday. But when I went up nobody was there, and the shed was locked up. Nobody came near it that day; no Chissick, no workmen.

I held my tongue about this until Trace came home on Sunday evening, when I told him all that I had seen and heard. We sat up late, theorising about the whole thing, and when at last I went to bed I dreamt that I was in the shed, and that somebody was knock, knock, knocking at the door—no end of knocking. Then I woke to find the light just breaking, and Trace at my bedside, shaking me.

"Get up, Tom!" he said, as I started from my pillow. "Didn't you hear Preece thumping at our door? Here's murder again!—murder! It's Chissick!—murdered in his own house!"

# CHAPTER TWELVE

## THE DEAD MAN'S SAFE

I was out of bed and bundling into my clothes before I found words with which to reply to Trace. In the end I only found one, and my voice sounded queer and thick as I stuttered it out.

"Murdered!"

"So Preece says, Tom! Found murdered in his own house, not an hour ago. And, by the look of him, dead for some little time," replied Trace. "When did you see him last?—Friday afternoon, wasn't it?"

"Friday afternoon, about five o'clock," I answered. "He was all right then."

"No doubt!" said Trace dryly. "Well—that's where it is! Come on—Preece is waiting for us; he wants our help."

We hurried downstairs, to find the sergeant, himself half dressed, pacing up and down at the garden gate. Without a word he turned off towards Chissick's house, which stood two or three hundred yards away, at the end of the village, in a lonely place at the foot of the hill. But before we had gone many yards, he began to talk.

"Whether this is all of a piece with the other affair or not, I don't know, Captain!" he said, with the air of a man who finds himself up against a bewildering problem. "But it's murder, right enough! No possible doubt of it!"

"You haven't told me much about it yet, you know," remarked Trace.

"Don't know much myself," answered Preece. "Only sufficient to know that it's murder! How was it found out? Well, you know Stephens, the gamekeeper? He and one of his watchers have been out all night in the preserves. Early this morning they were coming home, and their way brought them past Chissick's garden gate. They heard that little black spaniel of his whimpering at his front door. So they went in and looked through the windows. They saw nothing from the front—the blinds and curtains were drawn there. But through the kitchen window they saw Chissick lying on the floor, half in, half out of a passage-way communicating between kitchen and parlour. And—they saw blood! So Stephens forced the scullery door and they went in and found Chissick was dead, and, as Stephens said, cold as ice—been dead some time. Then they fetched me, and I ran back there and just had a look. Then I came for you."

He paused for a minute, shaking his head as if in dislike of the recollection of what he'd seen; then he went on.

"You see, anybody who knows about Chissick and his mode of life, as I do, can get a ready idea of how this has been done. To start with, Chissick was a bachelor—lived alone too. He couldn't have a maid-servant in his house; he'd a charwoman, Mrs. Watson, who went there of a morning. Sundays she never went at all, because Chissick always spent his week-ends away, usually at Brighton, where he had a brother living. He generally went off of a Saturday afternoon to Brighton. And I think he was probably going to Brighton this week-end, for I did just notice on glancing at him that he'd his best suit of clothes on, and that there was a small suit-case lying on the kitchen table. That looks, of course, as if he'd been murdered on Saturday. Nice, black job! And also, of course, what one wants to know now is—has this anything to do with the last affair?"

Trace offered no opinion on that point; we were close to Chissick's house by that time, and I think he and I were nerving ourselves for our unpleasant task. I know I hated the whole thing. It was a beautiful morning; the sun was just rising, and the birds were singing gaily in the orchards and coppices. Chissick's garden was bright and smiling with flowers. Yet here was this awful sense of fell murder; at the house-door stood Stephens and his man, grave-faced and silent, and somewhere in an outhouse close by, where they had shut it up, we heard the spaniel crying for its dead master.

We went in very quietly and looked at Chissick. He lay, as Preece had said, half in, half out of a narrow passage; it seemed as if he had been struck down in coming from the parlour to the kitchen. And presently, when Preece made a closer examination, we saw how he had been murdered—by a savage blow, perhaps more than one blow, on the head with some heavy weapon; probably, said Preece, a bar of iron. No doubt he had been struck down from behind, by some man following him—a man whom he had admitted to his house and was most likely conducting to the door again. Indeed, as Preece said, it didn't seem difficult to understand what had happened from the fact that Chissick was in his best suit and that his suit-case lay on a table close by and an overcoat and umbrella on a chair near the door. He had been about to leave home; a man had come to the house; he had let him in; they had talked; Chissick was showing his caller out again and preceding him to the door; the caller had beaten the life out of him. And that was in all probability on Saturday afternoon; perhaps on Saturday morning, and nearly forty-eight hours had elapsed.

Preece went out to the two men at the door and sent one of them for the nearest doctor and the other to telephone to the police authorities. Standing at the door as they hurried off, he drew our attention to the situation of the house.

"Not another house near it!" he said. "At least, not within a hundred yards. And there, at the end of the garden, the woods come right up! The murderer had nothing to do but slip through the garden and into the woods and make off. But—what was his object in murdering Chissick? We'd best have a look round, Captain."

We went carefully over the house, leaving the dead man where he lay until the doctor could examine him. There was no sign of any fight or struggle. It was not a big house—an affair of some seven or eight rooms. Everything was in spick-and-span order. It was easy to see that Chissick had been one of those naturally orderly and methodical men who cannot bear to have things out of place: the most exacting old maid could not have found fault with anything there. And there was no sign that the murderer had searched for anything.

Preece looked at his watch and turned to me.

"The morning's getting on," he observed. "Mrs. Watson'll be up now. Just step along to her cottage, my lad, and ask her to come here at once. Don't tell her what's happened—I'll do that."

Mrs. Watson's cottage stood down an adjacent lane; I found her lighting her fire. She knew, of course, that something was wrong as soon as I gave her my message, but she asked no questions, and presently followed me in silence to Chissick's garden, where Preece and Trace were awaiting us. Preece told her the news, briefly. She was a phlegmatic woman, and, beyond an exclamation of horror, took it without any show of emotion.

"Well, of course, he lived alone, did Mr. Chissick, and he kept money in the house," she observed. "Many's the time I've said to him that there was danger in living like that! People gets to know of it."

"How do you know he kept money in the house?" asked Preece.

"Well, Mr. Preece, because I've seen him a-counting of it," replied Mrs. Watson. "Frequent I've seen him, for a many years. Fridays it was when he gen'rally had a lot of money about—used to count it on the table in his parlour, and didn't care about me seeing it, nor anybody else, neither, as happened to come in."

"Pooh!" said Preece. "That would be money for his men's wages! He'd have got rid of it by Friday night. It's not been for that, I think. Now, when did you see him last, Mrs. Watson?"

"Saturday morning, Mr. Preece. About eleven o'clock it would be. He was in the house all that morning; never went out. He'd his breakfast later than usual. Then he dressed himself up in his best clothes and packed his portmantle, and when he gave me my money for the week he said he was going to Brighton for the week-end, as was his custom, and I needn't come on Monday or Tuesday morning, for he was going on Monday from Brighton to London."

"To London, eh?" said Preece. "Did he give any reason—say what he was going for?"

"No, sir—he said no more than that," replied Mrs. Watson. "Except that he'd let me know when he got home—he might be home Tuesday, he said, or it might be Wednesday."

"And you left him in the house—alone?"

"Oh yes, Mr. Preece! There was nobody with him when I left. He was putting on his boots in the kitchen. That 'ud be about twenty minutes after eleven."

"You haven't heard of anybody being seen about the house, Mrs. Watson?"

"No, sir—I haven't heard anything. I've never been up this way, either, since Saturday morning."

There was nothing more to be got out of Mrs. Watson, and nothing to be done until the doctor arrived. Preece, evidently, was resolved not to move the dead man until he had been seen by a medical authority. But we had not long to wait; the doctor—the same man who had been fetched to Kest—was with us before eight o'clock, and close on his heels came a police-inspector and a couple of constables.

The doctor gave it as his opinion that Chissick had been dead since, at any rate, Saturday afternoon. Preece, hearing this, pointed out that he already had evidence that Chissick was going to Brighton, and that there was a train to Brighton from the nearest station at twelve-forty; it would take Chissick, he said, half an hour to walk to that station, and therefore the probability was that his intention was to leave his house about twelve o'clock. Mrs. Watson had left him at eleven-twenty; the murderer must have called between eleven-twenty and twelve. Did the doctor think the murder had taken place between these times? The doctor said it was possible; anyway, he was sure that Chissick had been dead for at least forty to forty-two hours. And he had been dealt two terrible blows at the back of the head, either of which was sufficient to kill him instantly. One blow, declared the doctor, had been dealt as he lay on the floor—to make certain.

The next thing was to examine Chissick's clothing. There was nothing unusual or remarkable there. There were a few business letters in a case in his inside pocket, and a considerable sum of money in his purse—considerable, that is, for a man to carry about him—and that and his handsome gold watch and chain had been left untouched. In fact, the murderer, it seemed, had never laid finger on his victim after striking him down, and it was difficult to think of him as thief as well as murderer. Everything that Chissick had on him appeared to have been left unhandled—it looked as if the murderer had done his work and gone straight away.

There was a small bunch of keys amongst the articles turned out of the dead man's pockets, and the inspector and Preece, accompanied by Trace and myself, went into the parlour to see if they fitted a roll-top desk and drawers that stood there. It was while they were examining this desk, in which they found nothing but account books and papers relating to Chissick's business affairs, that Trace noticed a small safe which stood under an occasional table in a recess: a safe so small that it might have been taken as a miniature specimen rather than an article for use. He suggested that they might try that, and Preece presently found a key on the bunch that fitted the lock.

"Very ordinary lock this, for a safe," he remarked, as he pulled open the tiny door, "and not much of a safe either. Not likely to find much here, I think."

The safe was comparatively empty. There were some ledgers and account books in it, and some bundles of papers, which, on examination, proved to be leases, conveyances, and the like. But on pulling open a small drawer, which lay beneath the shelf on which the books and papers rested, we saw two objects that instantly arrested my attention and made me start with eagerness to handle them; indeed, I half thrust out a hand to get hold of them. Preece, of course, was before me at that game; he had the things out in a trice and turned to the rest of us with them in his hand—a little packet of bank-notes and . . . a map.

I think that Trace as well as myself had an instinctive notion of what we were going to see. I know I held my breath as Preece unfolded the map. But I found my tongue quick enough when he had unfolded it.

"That's the map that Kest had in the mill!" I exclaimed. "I know it!"

The police-inspector eyed me closely.

"Sure of it, my lad?" he asked.

"Dead certain!" said I. "That's Kest's map! There's the black spot I told you of, and there are the lines. Oh, that's it!"

The three men—Preece, Trace, the inspector—looked at each other. I knew what they were thinking. How came Kest's map in Chissick's safe?

"Look at those notes, Preece," said the inspector suddenly. "They are notes, aren't they?"

There was an india-rubber band round the notes. Preece slipped it off and turned each note over.

"Two notes of ten pounds apiece, four notes of five," said Preece. "Bank of England notes—new ones."

Both Preece and the inspector had been present at the inquest on Kest. And now they looked at each other—a world of suspicion in their eyes.

"Didn't that bank-clerk who gave evidence about Kest say that Kest drew some money in notes and gold from the bank the Monday before he was murdered?" asked the inspector. "Runs in my mind he did."

"He did!" replied Preece promptly. "A hundred pounds. Forty pounds in notes, sixty in gold. He said they'd the numbers of the notes at the bank."

The inspector nodded and began to examine the map again. Suddenly he turned on me with a sharp question.

"No mistake?" he said. "You're certain about this map?"

"I can swear to it!" said I. "There's no mistake. That's the map I saw Kest examining in the old mill."

"Well, this is a nice state of things!" he exclaimed, looking at Trace and the sergeant. "Here we find Chissick murdered, and in possession of this map and these bank-notes which appear to have belonged to Kest, already murdered! This young fellow swears to the map; the question of the bank-notes we can soon settle by telephoning to the bank. But—how come these things in Chissick's possession? Seems to me, Captain Trace, this is a bigger mystery than the other! And are they both one?"

We went away from the house soon after that, Trace and I. I think we were both full of the same wondering thought—was Chissick, now murdered himself, the murderer of Kest?

# CHAPTER THIRTEEN

## SUSPECT

One thing and another, we were very late in sitting down to Trace's break-fast-table that morning, and we were still there when Preece and the inspector walked in on us. It was easy to see that they had more news.

"We've settled that point, Captain!" said Preece. "Those bank-notes, you know. They're the same!"

"You mean—the notes that were paid out to Kest?" exclaimed Trace. "You've ascertained that—definitely?"

"Definitely!—no doubt whatever about it," replied Preece. "I've just been on the telephone with the bank people. Those notes that we found in Chissick's safe are the identical notes paid out to Kest as part of the hundred pounds he drew! That's certain—no getting away from it. And now, then—how did they come into Chissick's hands?"

Trace pointed at me.

"I think Tom Crowe had better tell you both of certain mysterious doings on the part of Chissick during the last few days and nights," he remarked. "And," he added, turning to me, "don't forget the man you couldn't identify, Tom. Begin at the beginning."

I told Preece and the inspector of everything that had happened on the hill-side, from the time at which Miss Hentidge told me of the midnight visitant, to that in which Chissick locked up the completed shed. And I saw at once that what impressed them most was the conclusion of the story, in which I described the stealthy coming of the unknown man.

"You couldn't say who he was?" suggested Preece. "Couldn't make a guess?"

"I couldn't say, Mr. Preece. He wasn't near enough. But," I added, "I thought it was—I mean, I thought it might be Trawlerson."

"There's a difference between thinking it was Trawlerson and thinking it might be," said Preece uneasily. "You couldn't say positively it was Trawlerson?"

"No, I couldn't!" said I. "That's a fact!"

"Why did you think it might be?" he asked.

"Well, it was like his figure—just his height and build. But I'd other reasons," I said. "Trawlerson had never been away from that spot from the time Chissick started work on it! He was there all day long—watching. Chissick remarked on it to me—said Trawlerson was enough to get on his nerves. He'd some extraordinary curiosity about what was going on, Trawlerson."

"We shall have to question Trawlerson," observed Preece. "But first, this shed. I've got the map here," he went on, feeling in his pocket. "We've been studying it, me and the inspector—superficially, there's lines, figures, measurements on it. Look at it, my lad—where do you make this shed to be?"

"Right there!—where that line's drawn down from the black spot," I answered promptly. "This line, with the figures at the side of it."

"I take that black spot to be the mill," said Preece. "So the line evidently points to a place so many yards, so many feet, beneath it?"

"That's just what you'll find it does, Mr. Preece," I said. "And you'll find, too, that the line ends underneath the biggest oak tree up there, and it's alongside that oak, beneath the long lower bough, in fact, that Chissick built the shed."

"Well, we'll go up there," remarked Preece. "I've got a lot of keys that we found in Chissick's house, and if the shed's locked we must try them. That's the first thing to do—to see if there's anything in that shed that can throw any light on this affair. You say Chissick put a strong lock on the door?"

"And a very strong bolt—inside," I answered. "He didn't mean anybody to get in when he was busied inside, Mr. Preece. And—there's no window!"

We all set off, there and then, for the shed. I remembered what Chissick had told me—that active work on the foundations of the bungalows was to begin that morning. But there were no workmen there; the hill-side was left to itself. I glanced at the rock on which Trawlerson had been accustomed to sit for hours: it was untenanted. Preece quickly found the key which opened the door of the shed, and we all crowded in. There was nothing to see at first—nothing. I almost began to believe that I had been mistaken about the digging, for the floor looked as if it had never been disturbed. But Preece, growing accustomed to the light sooner than the rest of us, suddenly pointed to a corner.

"That's where the digging's been!" he said. "Look there!—it's plain enough. Somebody—Chissick, of course—has dug here, and when he'd found what he wanted, he's filled in the hole again."

We were all getting accustomed to the light by that time, and we saw what Preece meant. It looked as if Chissick had dug a cavity some two feet square—how deep, of course, we could not know—and having either found something in it or decided that there was nothing to find, had carefully filled it up again and levelled the turf.

"The thing is," said the inspector musingly, "the thing is—what was his object? What was he digging for?"

"I don't think there's much doubt about that!" said Trace. "The map's the key to all that! Something's been buried here. Why was Trawlerson so keen about finding this mill? Why has he stuck to the village and haunted this spot ever since he came here and heard that Kest had a map? Why did Kest come?—with the map?"

"Aye!" muttered Preece. "And how did Chissick get the map? And how did Chissick get Kest's bank-notes? The whole thing's——"

He broke off at the sound of a heavy step just outside the door. We all turned sharply. There stood Fewster, whom I knew chiefly as Chissick's friend and constant companion.

Fewster's big, flabby face was pale, and there was perspiration on it. It might be from hurrying up the hill-side, but I saw that his hand shook badly as he pulled out a huge bandanna handkerchief and began to mop himself. He looked anxiously at Preece.

"What's this I hear, Sergeant?" he asked, in a shaking voice. "Our milkman told me, and said he'd seen you coming up the hill. Chissick? Is it——"

"It's quite true, Mr. Fewster," replied Preece. "Found dead in his house, this morning. Murdered, sir! No doubt about it!"

Fewster seemed to grow paler, and I thought he trembled. He put a hand on the lintel of the door, as if to steady himself.

"No clue?" he asked sharply.

"None as yet, Mr. Fewster," said Preece. "I suppose you can't help us? You knew Chissick better than anybody, I think."

"I know nothing," answered Fewster. "Nothing! Chissick—he dropped in on me, latish, Friday night. He didn't stay long—just had a cigar and a drop of something. He mentioned that he was going to Brighton next day for the week-end. Nothing uncommon in that—it was his custom."

"Did he say anything to you about this?" asked Preece, waving his hand in a gesture that took in the shed and the piles of building material that lay about. "Make any reference to what he was doing here?"

"No more than that he was going to build a couple of smart little bungalows hereabouts," replied Fewster. "And nothing particular about that."

Preece nodded, and motioning the rest of us out of the shed, proceeded to lock the door and put the keys in his pocket.

"Well, there it is, Mr. Fewster," he said. "He's dead—murdered. That's the second murder within three weeks! We haven't solved the problem of the first yet. Now here's another—and perhaps a more difficult one. What is it, Mr. Fewster?"

For Fewster was showing unmistakable signs of anxiety to ask a question. He glanced, in a queer, speculative way, from one policeman to the other.

"There'll have been a motive," he said. "There must have been a motive! Was it—was it robbery, now?"

There was something underlying his curiosity, and I thought the policemen saw that there was, for they exchanged glances. But the inspector answered him readily enough.

"It doesn't look like robbery," he said. "He'd considerable personal effects on him, Mr. Fewster, and nothing was touched. But—why do you ask?"

Fewster was prodding holes in the turf with the ferrule of his stick. He kept his gaze on these as he made one after another, but suddenly he looked up and spoke in a low voice, as if he were telling a secret.

"I've been in a mind to see you about this, Sergeant, once or twice," he said, addressing himself to Preece. "But I'm not the man to spread rumours or make mischief. However, this is no time to mince matters. Murder!—come, that's the limit! The fact is," he went on, with a look that seemed to beckon us all round him in confidence, "the fact is—there's somebody about that shouldn't be!"

"How do you mean, Mr. Fewster?" asked Preece.

"I mean this, Sergeant," replied Fewster, with a knowing look. "This! You're not aware of it, though my doctor is, and my chemist is, but I suffer from insomnia—have done for a long time—and occasionally I try walking out late of a night as an inducement to sleep. Well, I know, as a matter of fact, that there's somebody lurks about this place at night in a fashion that shows he's up to no good!"

"You've seen somebody—or something?" suggested the inspector.

"More than once!" replied Fewster. "A man! I've seen him, late at night, cross Hentidge's lighted windows, down there, and disappear amongst Hentidge's outbuildings. I've twice or thrice seen him outlined against the sky, up there, moonlight nights. Once, as I came along Sweetbriar Lane, I saw him—it must have been the same man!—coming to meet me—he disappeared into a coppice and lay hid there till I'd gone by. And once, Captain Trace, I saw him listening and peering in at that little side-window of yours, overlooking the garden!"

"You've never been near enough to get a sight of his face?" asked Preece.

"No—but it's always the same figure—sturdily built, somewhat thick-set man," said Fewster. "One thing I do know about him—he goes about in rubber-soled shoes—steps soft, you know. And I don't want to mention names, but I think if I were you, I should get to know more about the man who's lodging at the inn—you're aware of who I mean, Sergeant!"

"I'm not afraid of mentioning names," said Preece. "You mean Trawlerson. That's the man you suspect of this midnight prowling about?"

But Fewster remained true to his principles, and with a nod which might have meant no more than a farewell for the time being, he went off. Preece turned to the rest of us, with a shake of his head.

"That's queer stuff!" he said doubtfully. "I'm out and about at night—no end!—and I haven't seen anything of this."

"You've a beaten track," remarked Trace.

"Well, more or less so, yes," admitted Preece. "But I've never heard any complaints from anybody. However, here's this lad says he saw a man at this shed when Chissick was digging whom he thought might be Trawlerson, and Mr. Fewster implies pretty plainly that he suspects Trawlerson, so I reckon we'd better go and hear what Trawlerson has to say for himself. But you know we've nothing to connect him with this, and he's a stiff nut to crack, and a hard man to draw!"

"I know what'll draw him, Mr. Preece!" I exclaimed. "And so does Captain Trace! Tell Trawlerson the map's been found!"

Preece looked at me with a dawning appreciation of the value of my suggestion, and a knowing look came into his eyes.

"Not a bad notion, my lad!" he said. "The thing is—if he knows we've got it, and that he's no chance of getting it——"

"Don't forget something that Trawlerson said at the inquest," interrupted Trace. "Do you remember?—he implied, to the coroner, that the map was his."

"He'll have to prove that!" said Preece. "I shan't let him handle it. But I think"—here he turned to the inspector—"I think we'd better see the landlord at the inn before we see Trawlerson, just to find out—eh?—what Trawlerson's movements were on Saturday and Sunday."

We went down to the village in a body. Near Hentidge's farm we met Halkin. Halkin had heard the news, and was hurrying to the inn as the distributing centre of all local information. But as soon as he saw the policeman he halted, and, waiting for us to come up, buttonholed Preece.

"This affair of Chissick's, now!" he exclaimed, so that we all could hear. "I've been talking to one of your men at Chissick's garden gate. He says that the doctor says that Chissick was murdered at noon—about noon, anyway—on Saturday. But it can't have been so, Preece, it can't have been!"

"Why can't it have been?" asked Preece, with a glance at the rest of us. "What do you know about it?"

"This much!" retorted Halkin. "I was past there on Saturday night—just about dusk—coming home from marketing. And I saw Trawlerson come away from Chissick's garden gate and heard him say good night. That 'ud be to Chissick, of course! So—Chissick must have been alive then, d'ye see? But you ask Trawlerson."

"You're sure it was Trawlerson you saw?" demanded Preece.

"Sure? Certain! You ask him," replied Halkin. "Come down to the inn—he'll tell you."

We all walked along to the inn. The landlord, in his shirt-sleeves, and with a straw in his mouth, was standing at the front. He gave the police a shrewd glance as they drew near him.

"I know who you're after," he said, with something like a wink. "No good, gentlemen! He's not here! Never seen head nor tail of him since Saturday night!"

# CHAPTER FOURTEEN

## THE MAN WHO BOUGHT FOOD

I don't think any of us were prepared for this intimation; the two police-men, I am sure, were taken aback by it; Preece looked as if he wanted to start out there and then in search of Trawlerson. Before either inspector or sergeant could speak, Halkin pushed to the front.

"Ah!" he said, with a sly chuckle that was meant to signify a great deal. "Made off, has he? And when—at what time was it on Saturday night, I mean—did he make off, now?"

The landlord, scratching his elbows and chewing his straw, looked at Halkin pretty much as a mastiff might look at an officious cur, and looked away again. He turned to the police.

"In and out he was all Saturday," he said. "It was only Saturday morn-ing I said to the wife as how he was getting stranger and stranger in his goings-on. Like one o' these figures in an old-fashioned weather-glass he was—always either out or in, and you never knew which! But quiet and well-conducted, even when he'd had his rum—and he was a good hand at that! and always down on the nail with his money. However—there 'tis! Gone!"

"What time did he go, Saturday?" asked the inspector.

"As I say, he was in and out, all Saturday," continued the landlord. "I see him last some time after he'd had his supper. He was in the parlour, then, in his fav'rite corner, where it was his custom to sit. That 'ud be about half-past eight—he took his supper at eight, reg'lar. He was in that there corner one minute, and gone the next. Never saw him go out—and ain't seen him since."

"What time was it when you saw him, Halkin?" asked Preece.

"It would be about nine," replied Halkin promptly. "I came from Chich-ester by the 8.21. That's due at our station at 8.37. It would take me nearly half an hour to walk up. Say all about nine."

"You're sure it was Trawlerson?" asked Preece.

"As sure as that I see you!" asserted Halkin. "He was coming out of Chissick's gate. As you're aware, that gate's set at the end of a thick holly hedge that leads up to the front door. He'd his head turned that way, and he was calling a good night to somebody that I couldn't see—somebody behind him hidden by the hedge. I took it to be Chissick, of course."

"Which way did Trawlerson go, then?" enquired the inspector.

"I didn't see him go any way. I'd turned my head as it was, to see him at all; I'd heard his footsteps on the gravel walk, d'ye see?" explained Halkin. "When I saw who it was, I didn't look round again, so I don't know if he came after me or where he went. But I say, you know," he continued, in his customary fussy manner, "if that was Chissick that Trawlerson called a good night to, Chissick couldn't ha' been murdered on Saturday noon! Those doctors——"

The two policemen ignored Halkin. They went into the inn, to question the landlord and his wife, and Trace and I turned homeward. Murder or no murder, there were the fowls to attend upon. Of course, we talked of the events of the morning; everybody in the neighbourhood would be talking too. Trace discussed the affair from every possible point of view. He had theories—suggestions. Taking Halkin's story about Trawlerson and Chissick's cottage to be true, perhaps the doctors had been wrong, and Chissick's murder had taken place at night. Perhaps Trawlerson was the murderer. Perhaps the good-night call which Halkin heard was a piece of bluff on Trawlerson's part—to deceive anyone who, like Halkin, happened to be about when Trawlerson was coming away from the scene of his crime. It looked, putting one thing and another together, as if Trawlerson had murdered Chissick. Trawlerson had stuck like a leech to his post on the hill-side while Chissick and his men built that shed. It must have been Trawlerson whom I had seen prowling about the shed when Chissick was digging inside. Trawlerson had come to the conclusion that Chissick had unearthed something in that shed, and he had gained admittance to Chissick's house and murdered Chissick in order to possess himself of that something. And now Trawlerson was away—probably, in the words of the old song, over the hills and far away; very far away, indeed, it might be.

I wasn't very much interested in these speculations. Ever since we had witnessed the opening of the safe in Chissick's prim parlour, one and only one question had obsessed me—how did Chissick get hold of Kest's map and Kest's bank-notes? Was Chissick the man I had seen in the sea fog, who first struggled with Kest and then knifed him? Letting my mind go back over everything I could remember about Chissick, I could scarcely bring myself to regard him as a murderer. He might be shifty, sly, crafty, unscrupulous, all that, but I couldn't see him as a man who would drive his knife into another man's throat. Still, there were the facts, Kest was murdered. I had seen him murdered. And Chissick had been proved to be in possession of things taken from Kest's body.

But we got some light on this two days later, when the inquest was opened on Chissick. There was no other light thrown on anything else, though. I suppose that all the police in the county, and perhaps some from outside its boundaries, had been hunting for Trawlerson during the forty-eight hours which had elapsed since the discovery of Chissick's murder, but they hadn't found him, nor had they come across a single trace of him. Preece, who had a commonsense way of looking at things, said that in his opinion Trawlerson had gone up to London by the last train from a neighbouring junction on the Saturday night, and was safely hidden in some sailors' haunt in the East End.

But we got this sidelight on Chissick. There was a disposition on the part of the officials to shorten the initiatory proceedings of the inquest on him; somehow or other they gave you the impression that at that stage they didn't want very much to get out. Still, they put a witness before the coroner whose evidence, when all was said and done, had nothing to do with the actual murder of Chissick—directly, at any rate—but was extremely pertinent as to the mystery of the bank-notes. This was a cattle-drover, a rough-looking but intelligent fellow, who said that, having seen all this stuff in the newspapers about first Kest, and then Chissick, he thought he'd better come forward and tell the police of certain things that he knew.

What this man—Solomon Cole—said, amounted to this: On a Monday afternoon (the Monday being at once settled by date to be that on the morning or early afternoon of which Kest drew one hundred pounds out of his bank) he, Cole, was in the parlour of the Prussian Hussar tavern at Chichester. That was about four o'clock. Everything was very quiet; he, in fact, was the only occupant of the room. Chissick came in; he knew Chissick well by sight. Chissick had with him a sharp-faced, red-haired man, with a goatee beard, who looked like a sailor: him Cole did not know, and had never seen before. Chissick and his companion sat down in a corner. Chissick ordered and paid for two glasses of whisky and two cigars. He and the red-haired man seemed to be talking business. He, Cole, now and then caught a stray word or two. The business appeared to relate to land: he heard something about freehold property, conveyancing, and the like. Eventually, when the two seemed to have reached an agreement, he heard a more definite remark from Chissick. Chissick said, as near as he could remember, "Ten per cent. deposit on the agreed price is the usual thing." He then saw the red-haired man produce a pocket-book, and from it take some bank-notes which, after counting, he handed to Chissick, who in his turn counted them before putting them in his purse. After that Chissick rang the parlour bell and borrowed pen, ink, and paper from the landlady, and when he had got them, wrote out what he, Cole, supposed to be a receipt. He gave this to the red-haired man, and soon afterwards the two men went away, Chissick having first paid for two more glasses of whisky.

Chissick's brother from Brighton was at the inquest, and he had a solicitor with him; this solicitor asked Cole questions when he had finished his evidence-in-chief. Was he watching Chissick and the red-haired man very closely? Not particularly, said Cole; he was—well, just noticing. Did he see the red-haired man give Chissick anything else than the bank-notes—a folded paper, for instance? No, replied Cole; he did not. Might the red-haired man have handed over such a paper—with the bank-notes or afterwards? He might, said Cole, but he didn't see any such paper handed over and he didn't believe it was ever shown. Mr. Chissick—he had a paper, a great roll of paper, which he spread out on the table at which he and the red-haired man sat. But the red-haired man never produced any paper that he, Cole, saw—except the bank-notes.

We all knew what Chissick's brother's solicitor wanted. He wanted to convince coroner and jury that the red-haired man, who, without doubt, was Kest, handed over to Chissick, in addition to the bank-notes, the map that was found with them. But the coroner was quick to point out that I, as witness in the Kest case, had sworn that I saw the map in Kest's possession more than twenty-four hours after the meeting at the Prussian Hussar.

"And it comes to this," said he. "I see no reason to doubt Cole's evidence. The man who was with Chissick at the Prussian Hussar was, no doubt, Kest. Kest, it would seem from Cole's evidence, was buying some land from Chissick; we know, from the evidence of the bank-clerk, that Kest had said that he was going to buy some property. Apparently, he paid Chissick a deposit on the agreed price. That accounts for Chissick's possession of these particular Bank of England notes. But it does not account for Chissick's possession of the map which the witness in the Kest case, the young man Crowe, saw in Kest's hands on the night before Kest was murdered."

Things were left at that, for the time being; that is, the inquest, as in Kest's case, was adjourned for the production of more evidence. And now, where there had been half a dozen police folk on the scene of Kest's affair, there were at least twice and at times thrice as many in Chissick's. Men came down from London—real Scotland Yard men. There was the usual examination and re-examination of village people, and especially those who lived nearest to Chissick (nobody did live very near; his charwoman, I think, was his nearest neighbour). As for me, if I told my tale once to police authorities, big and little, I told it fifty times. There were all sorts of mysterious doings at Chissick's house: searchings for finger-prints on wood and metal-work; microscopic examination of the garden for footmarks; inspection on account books and papers and letters; a general turning over and inside out of everything. It all came to nothing, by which I mean that at the end of a week the police were no wiser than before. And Trawlerson, for whom the hue-and-cry was out, was as if he had been bodily snatched up by a jinnee and set down amongst the Mountains of the Moon. Not a whisper of news about him came to hand.

Then one day, as Preece was talking to Trace and me at our garden gate, we saw a man, a stranger, come along the street and go to Preece's cottage, over the door of which, of course, were the insignia of the county constabulary. We saw him knock; we saw Mrs. Preece come out, talk to him, and then looking up and down and catching sight of her husband, point him out—Preece was in plain clothes. The man came along in our direction—an elderly, respectable, small-tradesman-looking sort of man—eyeing my two companions questioningly.

"Sergeant Preece?" he asked, looking from one to the other.

"My name, sir," replied Preece promptly. "What can I do for you, sir?"

The man took off his hat, wiped his forehead—it was a hot June morning—and leaned back against our wall.

"I've come a long way to see you, Sergeant," he said. "My name's Scale—I keep a grocer's shop over at Barlaton—other side of the hill there. Not in your district, that, I think. However, I believe I've got some information that may be of use to you. You're looking for a man called Trawlerson?"

"We are, Mr. Scale—and wanting him badly!" exclaimed Preece. "If you can tell us anything about him——"

"I don't know whether I can or not," interrupted Scale. "But it's in my mind that I may be able to. It's like this—last night, just before I closed, there was a man came into my shop who was a total stranger to me, and who, moreover, wasn't a man of our parts. He told me that he was in charge of a steam-roller on a road away up in the hills, and had to camp out for awhile, and he wanted some provisions. He bought a quantity—chiefly tinned stuff: tongues, beef, sardines, preserves; that sort of thing, that doesn't need any cooking. Biscuits too—a lot. Bread, tea, coffee—altogether as much as ever he could carry in a sack that he'd got with him. I said to him jokingly that he must be going to make a long job of it; he replied that he didn't know when he'd get done, and he didn't want to come foraging again. It was dark when he went off, and I didn't see which way he went. But I heard, later, that he called in at our public-house and bought three bottles of rum."

"Paid for everything, I suppose?" asked Preece.

"Oh, on the nail!—made no difficulty about that," replied the grocer. "He'd plenty of money on him—I saw that. And he'd something else too—a revolver! I saw it sticking out of his hip-pocket. Well, this morning I was talking to some of my neighbours, and there's nobody knows of any steam-roller at work anywhere amongst our hills, nor in our district. And they suggested this man might be Trawlerson, driven out of some hiding-place in search of food and drink, and that I should walk over and see you."

"Much obliged to you, Mr. Scale," said Preece. "And now, sir—what like was this man? You'd no doubt take stock of him?"

Scale had evidently taken stock of his customer to some purpose. He described him with great particularity of detail. And our faces fell and we shook our heads. For the grocer's description of his mysterious customer was not one that fitted in with our knowledge of Trawlerson.

It was at this juncture—in fact, while we stood talking there—that Macpherson came back.

# CHAPTER FIFTEEN

## BLACK MILL BOTTOM

I knew at once that Andrew Macpherson had come to stop. He had a certain old brown leather portmanteau in his left hand and a bunched-up umbrella, equally ancient, in his right; they were familiar to me as being articles that he dug out of his boxroom whenever he was going to stay more than a night from home; for a mere one-night stay he carried his luggage in his pocket—a collar, a handkerchief, a comb, and a tooth-brush. Preece and the grocer-man leaving us as Andrew came up, we took him in, and he told us at once that, his holiday being due, he had come to help in the solution of these problems.

"For there's no denying that it's an uncommon and interesting case," said he, "and'll tax the brains and the ingenuity of as many folk as can give their time and attention to it. And Tom there being mixed up in it—losh, man, ye've fallen full length and head over ears into a wealth of those adventures you were longing after!—it becomes a sort of family affair. And so, if ye'll give me bed and board for a few days, Captain——"

"Both—and delighted!" responded Trace. "Two heads are better than one, and three than two, you know!"

"I'm no so sure about that, as a proposition," said Macpherson. "It's like a lot o' those old saws—there's a flaw in it. But, man, ye've been through strange experiences! And what body was that, going away with the policeman? A detective, likely?"

"No—a man in your line of business," replied Trace. "Came with what he thought might be some information. But you'll want posting up, Macpherson. Wait till we've had dinner, and we'll put you wise, as they say across the water. There's a lot for you to ruminate over."

"Aweel, I ha' read all the newspapers," said Macpherson. "Very pretty reading it makes, and gives rise to some strange reflections! But I'll not be the worse for hearing it all at first hand."

We told him all we knew, either at dinner, or as he and Trace smoked their pipes in the window-place when dinner was over. He was a good and a shrewd listener, Macpherson, only interrupting a story to ask some very pertinent question, and he took in all we had to tell him on this occasion with unusual attention. And at the end he knocked the ashes from his pipe with a firmness of gesture which showed me, who well knew his various tricks, that he had formed some opinion.

"Captain!" he asked, giving Trace an earnest look. "Is there an ancient man or woman in this place, in full possession of what you might call his or her intellectual faculties, that's thoroughly acquaint with its history for years past?"

"I should think there is!" replied Trace, with a confident laugh. "Old Hentidge!"

"And who may old Hentidge be?" asked Macpherson.

"Farmer—one of the last of the old sort," said Trace. "Well over eighty—fine old fellow. He's in full possession of his faculties, if you like!—clear-headed as ever they make 'em. Eyes, ears, teeth, all sound—nothing amiss with the old chap except that he's lost the use of his legs and has to go about in a wheel-chair. But as to his memory—wonderful!"

Macpherson rose and picked up his hat. He beckoned us to rise too.

"Take me to that man!" he commanded solemnly. "We'll ha' speech together!"

We led him up the village to Hentidge's farm. As we came near the garden gate we saw the old man sitting in his wheel-chair in the sunlight amongst the apple-trees. Chrissie sat near him, busied, as usual, with some woman's job of knitting or sewing.

"Is the old gentleman well acquaint with these recent happenings?" enquired Macpherson, as we went in. "Posted up to date in them, eh?"

"Oh, he'll know all about things!" asserted Trace. "We haven't been to see him for some days, but his daughter reads the papers to him, and he reads them himself, and he gets all the news of the place—he'll know. And you needn't be afraid of talking, Macpherson—the old man likes it."

"It's him I'm wanting to talk," said Macpherson. "I'll do the listening." He sat silently regarding old Hentidge for some minutes after Trace had presented him to father and daughter. "Ye were no born yesterday, Mr. Hentidge, I'm thinking!" he blurted out suddenly. "No, nor the day before that, neither, eh?"

"No—no—no!" chuckled Hentidge. "Eighty-five!—according to the family Bible."

"Aye, just so—not that you look it," said Macpherson. "Still, you're an ancient man. And, like some of 'em, I'll warrant ye've a good memory for past events?"

Hentidge chuckled again.

"Remember things of my young days better than things that happened last year!" he answered. "More clearly!"

"Ye will—it's an infirmity of nature," remarked Macpherson. "And a highly useful one, whiles. Well, now, Mr. Hentidge, can you no recall anything that happened in this village that in your opinion bears on these recent tragedies? I'm thinking it's very likely you can, Mr. Hentidge."

Hentidge smiled, and lifting the ash-plant stick which he always carried across the rug laid over his knees, pointed it first at Trace and then at me.

"I was going to say something to those two boys about that the other day," he said. "Going to tell them a story. But they ran off—after that man Trawlerson. So it never got told. May have something to do with these recent affairs, Mr. Macpherson—and it mayn't. I don't know. Perhaps it has—if so, it wants careful thinking."

"Man, I'm a born genius at that!" exclaimed Macpherson. "In a business like mine, there's opportunities for cultivating the science o' pure reflection. If you'll tell us your tale, now, I'll reflect and meditate on it till I've reduced the component parts to a congruous whole. Ye'll no doubt have it at your tongue's end, Mr. Hentidge?"

"Oh, I can remember, I can remember!" said Hentidge, with one of his dry chuckles. "Dates and all, Mr. Macpherson—I've a fine memory for dates. Well, now, look this way." He raised his ash-plant and pointed up the hill-side to where a fringe of woodland rose on the sky-line. "You see that coppice up yonder?" he went on. "If you go up there, and through those trees, you'll see, just below you, on the far slope of the hill, a farmstead—Highmeadow Farm. Man named Mellin has it now, Tom Mellin, but fifty years ago it belonged to a family called Welgrave, and it had been in their hands for a couple of centuries at least. However, fifty years ago, that family was on its last legs. They were a queer lot, those Welgraves; some said, a bad lot. I don't know about that, but as far back as I can recollect, they were steadily going to ruin."

"That 'ud be the drink, Mr. Hentidge?" suggested Macpherson. "It's a catching thing, that, for folk living in solitudes!"

"Drink for one thing," assented Hentidge. "Gambling for another—they were great horse-racing folk—always off at some race-meeting or other. And card-playing too. A loose, fast-living, rackety lot—all of 'em. There was a father, two grown-up sons, and a grown-up girl or two—the mother was dead. They were all tarred with the same brush—loose-lived! And when the father died suddenly—he fell off his horse, dead, out hunting one day—the whole thing came to the smash-up that we'd all foreseen. He left nothing—but debts. The two lads went off somewhere; the girls, somewhere else; all disappeared. That was in the year 1868."

"Forty-four years ago!" remarked Macpherson. "Ye'd be a man o' middle age yourself at that time, Mr. Hentidge."

"In my prime!" said Hentidge, nodding. "And living here, of course—we've been on this land longer than those Welgraves had been on theirs. We're here still!" he chuckled. "But they!—as I say, they all disappeared. Nothing's ever been heard of them since they left the parish—with one exception. That was in the case of Daniel Welgrave—young Dan, as he was always called; his father was known as old Dan. Three years after they'd all left, young Dan Welgrave came back—for one night. And it's about what happened on that night that I want to tell you."

"Three years?" remarked Macpherson. "That would be in 1871, Mr. Hentidge?"

"1871 it was—the date's important, as I'll show you," asserted Hentidge. "1871 the year, and the month was November. One November afternoon, late, young Dan Welgrave walked into the inn down yonder. Up to recently there were men in the village who'd have remembered it, and who saw him, but they're dead. I didn't see him, but I heard all about his coming and his doings. They said he was dressed like a gentleman and sported a gold watch and chain and had rings on his fingers. He soon got a crowd of them round him and treated them all to drink—it was said they nearly finished all the best liquor the landlord had in his cellar. Young Dan himself, they told me, was foremost of the lot in that sort of thing, and the more he drank, the more he talked. He told them he'd been out to South Africa, to the diamond-fields—I said the date was important, and so it is, because I'm given to understand that it was just about that time that the great rush to those South African diamond-fields took place, so that seems to prove that young Dan was telling the truth—and that he'd made his fortune. Money in plenty he had on him, they said—he was throwing sovereigns about like ha'pence, and showing rolls of bank-notes whenever he paid for anything. He boasted that he was going to buy the old place and turn it into a gentleman's residence. And so on, and so on—you can guess, Mr. Macpherson, what sort of a riotous evening it was down yonder at the inn. And about ten o'clock young Dan left it, to walk over the shoulder of the hill to see an old friend with whom he proposed to stay that night. He went off alone—and nobody heard any more of him until next day, when, late in the afternoon, a man found him lying in a lonely place in Black Mill Bottom, dead. And—murdered!"

"Aye!" murmured Macpherson, with a sage nod. "Aye, I was thinking that would be the next news! Murdered! Aye—that would be the way of it!"

"Murdered!" repeated old Hentidge. "He'd been struck down—battered to his death. And of course, robbed. The fine gold watch and chain, the rings, the money in his pockets—all gone. They made out the exact spot where it had happened: near a stile that he had to climb over. They traced the line through the grass over which his body had been dragged into the cover of the undergrowth. But they got no clue to the actual murderer. Perhaps they weren't as clever in those days as they are now, sometimes, but there's the fact—the police never made any arrest. It was like a good many other things that happen in the country—talked about for nine days, you know, Mr. Macpherson, and then . . . dropped."

"Was there nobody that you'd call suspect, then?" asked Macpherson.

"Well, you'll see the difficulty of suspecting anybody," answered Hentidge. "There'd been a crowd of some twenty or thirty men down there at the inn, all drinking and carousing at young Dan Welgrave's expense. Some of them lived in the village, some on the hill-sides, some in the valleys. When they separated they went their various ways. Most of them, you may be sure, had had more than enough liquor; none had over-clear ideas of anything next morning. But in addition to these roysterers, gathered about Dan in the parlour, there were other men, of a lower sort, in the place, who were well aware of what was going on and heard Dan's boasting of his wealth and doubtless saw enough to assure them that he'd a lot of money on him. And we had some black sheep in the parish in those days. The thing was to get evidence against anybody, and the police couldn't get any evidence—none whatever. But, amongst the village folk, one man was suspected."

"Aye, and who would he be, now?" asked Macpherson.

"A young fellow named Flinch, Kit Flinch," replied Hentidge. "He came of a bad lot and he was a bad lot himself—he'd been in trouble for poaching several times. Whispers went round that Kit Flinch was the man, but they couldn't get a scrap of evidence against him, and though he knew people were talking he took no heed, and showed himself in his usual haunts as impudently as you like, as if daring the police and the public. But—all of a sudden he disappeared!"

"Aye!" muttered Macpherson. "Aye, he would! Aye, he would, indeed! Losh—it's wonderful, fair wonderful, how things join together! To be sure, he would disappear! That would be the way of it. Aye, it fits in—amazingly!"

I don't think old Hentidge had the least idea of what Macpherson was muttering about; it was easy to see that the story he was telling was chiefly interesting to him as a story.

"Yes," he continued, "he disappeared, Kit Flinch. Suddenly and completely too—he was drinking and smoking at the inn one night with certain cronies of his own sort, and next morning he wasn't to be found. Of course, he'd gone off in the night, but nobody knew where. He never came back—never!"

"That'll be as far as you're aware, Mr. Hentidge," remarked Macpherson, with a sly glance at me and Trace, which I, for my part, couldn't comprehend. "As far as you're aware, that'll be. For, you see, I've a notion of my own about it—and a man that can run away from a place unperceived can come back to it without anybody knowing!"

"Well, he was never known to come back," said Hentidge. "And nobody ever heard a word of him again. And what might your notion be, now?"

But Macpherson was not going to be drawn. He shook his head and looked wiser than ever.

"It's a shapeless and inchoate and nebulous thing, my notion, Mr. Hentidge," he answered, "and'll need a deal o' reflection and perpending before I can put it in such poor words as I have at my command. But yon's a grand story, and as entertaining as any I ever read in the books—man! ye'd never think such deeds o' blood and blackness could be done in the midst o' this beautiful scenery—eh, it's a sad, sad world that ye've been spared so many days in, Mr. Hentidge!"

Presently we went away, and, once outside the garden gate, Macpherson clapped Trace's shoulder.

"Captain!" he said in a low voice. "I don't know what ye think, but, eh man, in my opinion I ha' learnt the secret o' these murders!"

# CHAPTER SIXTEEN

## MACPHERSON

I think Trace and myself had an almost infinite belief in Andrew Macpherson's powers; there was that about him which made you think that he could see deeper into things than most people. But at this announcement we turned incredulous eyes on him, and Trace, after a start of surprise, let out what we were both thinking.

"What!—already?" he exclaimed. "Out of an old man's tale!"

"Ca' canny, my lad!" replied Macpherson. "We'll talk!" He kept silence himself until we were back in Trace's garden, where he perched on a rustic bench that stood beneath the parlour window and motioned us to seat ourselves on either side of him. "Now, you'll conceive of me as one of those gentlemen of the wig and gown," he said, "arguing a case before a judge and jury—I've sufficient good conceit of myself to think I'd ha' made a good figure at that work! Well, we've heard what the old gentleman up above had to tell us, and a very clear and concise job he made of it. Now, we'll recapitulate a little. Daniel Welgrave the younger came back to this village, flashing his money, and communicating the notion that he'd a deal of that about him. He was murdered—for what he had on him. But I opine, from evidence adduced, that the man who murdered him found not only money on his victim, but something else. What, now—in view of what we've heard about where Daniel Welgrave the younger had come from?"

"Diamonds!" said Trace.

"Man, ye're in the right of it!" exclaimed Macpherson. "Diamonds it would be! I've heard stories myself, many's the time, of how these first prospectors that went out to the diamond-fields when the boom arose, in 1870, would come back to England with packets of uncut stones in their pockets. I think this young Dan had diamonds on him when he came back to this village and caroused in yon public tavern. I think that when he was murdered, late that evening, the diamonds were found on him, as well as the money which was the murderer's first objective. And I think the murderer, perhaps not there and then, but at any rate not so long after, buried those diamonds at the spot over which, only the other day, Chissick built his bit of a shed—without a window, and with a stout lock and a weighty bolt! Aye!"

"Aye!" echoed Trace. "A good theory!"

"Now, then, who murdered young Daniel Welgrave?" continued Macpherson. " 'Tis forty years ago and more, and we've no details except those given us, after all that time, by the old man up the street—Hentidge. There are all sorts of things I would like to know. One is—who was the man that young Dan set out to spend the night with on the other side of the hill?"

"That could be found out, even now," said Trace.

"And it might be well to find it out," remarked Macpherson. "And especially if that man's alive, as he might be, for we'll consider him as having been at that time of about Dan Welgrave's age, and Dan was a young man. However—for another thing, the murder may not have been the work of one man. There may have been two of them at it—there may have been a gang. But for the sake of a logical argument, let's conclude it was the fellow called Flinch—Kit Flinch. Now, what does Flinch do after he's buried those diamonds?—of the exact value of which, of course, he knows nothing, or, at best, can only guess at. He finds out that he's being suspected, and one night he makes off, quietly, and effects a complete and successful disappearance. No doubt he went to sea; we'll assume that he did. At some time or other, he made that rough map, or chart, or drawing, that's figured so largely in this affair—or, he got some mate of his, better equipped for the job than himself, to make it for him. And, no doubt, on occasion, as sailor-men will, he talked, boastingly perhaps, of his buried treasure to those about him, without, of course, giving details, and Kest on one hand, and Trawlerson on another, got to hear of it. Eventually, Kest got hold of the map—in quite recent times. We know how Kest got it. He found it in the sailor's ditty-box that he bought of Silvermore, the jeweller-pawnbroker, at Portsmouth. That's established! But there are three questions I'd like answering about that. When Kest found, when he first saw, that map in the ditty-box at Silvermore's, did he recognise it? That's one. Did the recognition come from having actually seen it before? That's two. Or—did he recognise it from having heard talk of it? That's three!"

"You can't answer any of them," remarked Trace. "Or get answers to them!"

"You can't! But you can form your own opinions," said Macpherson. "I opine that Kest knew that map! I think he bought the ditty-box because the map was in it. Anyway, he got it. And from the testimony of Tom here, Kest had that map in his possession when he came to the mill up yonder. Now, two days before Kest was seen at the mill by Tom, he'd bought, or agreed to buy, from Chissick the particular bit of land on the hill-side on which we conclude the diamonds had been buried. What does that prove? That Kest had already found out where the exact spot was! He wanted to get that land into his own hands so that he could dig in peace. Well, Kest was murdered, and the map was stolen from him at the time of the murder, either just before he woke from his sleep in the mill, or after the murder during the half-hour or so that elapsed between Tom finding Kest dead and coming back with you, Captain, to the dead man's side. The map disappeared—and nothing's heard of it until it's found in Chissick's safe, after the murder of Chissick."

"In company with the bank-notes which Kest undoubtedly handed to Chissick!" murmured Trace. "Which is——"

"Extraordinarily strange!" said Macpherson. "But we'll leave the bank-notes alone—we know how and why Chissick got them. But we don't know how Chissick got the map! Did he murder Kest? Did he rob Kest's dead body? Was it somebody else, somebody we know nothing whatever about, who knifed Kest, and made off in the morning sea fog? Did Chissick, who might be out for an early walk, or up there on some of his prospecting business, emerge from that sea fog, when Tom had run down the hill, find Kest lying dead, and go through his pockets? That may have been the way of it. Tom can't say definitely, for he doesn't know at all whether Kest was robbed before or after he was dead."

"No!" said I, reflecting on that misty morning and its horrors. "And that's a fact, Mr. Macpherson."

"Aye, it's a fact, my man, and a deplorable one!" he answered. "However, Chissick came into possession of that map. Now, then, here's the greatest question of the lot that crowds upon my mind, Captain! When did Chissick master the secret of that map? He'd agreed to sell the patch of land to Kest, and Kest had paid him a deposit to clinch the bargain. Kest was dead; nobody knew of the transaction; no papers had been made out and delivered; Chissick decided to say nothing. He had the map—how soon after Kest's death we don't know. But—when—when!—*when* did he find out what the map signified?"

He looked from one to the other of us as if seeking an answer from either or both, though I am sure he expected none; the look was merely a forensic trick. He answered his question himself—with an air of triumph.

"I'll tell you!—that is, in my opinion," he exclaimed. "He found it out when Trawlerson was in the witness-box at the opening of the inquest on Kest! You'll remember, both of ye, that there was a rare to-do between Trawlerson and the coroner over the question of why Trawlerson wanted to find the mill, and the map came into the arguments. Now, Chissick was on the jury and heard all that, and no doubt he saw, as most other folk of any perception saw, that there was a particular secret about this mill and its vicinity, and that the secret was confined in the map. But had he the map *then*—at the time of the inquest? If he had, I think he either murdered Kest or robbed Kest after the murder. If he hadn't, then I think somebody else did the murdering and robbing, and sold the map to Chissick."

"That's a new idea," remarked Trace. "I don't like it, Macpherson. Nobody could sell Chissick the map but the actual murderer and thief. Do you think he'd give himself away by letting Chissick know that he had the map?"

"Aye, man, but I don't see that way at all!" said Macpherson. "We're well aware, we three, that whoever got the map in the first instance took it out of its wrappings in yon wood at the top of the hill, and threw the wrappings away—that is, we're well aware of the seemingness of that, on surface facts. But is that right? It mayn't be!"

"We found the wrappings, Mr. Macpherson," I reminded him.

"Aye, surely we did, my lad," he answered. "But we don't know that the map had been taken out of them by the murderer. Now, put it to yourselves this way. The murderer, after knifing Kest, gets away into those woods. He's either robbed Kest before or after the murder—of everything that he had on him. Let's take it that what he was after was valuables—money and the like. Well, in the wood he examines what he's got. He finds the map— that's no use to him! He throws it away, with the wrappings. It's picked up later by some man passing through the wood—perhaps after the inquest, at which the map's freely enquired after. That man, the man who picked it up, sells it to Chissick. He'd say nothing. Chissick did say nothing!"

"What was Chissick murdered for?" said Trace, after a short pause.

"Aye, do you ask me that?" answered Macpherson. "Man!—for what he'd dug out of that hole in the hill-side, the night before! Man!—Chissick had been watched!"

"Then it's Trawlerson!" I exclaimed. "It's Trawlerson! Trawlerson did nothing but watch from the moment Chissick began operations on those bungalows! And I'm sure it must have been Trawlerson I saw prowling around the shed that night."

"Aweel!" said Macpherson, in his driest manner and relapsing into his native manner of speech. "The man's no here to answer for himself, and I canna say. Ye'll no get a reply from him either, Tom, my man, if they catch him."

"Did Trawlerson murder both of them?" said Trace musingly. "I don't mean did he actually murder Kest, for we know he was in bed, miles away, at the exact hour of Kest's murder. But—had he an accomplice? Was Trawlerson an accessory? He professed utter ignorance, but Trawlerson, in my opinion, is a good actor, or an expert at dissimulation. Nobody's gone into that accomplice idea!"

"Barring my own self!" remarked Macpherson. "And what I think about that, my lads, I'm not going to tell to anybody—yet! I'm engaged in serious cogitations about that, and I'll walk now under your apple-trees, Captain, and cogitate some more."

He left us then, and we saw no more of him until it was time for tea, over which meal he was unusually silent. And as soon as it was over, he took up his stick and went out into the road. Out of inquisitiveness, I got into the window-place and watched him. He made for Hentidge's farm, and I saw him turn in at the garden gate.

It was growing dusk when he came back and joined us again in Trace's parlour. He gave us glances that had something of sly triumph in them.

"I ha' found out more about yon matter o' two-and-forty years ago!" he announced. "He's a more than by-ordinary memory, yon Hentidge, and improves with acquaintance. Now, I'll tell you still more about what happened to young Dan Welgrave—man! I'm now doubtful if the fellow Kit Flinch should ha' been suspected at all, though I think he knew things that he never told. It just shows how things that didn't occur to people at the time occur to impartial listeners a long time after."

"You've got further information on that affair?" asked Trace.

"And weighty information too, bearing on later things than it," said Macpherson. "I daundered up the road there while you were still finishing your teas and dropped in on Hentidge and his daughter at theirs, and I ha' had more talk with the old man, and got him—small effort on his part, for, as I say, he's a fine hand at recalling things—to tell me still more about that Dan Welgrave affair. Now, you'll recollect that when Dan Welgrave left the inn down here after his evening's carouse, it was to go over the hill to spend the night with an old friend? That friend was a young farmer, a bachelor-man, of about his own age, which, Hentidge thinks, was about four-and-twenty years. His name was Ralph Charlesworth, and the farmstead he had is still there, and its name is Blackponds—ye'll maybe acquaint with it, Captain? Very well—now this Ralph Charlesworth was of the same kidney as Dan Welgrave and his lot, wild, rackety, fond of his glass, and given to spending a deal of his time at inns. He was in this inn down the village here when Dan Welgrave turned up that night; he was one of the gang with whom Dan caroused. But—he didn't stay to the end! He settled with Dan that Dan should stay the night with him, but he himself left the inn at nine o'clock, saying he'd got to see another farmer on his way home, on business. Dan wouldn't go with him then; they arranged that he was to go on to Blackponds later. Now, this Ralph Charlesworth said, when the discovery of Dan's dead body was made next day, that he sat up for Dan for a good two hours, till past midnight. When Dan never came, he concluded that Dan had either become too drunk to walk over the hill, or that he had decided to stop where he was for the night, or had gone home with some man who lived in the village. Nobody questioned him, or suspected him, this Ralph Charlesworth. But I do!—from two very significant facts remembered by old Hentidge. The stile by which Dan's body was found was between two meadows on Charlesworth's farm, in a very lonely place; a man well knowing the district could easily have lain in wait there. That's one. The other is, that, after this happened, Charlesworth took to drinking hard, *at home*, and whereas he'd been a great hand for raking out at nights, could never be persuaded to go out again after dark! And not so long after Kit Flinch disappeared, Charlesworth disappeared too—and they found that, financially, he was in a bad way and there was nothing much for his creditors. Man!—I think Charlesworth murdered Dan Welgrave, and I think Flinch knew it!"

Before Trace could find words to comment on this, and while I sat, open-mouthed, wondering at this story of the past, a knock came at the door, and I went to answer it. There, in the porch, stood a man whom, from his blue pea-jacket and blue jersey, I knew to be a sailor.

# CHAPTER SEVENTEEN

## THE CHINA SEAS

I was getting pretty quick of perception by that time, having had my wits sharpened a good deal by the recent happenings, and I saw at once that this new-comer had some message to deliver and that it was probably of a confidential nature. He looked at me with a sort of shy doubt, as if wondering who I was, and having thus inspected me, his eyes shifted to either side, peering into the hall beyond as though in search of something.

"Well?" I said, curtly enough. "What is it?"

He was standing on the step, but at this he summoned up courage and put a foot on the mat inside, taking off his cap as he did so. And he sank his voice to a whisper.

"Captain Trace?" he said. "Is this where he lives?"

"This is Captain Trace's," I answered. "What do you want with him?"

"And he's in?" he asked. "To be seen?"

"That depends," I said, "on the business! What's yours?"

Turning his cap over and over in his hands, he gave me a look that, I am sure, was meant to carry an impression of great delicacy and secrecy.

"If so be as he's in—and to be seen—and'll see me," he whispered, "say as how it's a man from Jim Swaddle's, of Bosham. You might say, a relation of Jim's. Cousin—on the mother's side."

I let him in then, further. I knew Jim Swaddle—by name, at any rate; he was the man who looked after Trace's small yacht. I beckoned the stranger to follow me into the parlour.

"Here's a man who says he comes from Jim Swaddle, at Bosham, Captain Trace," I announced. "He's Jim Swaddle's cousin."

"On the mother's side," added the visitor, as if anxious to be correct in detail. "Servant, gentlemen! Which my name is Pyker—John Pyker. Of Brixham, in Devonshire. But now holidaying, as it were—come to see Cousin Jim a bit."

"Glad to see you, Pyker!" said Trace. "Any relation of Jim's is welcome. Sit down—and have a drink after your walk. Tom!—the spirit-case."

I got out the spirit-case, and, at his own request, obliged Pyker with a drop of gin.

He took a swallow of it, prefaced by a polite expression of his best respects to all present, and, having set his glass down at his elbow, folded his hands and looked at Trace in the way in which I have often seen preachers look at their congregations—as if he had a lot to say, but scarcely knew how to begin saying it.

"Something to tell us, Pyker?" suggested Trace.

Pyker swallowed two or three times, nodding his head at each swallow.

"Which I told it all, first, to Cousin Jim Swaddle," he said, suddenly making a violent effort at speech. "Ah!—from start to finish. Cousin Jim Swaddle, he said—go straight away and tell all that to Captain Trace! Which I now do so!"

"Glad to hear it, Pyker, whatever it is," said Trace. "Take your time."

Pyker took his time. He seemed to reflect for a moment or two; then bending forward and looking from one to the other of us, he rapped out these words:

"This here Trawlerson!"

"Just so!" said Trace. "What about him, Pyker?"

Pyker prepared himself for a longer effort.

"When I come into these parts, three days gone by, to Bosham, to see Cousin Jim Swaddle," he said, "what do I find him, and all his mates, and all the people I meets, in street and in public-house, a-talking of? Murders!—these here murders! What do I read in the newspapers, day by day, me being a fair scholard, fair? Murders!—these here murders, in this here village! And what else? Trawlerson! 'Where is Trawlerson?' says everybody you talks to. 'Where can Trawlerson be?' says the newspapers! Very well! For, mark me, I know Trawlerson! Or, to speak correct, did know him! See?"

"When?" asked Trace.

"Years ago! I think seven. It might be eight. I can't swear. But—knew him well enough, whenever it was."

"Where was that, Pyker?"

"China seas, knocked about a deal in them quarters, I have. And, I should say, Trawlerson too. But that time, when I knew him—and it's the same christened name, which is Hosea, and a mighty bad-sounding name, somehow, is that, I reckon, and seems to fit in with Trawlerson, as was a bad 'un hisself——"

"Oh, you thought him so, did you, Pyker?" interrupted Trace. "Bad lot, eh?"

"Terb'le bad lot, in my opinion. Howsumever, that time I knew him, I shipped with Trawlerson at Hong-Kong, on a crazy old wind-jammer, name of the *Martha Marshall*, bound from Hong-Kong to Nagasaki. Scratch crew, you understand—queer lot, too. Various colours. Come to grief, the *Martha Marshall* did—and no wonder!"

"How did she come to grief?" enquired Trace.

"Shipwrecked we were! Bad ship—bad weather. Struck a reef, or a rock—something, anyways—some days out from Hong-Kong. Went down. There was two boats loads of us got away. One of 'em—captain was in her—I don't know what became of it—went down, like the old wind-jammer, I reckon. Never see or hear of it again, anyway. The one I was in, she made one of those small islands, north of the Loo-Choos, as they call 'em, in the Tung Hai sea. Trawlerson was in my boat. And also another fellow. Which, because of what's being said in all these papers, and amongst folk hereabouts, is what I wanted to tell you."

"Yes?" said Trace. "About—another fellow, eh? Who was he, now?"

"Never knew his proper name," replied Pyker. "Lor' bless you!—that crew on the *Martha Marshall*, it was of that sort that names didn't matter or count! Reckon they stuck down anything on the ship's books, if they stuck anything at all. This fellow, they called him Smarto. He was a sort of better stuff, d'ye see—looked like he'd been, well, a bit of a decent-bred chap. Bad 'un, though—bold, dare-devil sort! Looked it—a black-haired, black-eyed man—queer-tempered."

"Black-haired, black-eyed," said Trace, glancing at Macpherson. "We'll make a note of that! What else was he like, Pyker? Tall—short—what?"

"Tall, slim fellow—all muscle and sinew," answered Pyker. "He could do things—strongest man we had; though, to be sure, he was getting on a bit in years. And him and Trawlerson, they was chums. Always together. I made out they came from about the same part, here at home—south country. Kept themselves a good deal to themselves, those two. That is, until we was cast on that island—which, to be sure, was little better than a reef. They were a bit more companionable, like, after that. And Smarto, he used to talk more. And now and then, when he was feeling it more than usual, he'd say that he only wished he was back in England, for he'd something put there in a safe place that 'ud be enough to bring him roast beef and sound ale every day for the rest of his life, and didn't he wish he'd the handling of it then!"

"Did he say what it was?" asked Trace.

"He did not! But I made out—for he talked often of it in the last days on that island, and would ha' talked more if Trawlerson hadn't checked him—that it was something he'd put away, hidden, buried, or something of that sort. I know what I thought—and what other of my mates thought!"

"Aye, and what did you think, man?" asked Macpherson, suddenly showing great interest. "What were your impressions, now?"

"We thought Smarto had been one of these here burglars and had placed something," replied Pyker. "He wasn't a real sailor-man, Smarto, though he could do his job. He hadn't been trained to the sea, you understand—he was just a landsman that had picked it up."

"Well, and how long were you on that island?" asked Trace.

"Not so long, but long enough to make us thankful to get off it! Of course, there never was any great danger of being left there—it was in the way of ships. We could ha' got away in our own boat, only it got smashed through careless handling just after we struck land. We was took off by a vessel that carried us to Shanghai."

"And—there?" enquired Trace.

"There?—oh, there we all parted. Some got a job here, and another there. I don't know where Trawlerson and Smarto went—whether separate or in company. Never saw either of 'em again. Didn't want, neither."

"Never seen them again at all, eh?" said Trace. "Nor heard of them?"

"Not till I heard all this about Trawlerson—no! I come home, d'ye see, after that do. And to home I've stopped—down there at Brixham. Didn't want no more high-seas life! Took up wi' fishing—peaceful."

"Did you ever know a man named Kest?" asked Trace.

"No—never!" replied Pyker. "Not by that name, anyway. I've read about him, though, in the newspapers, along of his being murdered hereabouts. Can't say as I can reckernise him from the descriptions. Know a many men as would fall in with the description o' Kest as given in the papers—sharp-faced, red-haired, goatee-bearded man. Lots on 'em like that, in my time. Goatee beards is fashernable."

"Did you ever see the man you call Smarto show anything like a map to Trawlerson?" enquired Trace. "Think, now!"

"Not a map—no! I've read about that map. I never see it, nor hear of it. But I do rekerlect this here—Smarto, he had a pocket-book, a leather-bound affair, what he kept in a hip-pocket. I seen him showing that book, opened at a certain page, to Trawlerson. Looked to me as if there was a list o' something in it, where it was opened."

"A list? What sort of a list?"

"Well—words, and figures. Like—like a bill. Leastways, when he had his pocket-book open once, near me, a-showing of it to Trawlerson, I see words in one column, and figures in another. Like you see in bills."

That was the sum-total of what we got out of John Pyker. Macpherson and Trace seemed to think it a decided step to have seen him. Macpherson said that light was beginning to be thrown on several dark places all at once. And next day, when he and Trace and I were up at Hentidge's again, discussing things, he asked old Hentidge a sudden question.

"Mr. Hentidge, it'll be no great effort o' that grand memory o' yours to tell me this—what like was yon Kit Flinch ye've told us of?"

Hentidge chuckled, as he always did when any question about the past was put to him.

"I can see him now!" he said. "He was a tall, spare, black fellow! I should say he'd gipsy blood in him: he'd that look."

I could see that Macpherson was highly delighted at this discovery. He wanted to identify Flinch with the man called Smarto. But a moment later his face fell.

"And what like was yon Charlesworth, now?" he asked. "You'll remember him too?"

"Well enough!" replied old Hentidge. "He was of a similar sort—tall, thin, black. He might have had gipsy blood, as well. I don't know if you've noticed it, Mr. Macpherson, but there's evidences of mixture with that blood all the way along this country, from Kent through Sussex into Hampshire—black hair, black eyes, the gipsy look. You'll have seen it?"

But Macpherson only grunted an uninterested affirmative. He was disappointed—as he always was when he wanted to fit things together and encountered a difficulty.

"That's unfortunate!" he said grumblingly, when we went away from Hentidge's. "Both those young fellows, according to old Hentidge, were much alike! Now, as sure as my name's what it is, that Smarto was one of 'em! But—which? Both disappeared from here about the same time. Both, I'm convinced, knew a lot about the Dan Welgrave affair, and about what he had on him and was robbed of. Was Smarto Kit Flinch, or was he Ralph Charlesworth? And is Smarto alive?"

"He'd be getting on when Pyker knew him," remarked Trace. "And now, if he was a young man of twenty-three or four at the time of the Welgrave murder—that is, if Smarto was either Flinch or Charlesworth—he'll be well over sixty."

"That makes no difference to what I'm thinking about," said Macpherson.

I don't think either Trace or myself had any clear notion of what Macpherson was thinking about. But he was always busy. He passed a good deal of his time with Preece; whether he communicated his ideas to Preece, I don't know. But he and Preece spent hours in examining various places on the hill-side—I believe they went over Blackponds from garret to cellar. And Macpherson, at great trouble to himself, managed to rake up and copy out of old files the contemporary newspaper accounts of the Welgrave affair, and he devoted his evenings to studying his copies. He was certain, he said, that the secret of the recent murders lay in that of the one of forty years before.

I don't think Preece cared much about these researches. Preece had got it into his head that Trawlerson murdered Chissick, and that Trawlerson had disappeared in such clever fashion that he would never be traced. The local police had done everything in their power to trace him, and nothing had resulted. Preece, talking to us one night when he dropped in about something or other, said that, in his opinion, Trawlerson, whom he regarded as a past-master in craft, was already beyond the seas, and would never come back again—never!

"That I don't believe!" said Trace. "Trawlerson, according to his own account, owns a house at Fareham, with, you'll remember, a mast in the front garden and a bit of glass at the back. He insisted on the mast and the glass—which was his way of showing himself proud of his bit of property. I don't think Trawlerson is going to lose his property! Moreover, if I read Trawlerson's character, I don't think Trawlerson was the sort of man who'd risk his neck by murdering anybody, or his liberty by robbing anybody. I'm off the Trawlerson notion!"

"What's Trawlerson disappeared for, then?" demanded Preece. "He's advertised for outside every police-station in England! Where is he?"

Nobody could answer that, of course. Macpherson, who was fond of airing his knowledge of languages, said we were in a cul-de-sac. So we were—but just then Silvermore appeared again.

# CHAPTER EIGHTEEN

## DITTY-BOX AND 'BACCA-BOX

Silvermore turned up at Preece's one afternoon in company with a little elderly man who had all the unmistakable signs of the seafarer on him. Preece brought the two of them up to Trace's; we could talk more freely there, he said, than in his cottage, where there were women-folk about. And Silvermore introduced his companion as Silas Cushion.

"The man that pledged that ditty-box with me," he explained. "He's been knocking about all over the world since then, and has only just come back. And—he's been reading the papers, and came to see me in consequence. There isn't much those newspaper chaps have left out, I think!"

Silvermore was right there. The newspaper reporters, or correspondents, or whatever they called themselves, had made the most of what they termed the South Downs Mystery. It constituted a fine story, and they had given every detail they could lay hands on about it. I think the police authorities encouraged them, under the impression that publicity of the widest sort would be a good thing.

"Yes?" said Preece. He sized up Silas Cushion with a comprehensive inspection. "That ditty-box, now?" he continued. "I suppose you know all about it? Previous history, eh?"

Cushion was one of those men who appear to be always chewing something. It may have been that he had a quid of tobacco in his cheek, but his jaws were for ever working. This gave him a meditative expression.

"Well," he answered ruminatingly, "from the time I got it. Not before—though, to be sure, I know where it came from."

"That's just what we'd like to know," said Preece. "Where did it come from?"

"To me," replied Cushion, "from a man that I knew years ago. Him and me was shipmates. In the Pacific, that was. Merchant vessel—from Valparaiso to Sydney. He was took bad, uncommon bad, just before we made Sydney. And, of course, they put him in hospital. I used to go to see him there. But he was mostly past speech. Never got nothing much out of him, nohow. Nothing about his private affairs, you understand. And one day when I goes up to the hospital, they tells me he'd died. In the night—a bit sudden, at the last. There was a few things of his that had been taken to the hospital with him. The hospital folks, they give 'em to me, d'ye see, as being the only man that knew anything about him. That ditty-box, it was amongst 'em."

"What was this man's name?" asked Preece.

"Cossin—Dave Cossin. Name I knew him by, anyway. Some of 'em, of course, has a many names in a lifetime. But from what I see of him, I should say that was his right name."

"What like was he, can you say?" demanded Macpherson eagerly. "Was he a tall, dark, spare fellow, now?"

But Cushion shook his head—with signs of a decided negative.

"No, mister, he was not!" he answered. "He was a little, sandy, weechy sort of a chap! I never rightly knew whether he was Scotch or Irish—one of 'em. I did hear him say once he was born in Liverpool. But there's a sight of Irish there—and Scotch too. No!—he wasn't at all what you say. An offal sort o' little man."

"Did he ever tell you where he got that ditty-box, or what was in it?" enquired Preece.

"He did not. Never mentioned it to me, as I remember. I never see it, neither, till it was give to me by the hospital folks, when he was dead. You see, when they took him off from the ship to the hospital, I reckon they bundled up all the bits o' things he had in his locker, and sent 'em with him, and the ditty-box was amongst 'em. No, I never had no word from him about it."

Macpherson was obviously intensely disappointed to find that the man who died in hospital at Sydney did not answer to the description of either Kit Flinch or Ralph Charlesworth, and he muttered something about an impasse. But Preece, as became an intelligent policeman who had kept his ears open at quarter-sessions and assizes, proceeded with his examination-in-chief.

"Well, you eventually pledged that ditty-box with Mr. Silvermore there, at Portsmouth, didn't you?" he suggested. "You, yourself?"

"Oh, I pledged it!" said Cushion. "With other matters. A bit down on my luck at that time, I was. Yes!"

"Well, now, Mr. Silvermore says there were a lot of small articles, curiosities, and the like, in the box. Were they all what you'd found in it, when it was given to you after Cossin's death?"

"No! Some were what was in it then; some was what I put into it time and again. Bits o' things. Such as a man what uses the sea picks up, you understand."

"Well, about this map," continued Preece, producing his pocket-book. "You've read about it in the newspapers? Just so! Was it in the ditty-box when that came into your possession?"

"Oh yes—the map was there! Lying at the bottom—a lot o' little things atop of it."

"Had you any idea as to what it meant—what it was about?"

"Not I! I've seen that sort o' thing before. I thought it was something Cossin had drawed out, or somebody'd drawed out for him—'maginary stuff, I reckoned! I never gave no particular heed to it."

"But you left it in the box?"

"Never took it out but once, when I examined what was in the box. I put it back then, and t'other articles on top of it. There it stuck, and there it was when I pledges it at Mr. Silvermore's."

"Would you know it again if you saw it, Cushion?"

"Oh I should know it—remember it, and how it was drawed, well enough!"

Preece produced the map from his pocket-book, and spread it on the parlour table.

"Is that it?" he asked.

"Oh, that's it, right enough!" declared Cushion. "Don't look no worse, neither."

"You can swear that's the map you found in the ditty-box at Sydney?"

"Swear to it, yes! No doubt about it!"

Preece put the map away again.

"Have you ever known a man named Kest?" he asked abruptly.

"Not as I'm aware of," replied Cushion. "I've read about him, of course, in these here newspaper pieces, but I can't recall him nohow. He may ha' been known to me at some time or other, under another name, d'ye see? But as Kest—no, don't know him at all."

"Did you ever talk to anybody, any of your shipmates, anybody at all, about this map?"

"I can't recollect as I ever did. I don't remember doing so at any time. You see, I never attached no importance to it. I thought it was just a trifle that Cossin had picked up—sailor-men has a habit of picking up and keeping things that landsmen 'ud throw aside. No—I never talked about it."

That was all we learnt from Silas Cushion. The problem arising out of it, discovered at length by Macpherson when Preece and his visitors had gone, was—who was the man Cossin?—how did he get hold of that map?—was he a man who originally hailed from these parts?—he might have been in these parts at some time or other, said Macpherson, even though he was born in Liverpool.

"Well, there's one thing certain, Macpherson," said Trace. "He wasn't Kit Flinch, and he wasn't Ralph Charlesworth, the two men you're anxious to know more about. He was a little, sandy, weechy man! That settles you!"

"It's but another obstacle," replied Macpherson. "It can be overcome. I think Cossin got that map from the man called Smarto. Maybe he stole it. Maybe he bought it. Maybe he found it. But anyway, Trace, I'm sure it came from Smarto. And Smarto was one or other of those dark, spare fellows that went away from this quarter after the murder of Dan Welgrave the younger! Man, I contend that bit by bit we're progressing to the grand climacteric!"

"We certainly keep learning a bit!" agreed Trace.

We heard a bit more, two or three days later—again through Preece. Preece, in company with another local policeman, put in an hour or two now and then in examining the surroundings of Chissick's house. That house, as I have said, stood in a lonely situation: at least a hundred yards from its nearest neighbour. It had a garden in front, a flower garden, well shielded from the lane by thick hedges; there was another garden at the back, also well hedged, in which Chissick grew vegetables and cultivated fruit-trees. And there was a fenced-off yard, in which there were two refuse-bins, one reserved for stuff thrown out of the kitchen by the charwoman, Mrs. Watson, another sacred to ashes, waste paper, and the like. Preece took it into his head to examine this ash-bin and its contents; he had already gone through a waste-paper basket in Chissick's parlour, and had also raked out the parlour grate, without finding anything. It was difficult to imagine his finding anything, it seemed to me. But one day he turned up at Trace's with a small parcel in his hand, carefully done up in brown paper.

"See here!" he said, as he set it down on the sitting-room table. "If this isn't a find, I don't know what could be! Unearthed this, myself, in a refuse-bin at Chissick's back door, amongst a lot of torn-up paper and stuff that he'd evidently emptied out of a waste-paper basket. If this doesn't refer to that business of forty years ago that you're always nosing into, Mr. Macpherson, I'm a Dutchman! And I'm not a Dutchman!"

He was plainly highly elated at his discovery, and he enjoyed our suspense and curiosity as he undid the wrappings of his parcel. Eventually, having stripped off various folds of brown paper, he revealed an old tin box, about five inches in length, three in width, and two in depth. It bore unmistakable signs of age and of rust, but the lettering on it, in block letters, not on a paper label, but on the lid itself, was still plain enough. And that was: *Soldans and Sandberg, Tobacconists and Cigar Merchants, 85, Alderley Street, Cape Town.*

The depth of Macpherson's delight at the sight of this ancient relic—for it was obvious to all that the box was by no means of recent manufacture—was evidenced by the way in which he seized on the thing.

"Man, Preece!" he exclaimed, his voice hoarse with emotion, "ye've made a most important discovery!—the most important, in my opinion, of any that's been made in the whole procedure of investigation into this truly amazing mystery! Man!—this is a grand day!"

"Aye—and how do you make all that out, Mr. Macpherson?" asked Preece, with a wink at me and Trace. "Something—perhaps a good deal—in it, no doubt, but——"

"Something in it, you say?" interrupted Macpherson excitedly. "Man!—do you tell me that you don't see what's in it? Man!—I'm telling you! This is the box yon Dan Welgrave carried his diamonds in when he came to the inn down below! This is the box was taken off him when he was murdered! This is the box was hidden by the murderer under yon old oak tree up the hill-side, where Chissick built his bit shed! This is the box Chissick dug out o' that hole he made in the floor of the corner of the shed! Losh, man!—I see it all as plain as I see your fat face, Preece! And the great question, great, great question"—I cannot presume to describe how Macpherson rolled his r's, and broadened his o's and a's during this speech—"is—where are the diamonds?"

He gazed from one to the other of us as if demanding an instant reply. But Preece and I only stared at him. Trace, however, who had got into a way of chaffing him about his newly developed passion for sleuth-work, smiled good-humouredly.

"Better theorise a bit more, Macpherson!" he said. "It's amusing!"

"No, but I'm serious, Captain," protested Macpherson. "Man!—it's a very serious matter! And ye'll get no practical result in anything, in my opinion, unless you theorise first. Now, it's my theory that whoever killed Dan Welgrave forty-two years ago found this very box containing diamonds on him. They may have been uncut; they may have been cut. I think they were uncut. Didn't he tell his cronies at the inn that he'd come straight from the diamond-fields? Anyway, this box and its contents o' diamonds was found by the murderer; he didn't know exactly what to do with them then, and he buried the box for safety. Now, I argue that the diamonds were in the box when Chissick dug it up, and that Chissick took them out of the box in the privacy of his own house, and flung away the box where friend Preece here has just discovered it. Then Chissick put the diamonds in his own pocket! And now I'll just ask you to recall a highly important matter. D'ye recollect, all of you, what yon charwoman body, Mrs. Watson, told us when the lad Tom here fetched her to Chissick's house that morning he was found murdered? Whether it's escaped your poor mem'ries or not, it's no escaped mine! What did yon woman say Chissick had told her that Saturday morning she last had speech of him? That he was going to Brighton! Aye, but that was his usual custom; there was nothing in that. But more—from Brighton he was going to London, on the Monday, and might be away till the Tuesday or Wednesday. What for was Chissick going to London—which, as I've made out, was not usual with him? Man alive!—I could take my oath on what he was going for! He was going to London to sell those diamonds!"

I am sure that Preece and myself were vastly impressed by Macpherson; we saw it all as plainly as if it had been printed in a book. And even Trace seemed struck.

"Excellent theory, excellent, Macpherson!" he said. "You'd make a detective, I think. And——"

But that caused Preece to interrupt.

"Why, talking about detectives, Captain," he remarked, "Mr. Macpherson'll be glad to hear that we're going to do just what he advised some little time ago. There's a still bigger man coming down from Scotland Yard to-morrow, to take special charge of this Chissick case—the famous Detective-Sergeant Parkapple."

# CHAPTER NINETEEN

## DETECTIVE-SERGEANT PARKAPPLE

I first set eyes on the famous Detective-Sergeant Parkapple in the parlour of the village inn, where, with a glass of bitter ale in front of him, and a crust of bread and cheese in his hand, he was arguing with the landlord and Sergeant Preece about the best methods to be adopted in the successful growing of vegetable marrows. He was not a bit like a detective; at any rate, not a bit like my idea of a detective. I had always thought of detectives as men whose appearance suggested mystery: there was nothing mysterious about Parkapple. He was a little, plump man, with a cheery, pink face and mutton-chop whiskers; very smartly dressed, in a black morning coat, fancy waistcoat, and fashionable striped trousers. He wore spats to his shoes and had a shiny silk hat and a neatly rolled umbrella. And his manner was frank, chatty, and jovial—when conversing about vegetables, anyway. I made out, from his talk, that he lived at Surbiton, and possessed a garden in which he spent all his spare time, and, young as I was, it struck me that gardening was probably his proper job in life, and that he had got thrown into police work by accident and had somehow stuck where he was thrown.

When this great man (of whose fame and deeds, in the way of criminal-catching, Preece had told us a lot, the night before) had finished his refreshment, he went with Preece and me to Trace's, whose house by that time had come to be regarded by the police as a highly convenient centre for discussions. We had a sort of informal committee meeting there, at which Macpherson and Preece did most of the talking. As for Parkapple, he lighted a cigar, folded his plump hands over his fancy waistcoat, and listened. He was a good listener, but though, boy-like, I watched him with absorbed attention, I could not see a flicker of anything like interest in his face. He just listened, politely. And after Macpherson had said all that he had to say, and Preece had followed suit, Parkapple said a few quiet words which showed that he already knew pretty well everything they had told him. I was not surprised at that, when, a few minutes later, he opened a little dispatch-case which he carried about with him and drew from it a sheaf of papers, amongst which were quantities of sheets on which newspaper reports had been neatly pasted. Yet, to be sure, there were certain things with which he was not conversant, such as the Hentidge story, and the evidence of Pyker, and that of the man brought to us by Silvermore. What I, and, I think, Trace too (Macpherson certainly did), wanted to know was—what did Parkapple make of that aspect of the question?

Parkapple didn't tell us; for the time being, he seemed to regard all that as irrelevant; at any rate, he put it aside quietly. Out of his mass of papers he produced one, a folded sheet of official-looking foolscap. With this un-opened in his hand, he took his cigar out of his lips and looked round at Trace, Macpherson, and Preece.

"Which of you gentlemen lived here, in this village, when Chissick came to it?" he asked. Trace and Macpherson promptly shook their heads. Macpherson, of course, was not a villager at all. Trace was, comparatively, a new-comer.

"I lived here," answered Preece. "It's five years since he came."

"What did you know of him, when he did come?" asked Parkapple.

"Why, nothing! He was a stranger."

"Well, what did you learn of him? What did he do?"

Preece put on his thinking-cap.

"Let's see?" he said. "Five years is a long time—lots o' things happened in that time. Well, Chissick—first thing I knew of him, or anybody knew of him, he turned up here, a complete stranger, and bought that home in which he lived ever afterwards till he was murdered the other day. Bought it from an old man who had it to sell, and who's now dead. I think I seem to remember that they said Chissick gave eight hundred pounds for the house, garden, and orchard, freehold—it's not a very big place. And—well, then he settled down. Did nothing at first. Retired gentleman, you know, in the beginning, anyway."

"When did he begin to do anything?" asked Parkapple.

"After a bit," replied Preece, "he began speculating a time or two in land. Bought up a plot here and a plot there, d'ye see?—and, of course, sold them again. Then he began building a bit—and selling what he'd built as soon as it was finished. He kept on at that game. During the last two years he did a good lot at it; had a builder's yard, and employed a fair lot of men."

"I suppose you knew him pretty well?"

"As a resident, yes—no more. Never had any great amount of talk to him."

"You don't know, and never did know, anything about his past? Where he came from, for instance?"

"No! I do know this, though—he wasn't a native of these parts. You could tell that by his speech."

Parkapple turned, and, looking at me, gave me a close, searching in-spection.

"This is the lad, Tom Crowe, who's figured in this case a lot, isn't it?" he asked. "Very well—is he to be trusted thoroughly?"

They all spoke up for me. I began to think a lot of myself as I heard them. And Parkapple nodded.

"So I'd heard!" he remarked, with a smile. "I shouldn't have said as much as I have if I hadn't. Very well; as Master Tom there seems to be one of the cabinet, we can talk freely. This Chissick, now—I have his record here!"

I don't think any of us knew what he meant, with the exception of Preece. I am sure Trace and I didn't, and I believe Macpherson only guessed. But Preece, as a policeman of experience, started.

"Ah!" he exclaimed. "Record, eh? Just so!"

"Record!" continued Parkapple. "You see, when the fact came out about Chissick's murder, there was mention of his habit of going to Brighton to spend his week-ends. Very good! I went to Brighton! I got information at Brighton that enabled me to work back—a long way. To cut things short, I've investigated Chissick's past—I've only just finished the investigation. It's all here," he added, tapping his folded paper. "I'll give you the gist of it."

He searched for and found a pair of spectacles, and began polishing them, leisurely—too leisurely for me, and, I think, for Macpherson, who by this time was all agog with excitement and began to mutter.

"Aye!" he murmured, shifting about in his seat at the table. "Aye!—it'll be another digging up o' dry bones out o' the grave o' the past! Aye!—and maybe he'll be able to clothe them in flesh and blood—ye'll no doubt have some more than ordinary revelations to make, Mr. Parkapple?"

"Oh, so—so!" replied the detective. "Nothing very wonderful, Mr. Macpherson—just such facts as you generally get in such cases. Of course, you see, this man's real name wasn't Chissick at all."

"D'ye tell me that, now!" exclaimed Macpherson. "Aye, and what would it be, I'm wondering?"

Parkapple had fitted on his spectacles by that time. He unfolded his paper and began to give us bits from it, punctuating them with remarks.

"The real name of this man was James Creswick," he said. "His father was a small builder and contractor at Middlesbrough. He himself was apprenticed to that trade—to the building trade. But when he was about twenty he seems to have left it, and at twenty-one he was working as a clerk in the employ of a firm of shipping merchants at Newcastle. Three years afterwards he was secretary to a building society at Darlington: a building society the members of which were chiefly working-class people, folk who wanted to buy their own houses, you know."

"Aye, there's a deal o' societies o' that sort in the North," agreed Macpherson.

"Well, he evidently did very well in this capacity," continued Parkapple. "I mean well for the society—so well, indeed, that within a few years he was not only secretary but treasurer into the bargain, and had the entire affairs of the concern in his hands. However, when he was about thirty-five, some officious member began to suspect that something was wrong. He induced other members to join him in an enquiry; there was a drastic one, and the result was Creswick's arrest, on a charge of falsifying accounts, forging documents, and embezzling the society's money. Pretty bad, eh?"

"Aye—aye!" moaned Macpherson. "Aye—it's a grave matter!"

"Grave enough! Well, he was tried at Durham Assizes, and found guilty, and he got seven years' penal servitude," continued Parkapple. "He served part of that sentence at Dartmoor, and part at Parkhurst."

"That's where Kest was," observed Preece.

"Exactly!" said Parkapple. "Kest and Creswick were at Parkhurst about the same time. Creswick left first, some little time before Kest, but they certainly had some months together as fellow-guests in His Majesty's hotel, as they call it."

"They must have met!" exclaimed Preece. "In that case——"

"To be sure! But we haven't got to that yet," said Parkapple. "Continuing with Creswick—he proved himself, as his sort invariably do, quite a model and well-behaved prisoner, and earned the full period of remission. When he was discharged his friends sent him away—to Australia. He came back from Australia a few years after, called on his brother, who's a very respectable man at Brighton, and said he'd done well where he'd been, had saved a nice bit of money, and had come home to start life again in England under a new name—or, rather, under the name in which he'd left, which was Chissick. And then—he came here."

Parkapple uttered the last three words with a snap of his plump jaws, and, taking off his spectacles, put the paper back amongst his other documents. He picked up his cigar, which had smouldered at his side while he read, puffed at it for a minute, and then discharged a question, point-blank, at Preece.

"Know anything against him—as Chissick?" he asked.

But Preece shook his head, with definite decision.

"Nothing! Always a law-abiding man, I thought. Keen, they said, about his bargains, but—no, there's nothing whatever against him here."

Parkapple laid a finger on his newspaper extracts.

"I learn from these local accounts of the inquest on Kest that Chissick was one of the coroner's jury," he observed. "Did he show any particular interest in the case?"

"Not more than any other juryman," replied Preece. "That is, as far as I recollect."

"He was deeply interested, though," remarked Trace. "I can tell as to that. Kest was murdered in the presence of Tom Crowe here very early in the morning. By breakfast-time, the news had spread over the village. Before Tom and I had finished our breakfast, Chissick and Fewster——"

"Fewster—who's Fewster?" interrupted Parkapple sharply.

"A man who lives in the village, a retired business man, who was Chissick's great pal," replied Trace. "Chissick and Fewster, I say, before we'd finished breakfast that morning of Kest's murder, walked in here for news. They didn't get any!—I wouldn't allow Tom to speak. But—they were keen! Chissick especially. And, if we're going to be so confidential about it, I've come to a conclusion since—in fact, quite recently, since Chissick's death—why Chissick was keen, and what he really wanted!"

"Well, what do you think he really did want?" asked Parkapple.

Trace hesitated. Then he spoke firmly, more firmly than I had ever known him speak. "I think he wanted to assure himself that this boy was absolutely unable to identify the man who knifed Kest and ran away in the mist!" he answered. "Just—that!"

"And you wouldn't let this lad tell him?" suggested Parkapple.

"No! The lad himself refused to tell anything—then. But," added Trace significantly, "Chissick soon got to know!"

"How?"

"At the inquest. Tom told the coroner there, in his evidence, that he could not possibly identify the man."

"Did you notice if Chissick showed any sign of—well, anything, when he heard that?" enquired Parkapple.

"No! But he heard it. The point was emphasised," said Trace. "A good deal was made of it."

Parkapple turned to me.

"Sea fog, wasn't it, my boy?" he suggested. "Pretty thick?"

"Very thick, sir," I answered. "Thick, white, clinging!"

"But you saw the man who ran off after knifing Kest?"

"Oh, I saw him, yes, Mr. Parkapple—as a figure!"

"Well, now, as to a figure. Was his figure anything like Chissick's?"

"Well," I answered hesitatingly, "I should say—it was! A middle-height man, thick-set."

Parkapple began to put his papers in his bag. Suddenly, in the midst of a dead silence, he turned to me again.

"Are you a very sound sleeper, my lad?" he asked. "Real sound?"

"Yes, sir," I answered. "Especially when I've been out in the open all day."

"As you had on that occasion, I think," he remarked. "Do you think it possible that two men could have met and talked in the lower part of that old mill without waking you on the floor above?"

"Yes, sir," I said promptly. "I'm sure they could!"

He closed his bag with a snap of the catch and stood up.

"Looks to me, you know," he said, glancing at Preece and the other two, "as if Chissick, to give him his assumed name, had gone up there that morning to meet Kest, and as if they'd quarrelled and rushed out of the mill fighting, with the result we know of. Chissick may have been afraid of Kest giving him away as an ex-convict. I think, considering everything, that per-haps—only perhaps, mind you!—Chissick did murder Kest."

"But—who murdered Chissick?" muttered Macpherson. "Chissick!"

"Oh, that!" answered Parkapple, almost unconcernedly. "That is what we're going to find out!"

# CHAPTER TWENTY

## THE THATCHED ROOF

There was an air of jaunty confidence about Parkapple when he said this that made us all regard him with wonder. I suppose that what we all had in our minds was the fact that the local police and the previous detectives from London had done everything in their power to detect Chissick's murderer, and so far had failed. For the moment nobody spoke. But presently Macpherson found his tongue.

"Ye think that'll be an easy job, Mr. Parkapple?" he suggested.

"Don't know whether it'll be easy or difficult, Mr. Macpherson," answered the detective, with a laugh. "Difficult, I imagine! But it's what I'm here for."

"My opinion," remarked Macpherson, "is that this case needs a deal o' research. Whoever tackles it should go far back into the past, Mr. Parkapple!"

"Very likely, Mr. Macpherson, but I'm a man of the present! I can't—just now, at any rate—go raking up things of two-and-forty years ago. I want to find out who killed Chissick—perhaps we'll find out why later on."

"You're not concerned with the question of what Chissick dug out——"

"May have dug out, you mean," interrupted Parkapple good-humouredly. "I've no proof that he dug out anything!"

"Dug out, or may have dug out, o' yon cavity in the corner of his new shed," continued Macpherson imperturbably. "Do you tell me you attach no importance to that, now?"

"I'll attach no end of importance to it, Mr. Macpherson, if I find that it bears on the case," replied Parkapple. "You do, don't you?"

"My considered and deliberate opinion," said Macpherson solemnly, "is that the man Chissick dug up out o' that hole a parcel o' diamonds, contained in a tin box, which tin box, emptied of its contents, was discovered by Sergeant Preece in Chissick's waste-bin only recently, and that whoever murdered Chissick perpetrated that deed in order to rob him of those diamonds! Man!—we have the facts before us!"

"Well, let's see if we can spot the guilty man," said Parkapple. "When we've got him, we can find out what his motive was." He turned to Preece. "First of all," he continued, "there's the question of this man Trawlerson. You've failed to get any news whatever of him?"

"Absolutely!" replied Preece. "We've scoured the whole country-side for him! No good—none whatever! We've enquired at the place where he lives. It's quite true he's a nice little property there, at Fareham. He's known there as a quiet, respectable man. But the woman who acts as day-servant to him says he's never been home for some time; at least, if he has been, it must have been in the night, for she's never seen him. She says, indeed, she's never set eyes on him since a date that fits in with the time when all these things began. We've found out that he has a banking account at Portsmouth—well, he's never been at his bank for weeks, nor have they heard anything of him there, nor had any cheques of his presented, though they say that it had been his custom to get a small cheque cashed once a week at a tradesman's in Fareham. No!—we've heard nothing whatever of Trawlerson since Halkin saw him and heard him speak that Saturday evening at the garden gate of Chissick's house—nothing at all! He's clean vanished."

Parkapple took his papers out of his bag again and referred to something.

"Halkin, now?" he said presently. "Is he a dependable man?"

"Oh yes!" replied Preece. "Bit of a talker—I call him a humbug, myself—but you can depend on him. He's a village gossip, you understand—a sort of Nosey Parker—but in a matter of this sort I should believe his word."

"Well," said Parkapple, referring to his papers, "Halkin said that he saw and heard Trawlerson at Chissick's garden gate at dusk that Saturday evening, and evidently he thought, or wished it to be thought, that Trawlerson had been in Chissick's house. Now, according to the doctors, Chissick at that time had been dead some hours. That was what they said at the inquest, wasn't it?"

"They say so still," replied Preece. "I told them, of course, what Halkin said. They paid no attention to it. At least, what they said was this—Halkin may have heard and seen Trawlerson at Chissick's garden gate on that Saturday evening, but that makes no difference to their opinion. There were three doctors examined Chissick within an hour of the discovery of his dead body. They're all dead certain that when Chissick was found dead, he'd been dead not less than forty to forty-two hours. That shows that he was murdered Saturday noon."

Parkapple made no comment on this; he paid no attention to Macpherson's muttered remark that doctors were no more to be reckoned infallible than the Man of Rome. He put away his papers again, and turned to Preece.

"Well, I suppose nobody's interfered with that house of Chissick's?" he asked. "That is, nobody but yourselves?"

"No," replied Preece. "We've examined it pretty thoroughly, though. I don't think there's much likelihood of anything being discovered there."

"Perhaps not—but I'm going to examine it," said Parkapple. "I'll have a thorough look round it, this afternoon. You can all come and help, if you like," he continued, turning to the rest of us. "And," he added, addressing himself to Preece, "you must get me a carpenter—a man that you can trust to hold his tongue—and he must bring some tools with him. Knowing what I do know of Chissick, or, as he really was, Creswick, I'm going to know all I can about his house and what there is in it. We'll meet there at, say, two o'clock."

I was so excited at the prospect of actively engaging in real detective work that I could scarcely eat any dinner that day, and I was impatient enough to get off to Chissick's cottage when dinner was over. We encountered Parkapple and Preece as we went along the lane; they had Will Maddick with them, a young carpenter who had been employed by the dead man. Chissick's garden gate was secured by a padlock, of which Preece had the key; at Parkapple's instructions, he locked it again after we had all passed through. Preece had the keys of the house too; although summer was close at hand, it was cold and cheerless inside, and the silence that met us as we walked about was intensely depressing. Parkapple, however, was full of activity. He took a glance into every room in the place, upstairs and down; walked round the garden; examined the orchard and the yard at the back; and, having acquainted himself with the general aspect of the property, set to work on a more detailed inspection. He wanted a complete overhauling of everything, he said—just to satisfy himself about certain things. And having set Macpherson to one job, and Preece to another, and Trace to a third, and Maddick to a fourth, he tapped me on the shoulder and beckoned me to follow him outside to the back garden.

There was an old draw-well in a corner of that back garden; an ancient affair with a windlass and a bucket, and with a wooden covering over the top of the well-shaft. Parkapple led me straight to this, and himself lifted the cover. He peered down into the depths beneath. Standing beside him and peering down too, I could see the water shining far below.

"I wonder what the depth of that water is?" he said musingly. "Look in that outhouse, my boy, and see if you can find a rope and something heavy to fasten at the end of it."

I found a rope—which, to be exact, was an old clothes-line—easily enough, and a bit of old iron to act as a plummet, and went back to the well with them. Parkapple let the line down into the water until the weight touched bottom.

"Not much water in there," he remarked, drawing up the rope and showing me that no more than two or three feet of its length was wet. "Very poor supply, I should call that!—a dribbling sort of spring, if it is a spring. I should say it's nothing but drainings of surface water. Anyway, my lad, there's your bit of a job! You set to work and draw all that water out. There's the bucket—chuck the water away, anywhere, as you draw it."

This was not my idea of high-class detective work, but I didn't say so; instead, I took off my coat and waistcoat and rolled up my shirt-sleeves.

"What's the idea, Mr. Parkapple?" I ventured to enquire as I seized the handle of the windlass and pushed the bucket over the edge. "Do you think there's something down there, under the water?"

"Ah!" he answered, with a laugh. "Who knows? There's an old saying, my boy—truth lies at the bottom of a well! You clear all that water out, and when that's done, let me know, and we'll see about getting a ladder and going down to see if anything's lying in the mud."

He went off to the others in the house, and I set to work at my task. If I had read as much in those days as I have read since, I might have quoted something to Parkapple about:

> *"the toil*
> *Of dropping buckets into empty wells,*
> *And growing old in drawing nothing up."*

However, though there was but some two or three feet of water in it, that well was not empty, and I had to wind and unwind that old windlass a lot of times before the surface began to shrink appreciably. It was a hot afternoon, and a hot job. I had not only to hoist up each bucketful, but to unhook the bucket from the chain of the windlass and carry it—and it was heavy—across the orchard to a ditch that ran just within the hedgerow. Stiff work—but, after all, I was assisting in the detection, or attempted detection, of a crime.

We had had salted beef for dinner that day, at Trace's, and what with that, and the labour of drawing up and carrying that iron-bound bucket, I grew thirsty. So I went across to the back door of the cottage to get a cup or a mug, anything to dip into the next bucketful of water. And as I went, crossing patches of vegetables, and with no idea whatever of looking for anything, or seeing anything, or discovering anything, I suddenly saw—something!

Chissick's house, like a great many houses in that part of the country, was thatched—with straw. Thatching is a fine art thereabouts; a first-class roof of thatch will last you for two or three generations, perhaps longer. This house had been beautifully thatched. I was admiring the thatching as

I walked across the garden, between the beds of onions and beets. It was in two parts, that house. One, the principal wing, was tall, with a high, sloping roof; the other, the kitchen part, was low; you could touch the eaves of the thatch there with your hand. And at a corner of that part, just behind a thick holly-bush, I saw, slightly protruding from the thatch, something which I knew at once had nothing to do with it and had no place there, and looked like steel—it shone, though dully, in the sun. And I went up, and crowding in between the holly-bush and the wall, reached above me, and drew out from the thatch a length of steel, a sort of pick, or small crow-bar, on one end of which there were dark, thick stains, still sticky, and on them fragments of what I was sure was human hair.

I must have stood motionless for several minutes, staring at the thing in my hand. But I knew, all the time, that I was handling the weapon with which the life had been beaten out of Chissick. That was Chissick's hair!—Chissick's blood! It was as if the murder was being re-enacted.

A thrush suddenly perched in an apple-tree close by, and set up a loud song, and I started into activity at that and made for the house. There was no one in the kitchen. I heard Macpherson and Trace talking somewhere upstairs. I saw Preece examining a cupboard in the little hall. But I went straight into the parlour, where the detective and the carpenter were—literally—pulling to pieces an old bureau. I think my face must have gone pale, for they started as they stared at me.

"Mr. Parkapple!" said I, in a voice which I scarcely recognised as my own. "Look at this!"

He started afresh then, for he saw the stains and the bits of hair. But while he kept silent, staring, Maddick let out a cry:

"That's Mr. Fewster's! I know it! I've used it many a time when I've been working there!"

"What's Fewster's?" demanded Parkapple sharply. "That piece of steel?"

"Sure enough, sir! That's his—Fewster's! I've worked with it. More by token, look there—his initials stamped on it! He's a good lot of tools—a shed full of 'em, back of his house."

The other men had heard something unusual going on by that time, and they came crowding into the room in time to hear Maddick's last declaration. Parkapple took the piece of steel out of my hand gingerly.

"Where did you find this, my lad?" he asked.

"Thrust into the thatch, back of the house," I answered. "I saw it by accident—I think it had slipped down a bit from where it had been pushed in."

He turned to the other men, pointing.

"Look at that—and that!" he said, in a low voice. "Blood! Human hair! And Maddick says he recognises this bar as the property of that man you spoke of—Fewster!"

"No doubt about that, sir!" affirmed Maddick. "I tell you, I've used it many a time when I've been working there."

"Where does this Fewster live?" enquired Parkapple. "Just along here?" He hesitated a moment and then turned to Maddick. "Just run round there; see if he's at home. If he is, ask him to step along here to meet Sergeant Preece. But—not a word of this, you understand?"

Maddick nodded his complete comprehension, and hurried off. Parkapple laid the steel bar within a drawer and put a sheet of paper over it. He didn't seem inclined to talk, and the rest of us kept silence. And within a few minutes Maddick was back, with another nod at Parkapple. He had been running, and he panted out just one word:

"Coming!"

# CHAPTER TWENTY-ONE

## RECOGNITION

Fewster came bustling in at the gate a few minutes later. Maddick had left the front door open, and he walked straight into the hall, calling for Preece as he crossed the threshold. But Preece, at a sign from the detective, made no answer, and Fewster turned sharp into the parlour. The first man he set eyes on, standing right in front of him, was Parkapple.

I don't know why, but, quite apart from the discovery of the steel bar, I had a queer notion that something was going to happen when Fewster arrived—something out of the common. He couldn't see Macpherson, or Trace, or Preece, or Maddick, as he walked in; they were behind him, at the other side of the room. He could have seen me; I stood a little to Parkapple's right, between them. But he never looked at me; his eyes, starting, fixed themselves full on the little detective. And his big, flabby face turned white—a nasty, pasty white, and he caught his breath in a sudden gasp and half lifted a hand towards his heart. I realised then that Fewster knew Parkapple, and, glancing round, I saw that Parkapple knew Fewster.

I think the other three saw that too, and for a second there was a queer, dead silence. Then Parkapple spoke—and his voice was as hard and dry as ever human voice can be.

"Oh," he said. "Ah! So we meet again, Mr.—Fewster, eh? Just so! Some time since we last met, I think?"

It seemed like a full minute, or more, before Fewster replied. And before he spoke, he dropped into the nearest chair—suddenly. His voice was husky when it came, and he tapped his chest.

"I'll sit, if you please," he muttered. "Hurried here!—and I have—heart trouble. Some time, as you say, Mr. Parkapple—considerable time, sir."

Young as I was, I was sharp enough of wit to detect two dominant notes in Fewster's tones. One was obsequiousness, the other fear. And his actions showed that he was frightened. The big bandanna handkerchief of the sort that he always carried came out of his tail-pocket, and he mopped his pasty face; when he put the handkerchief away, his small eyes glanced furtively at the men standing on the other side of the room. He saw that they were all watching him, and I could see him shrink.

"Yes, but not so long that one can't recall everything about it," remarked Parkapple, still more dryly. "Um!—but I want to ask a few questions about recent events, Mr. Fewster. I understand that you knew this man Chissick, who's been murdered?"

"Yes, sir—yes, I knew Chissick," answered Fewster hurriedly. "Oh yes!"

"Known him long?" asked the detective.

"I was here when he came here, Mr. Parkapple—resident here."

"Just so—but had you known him before that?"

I could see that Fewster did not want to reply to that question. I could see, too, that he felt he'd got to. His answer came as hurriedly as before.

"Yes, yes, sir—yes, Mr. Parkapple, I had!"

"So it was a renewing of old acquaintance, eh, when Chissick came here?" suggested Parkapple. "Or—perhaps—it was due to you that he came? Was that it?"

"Well, sir, well—I certainly recommended this place to him—yes, you may say that was it, Mr. Parkapple—yes, I told him of the place, sir."

"As a likely sort of spot for a man to—retire to, eh?" observed Parkapple. "I see!"

"There was the chance of doing a little business in his line, sir," said Fewster. "That was the reason of my recommendation. I met him, accidentally, at Brighton. He wanted to do a bit of speculative building. I told him of this district. He came here. Nothing improper in that, I hope, sir?"

"No, I shouldn't think so," agreed Parkapple. "And, of course, you were very friendly after he came."

"We were friends, sir—we were friends. Both being bachelor-men, you see——"

"When did you see Chissick alive last?" asked Parkapple suddenly.

"The evening before his death, between six and seven o'clock," answered Fewster, with readiness. "Here!—in this room. I came to borrow a book he'd promised to lend. He mentioned that he was going to Brighton for the week-end. He often did that, Mr. Parkapple: he'd relatives there."

"Well, you say it was owing to you that he came here—to do a bit of building. I suppose you sometimes discussed his doings?"

"Oh, in just the ordinary way, Mr. Parkapple—just the ordinary way. He might tell me of his ideas, and I might pass a remark on them—no more than that, sir."

It seemed to me that Fewster's shade of fear was passing off. His voice was growing steadier, and the colour was coming back to his face. And when Parkapple put the next question to him he replied more readily than ever.

"When you were in here, then, the evening before his death, did he say anything to you about that latest job of his—building those bungalows on the hill-side?"

"No, sir! He never mentioned that job to me on that occasion."

Parkapple hesitated a moment; then he walked over to the bureau, lifted the sheet of paper, and taking up the steel bar, held it out to Fewster.

"Do you recognise that implement?" he asked.

Fewster's face paled again as he looked at the thing and saw what was on it. But he answered as readily as before.

"Yes—it's mine!" he said, "Chissick borrowed it from me a day or two before his death. He came and fetched it himself—took it with his own hands out of my tool-house; he said he wanted it to prise off the lid of a packingcase. The evening I called here—the evening before his death—I saw that tool; it was lying on that side-table there. He mentioned that he'd done with it, and I should have taken it with me, there and then, only I wasn't going home; I was just setting out for a walk."

Parkapple put the tool back in the bureau and closed the drawer.

"There's very little doubt that that's the thing with which Chissick was murdered," he remarked. "If it was still lying on that side-table—where, you say, you saw it the night before—on that Saturday morning, the murderer must have picked it up as he followed Chissick from this room on their way to the back door. But come outside, Mr. Fewster. Preece, come with us."

The three men went out; we heard them go to the back of the house. They were not long there; presently we saw them going down the front garden. Near the gate they paused, and for some time stood talking together. Fewster seemed to be explaining something to the other two. After a time, it was evident from their movements that all three came to some understanding. Fewster, looking much relieved, I thought, went away, and Parkapple and Preece came back to the house. The detective looked preoccupied; it was very clear that what had happened had given him a good deal to reflect upon.

"I think that's all we can do this afternoon," he said, as soon as he and Preece re-entered the parlour. "Of course, you'll all keep everything that's taken place to yourselves. Maddick, be careful not to say a word to anybody in the village! Well—lock the place up, Preece."

We all went away soon after that, Parkapple carrying the steel bar with him, carefully wrapped in paper. Outside the gate, Macpherson, who had been itching to speak for some time, nodded his head towards Fewster's house, the gables and chimneys of which we could see over his orchard.

"You'll be knowing yon man Fewster, I'm thinking, Mr. Parkapple?" he said, with a meaning glance. "You'll ha' set your eyes on him before?"

But Parkapple was not to be drawn.

"I've known and have set eyes on a sight of my fellow-creatures in my time, Mr. Macpherson!" said he. "And it wouldn't do for me to be answering questions about them. Well—thank you for your assistance, gentlemen."

He turned away towards the railway station, and Preece with him, and the rest of us went homeward. Macpherson showed signs of feeling affronted.

"Yon's a man o' the true-blood official sort," he muttered. "He gets what he can out of a body, and tells nothing in return! Where'll he be away to now, I wonder?"

"He'll be off to see the local police authorities, of course," said Trace. "To show them that bit of steel. It's a highly important discovery, that!"

"Aye, it's important!" agreed Macpherson. "But I'm thinking there's more important matters than yon to consider. When you take into account the fact that yon bit o' cold iron battered the life out of a living man, and that it's the property of Fewster, and that Fewster confessed it was his, there's a question I should have required a straight answer to before I'd let Fewster out o' my sight!"

"What?" enquired Trace.

"Oh, just this. I should ha' requested Fewster to give a circumstantial account of all his movements that Saturday, from his rising up to his lying down, and I should ha' wanted proof o' the truth of whatever he said in reply," answered Macpherson. "Aye, just that! But I suppose detective men have other notions."

"What you mean, Macpherson, is that you'd have made Fewster prove an alibi before you'd have let him go!" said Trace, with a laugh. "I should say—from what I've seen of Parkapple—that that's just what Parkapple did! When they were all there talking at the gate, Parkapple no doubt made Fewster tell his doings that Saturday."

"Man! Fewster could ha' told 'em as many lies as there's mites in an old cheese!" exclaimed Macpherson. "I said—proof! D'ye mind the look Fewster gave Parkapple when he walked into yon parlour? I do! D'ye recall the look Parkapple gave Fewster? Losh, man, I see it now! Those two had met!—aye, and where? And if you want my opinion, it is that when they last met, Fewster was in the dock, and Parkapple in the witness-box! Aye!"

"What—another revelation?" said Trace. "Come!"

"I'm telling you," persisted Macpherson. "Didn't you notice how very subservient yon big, fat man, a retired gentleman, as he's considered hereabouts, was to the detective, calling him sir and mister at every verse-end? Man!—yon Parkapple knows all about Fewster! Aye, it reminded me o' what I've seen, and you've seen yourself, Captain, at assizes and quarter-sessions, when the poor fellow in the dock's been found guilty—you know what happens then! There's a man appears with a bundle o' papers, few sometimes, and a many at other times, and reads out a record o' past misdeeds—previous convictions. Oh, man!—I'm afeard Parkapple recognised a naughty man in Fewster!"

I don't know what Trace was going to reply to this. We had just turned into the village street then, and our attention was diverted from the subject in hand by the sight of a group of people, mainly old men, women, and children, gathered in front of Sergeant Preece's cottage. They seemed to be listening to voluble speech on the part of a woman who, holding two children by the hands, one on either side of her, was addressing herself to all and sundry. She was an ill-dressed, haggard-looking creature, of a shrewish aspect, and her voice was strident and insistent. But at sight of us she grew silent, and Mrs. Preece, the sergeant's wife, who was standing at her garden gate, pushed her way through the throng and approached us.

"Have you seen anything of my husband, Captain Trace?" she asked. "Do you know where he is, sir?"

"I believe he's gone into town with Mr. Parkapple," replied Trace. "What is it, Mrs. Preece? Something gone wrong?"

Mrs. Preece indicated the complaining woman.

"It's Mrs. Halkin," she answered. "She's come down to the village to say that her husband's disappeared. He went out—when was it, Mrs. Halkin?"

"Night before last!" said Mrs. Halkin angrily. "Without a word to me, either. I've no idea where he was going, nor why! All I know is, he's never come back, and there I am left with these here childer up in that cottage, all alone, and what I say is, that what's the use of having policemen about if they can't find a woman's husband, and——"

Macpherson laid a hand on Mrs. Halkin's shoulder.

"Aye, just so!" he said soothingly. "And now let's be hearing all about it, my lass! What time o' night was it when Halkin went out?"

We heard the whole story; the rest of the folk listened, open-mouthed, for certainly the second, and perhaps the third time. There was not a great deal to tell, though Mrs. Halkin made a great deal of it. That day was a Wednesday. On the Monday night, Halkin, after having his supper at eight o'clock, had gone out of the house, and had never returned to it.

"Was it a habit of his to go out o' nights, now?" asked Macpherson. "Maybe he'd come down to the public and take his glass?"

But there an old man, who supported himself on two sticks, raised his voice.

"No, master, he wasn't a man for the public, wasn't Halkin! You'd see him there now and then, but very seldom. No—not a sociable man, he wasn't."

"Well, did he go out o' nights?" enquired Macpherson, again turning to Mrs. Halkin. "If that was his habit——"

But Mrs. Halkin suddenly froze into silence—on that question, at any rate. Muttering something about the police again, and that Halkin would have to be found, she dragged off her children and disappeared towards the hill-side, taking no further notice of Macpherson and his questions. The old man who had volunteered information as to Halkin's lack of sociability volunteered more.

"Her isn't goin' to say no more on that there p'int, master," he remarked with a sly look. "Her don't want no inconvaynient questions. Halkin!—ah, there be them as do know a bit about he! Halkin, he be a poacher! mighty clever hand he be at that, Halkin! I misdoubt he've come to some mishap in they woods. For there 'tis—he be a poacher!"

# CHAPTER TWENTY-TWO

## THE LIGHT IN THE MILL

We had plenty of food for thought and subjects for discussion over our tea in Trace's parlour that afternoon. The uppermost—being the last—was the disappearance of Halkin. Had it anything to do with the rest of things?—with the more important matter of Chissick's murder? Macpherson was quick to start a theory. It was his belief that Trawlerson was still in the neighbourhood, lurking about, and probably in a position to get news of what was going on. Supposing Trawlerson had heard what Halkin had said about him—that he, Trawlerson, had been seen leaving Chissick's garden on the evening of the murder? Supposing Trawlerson, prowling about the woods at night, and coming across Halkin, engaged in his poaching work, had gone for him—silenced him, as a man who knew a secret?

"I misdoubt we shall be hearing of a third murder!" he concluded lugubriously. "I misdoubt it!"

But Trace shook his head. He had never had any good opinion of Halkin, whom he had always regarded as a sly, canting rogue. His idea about Halkin's disappearance was that the man had cleared out to get away from his wife, who was well known to be a shrew. Halkin didn't interest him; he was wondering about the events of the afternoon, and if Parkapple and Preece would come back to us that evening with more news. But neither Preece nor Parkapple came; nobody came, until, long after dark, a timid tap at the back door summoned me to find Mrs. Halkin standing there, alone.

Mrs. Halkin had a big shawl about her head and shoulders, closely gathered around her sharp-featured face; her entire attitude suggested secrecy and mystery, and when she addressed me, it was in a whisper.

"Young man!" she said wheedlingly. "That housekeeper of the Captain's, now—is she in?"

"No!" said I. "She's out—it's her day out."

She came a bit nearer at that.

"Because," she went on, still whispering, "I don't want no women to hear what I've got to say—women, they talk! I don't mind you and the other gentleman. But it's the Captain I want to see. Confidential!"

Trace had overheard the whispering, and just then came to see what it was all about. I motioned Mrs. Halkin to come in.

"She wants to tell you something, I think," I said, turning to Trace. "Private!"

"Which I don't know anybody else in the village that I could tell it to, Captain Trace," said Mrs. Halkin. "I know a gentleman when I see one, and I was housemaid in an officer's family before I wed Halkin, and——"

Trace stopped her flood of talk by asking her into the parlour. I don't think he felt any pleasure at seeing her, and though he gave her a chair politely enough, his tone was curt.

"Well?" he said. "What is it, Mrs. Halkin?"

Mrs. Halkin showed more of her sharp features and inspected the three of us, especially Macpherson, who, stolidly smoking his pipe, took stock of her in return.

"Feeling as how I couldn't stop in that cottage up yonder one mortal hour longer," she said, "and there being neither sign nor sound of Halkin, I've brought the children down to my mother's in the village, and there they are and will be, and me too. And I came here, knowing as I do that here's a gentleman as a deserted woman can speak to, free! Not minding this here young man, nor the gentleman across there, busy with his bit of tobacco——"

"What is it you want to say, Mrs. Halkin?" asked Trace. "Out with it, now?"

"Which I wasn't going to say anything this afternoon, Captain Trace," she announced. "Not before that Mrs. Preece, though, to be sure, I want Preece to find Halkin—if he can, which I doubt. But this here is not for Preece, but for you, as can give better advice than what Preece can." She paused for a second or two, looking from one to the other of us as if in preface to some momentous announcement. "Captain!" she said, in a low, meaning voice. "Halkin!—he has money!"

We all stared at each other. I don't think any of us had the ghost of an idea as to what she meant. None of us spoke.

"Money!" she repeated. "And—them above alone knows where he got it from! I don't—and me his lawful wedded!"

"What do you mean about his having money, Mrs. Halkin?" asked Trace. "Do you mean he's got some large sum lately, or—what?"

She nodded her shawled head slowly two or three times.

"Halkin," she announced. "Halkin—he said to me, not so many days ago, that he'd come into a bit of the ready, and maybe we'd leave these parts altogether and go to a new country, across the sea. No more than that—and I didn't dare to ask questions, for Halkin, though he's as meek as a whipped dog when he's at that chapel, is not pleasant to deal with under his own roof, being of a strange temper. But one night I watched him, through a crack in the wall, when he thought I'd gone to bed, and I saw him count money. A fortune!"

"And how much might ye reckon that would be, my good woman?" asked Macpherson. "There'd be gold in it, no doubt?"

"There was gold money and there was bank-notes, mister," replied Mrs. Halkin. "I couldn't say how much there was, but it was more money than I'd ever set eyes on in my life, or Halkin either, I'll warrant! I say—a fortune!"

"Perhaps he's had a legacy left to him?" suggested Trace.

"I never heard of nobody as could leave him such, Captain," said Mrs. Halkin. "On no side at all!—neither father's nor mother's, nor uncles' nor aunts'. However, there it is! As I say, Halkin has money!"

"What did he do with it, mistress, when you watched him?" enquired Macpherson.

"He put it all in a belt—a new belt it was too—and fastened it round his waist, mister, next to his shirt, if I may mention such a garment to gentlemen," replied Mrs. Halkin. "And from that time to the time of his disappearance he never had that belt off of him! No!"

There was a moment's silence. Then Trace spoke.

"Mrs. Halkin! What do you think yourself?"

The woman fingered her shawl for awhile before she replied.

"I think it likely that Halkin's run away and left me and those children, Captain Trace," she said at last. "Halkin!—he's none the man he professed to be down here in the village! He's an oily tongue and a black heart. He hasn't treated me well. I think he's run away with that money. And I wanted to ask you, for I'm sure you'll know—isn't there some way of tracing people through them bank-notes? He'll have to change them——"

"You don't know the numbers of the notes, Mrs. Halkin," said Trace. "But if Halkin had all this money on him when he went away, you ought to let the police know. He may have come to some harm. Now come, Mrs. Halkin, look here!—it's no use keeping things back. Is it true that Halkin used to go poaching?"

She made no reply at first, but eventually she nodded.

"He went out at nights a deal, Captain," she admitted. "I dare say——"

"You'll know, now," said Trace. "He couldn't keep it from you."

"Well, of course, he'd bring a thing or two home, now and again," she said. "He was, as I say, out o' nights. And—it was night when he went off."

"You'll have to tell everything to the police," said Trace. "He may have been murdered for that money. Come with me, now, Mrs. Halkin. I'll go down to Preece's with you. It's the only thing to do."

He took her away there and then, but he was soon back with me and Macpherson, saying that Preece and Parkapple had not yet returned, and that he had sent Mrs. Halkin along to her mother's. Macpherson was already considering what we had just heard.

"Where did yon man Halkin live?" he asked.

"In a lonely cottage, up the hill-side," said I.

"Anywhere in the neighbourhood o' yon old mill?" he suggested.

"Half a mile from it—to the west," I replied.

Macpherson puffed slowly at his pipe for some time—in silence.

"Aye!" he remarked at last. "A man that's evidently double-dealing in his nature and actions, and that goes out o' nights, and lives in the neighbourhood o' yon awesome old ruin on top o' the hill—Captain!—it would no surprise me if Halkin hasn't been mixed up in these crimes! It would not!"

It was just what I had been thinking myself, ever since Mrs. Halkin had told us about the money and her husband's habit of night-strolling. Halkin, I thought, might, after all, be the man who ran away in the mist. But, to my surprise, Trace shook his head.

"In some indefinite, chance way—accessory after the facts—he might have been, Macpherson," he replied. "But actively, no! The man's an arrant coward! I know his sort—he hasn't the spunk to be a courageous criminal. If he thought of murdering anybody, the shadow of the gallows would fall heavy across his vision, and he'd slink and run."

"Aye, well, and I'm no so sure o' that," said Macpherson. "Meet a man in a straight fight for life—no, I'm not saying he'd do that. But yon Chissick was felled from behind—a coward's blow! And that—aye, I think Halkin would be the man to hit when 'twas sure he couldn't be hit back. Captain!—yon man has something more to do with all this than's been reckoned on!"

"It's all queer, and all suspicious," agreed Trace. "And this detective, Parkapple, should know. Tom," he went on, turning to me, "go down to Preece's after awhile and see if he and Parkapple have come back, and get them to come up here, if they have. Parkapple must be posted up."

I went along to Preece's cottage at ten o'clock that evening. He had not returned; his wife had heard nothing of him since his going out with the detective early in the afternoon. Still, she felt sure that he wouldn't be long. Instead of telling her what I wanted—for I was becoming wonderfully close and cautious amidst all these doings—I said I would look in again, later, and went away; not to return to Trace's house, but to wander up the village, in the darkness, wondering what the secrets were which, so far, seemed as impenetrable as the sea-fog into which Kest's murderer had vanished.

It had been a hot day, that, one of the first really hot days we had that summer, and the cool night air that swept about the foot of the hill was grateful and refreshing. I went wandering aimlessly up the hill-side, past the shed that Chissick had built; past the oak trees. I was scarcely thinking about where I went; anyway, I went higher up than I had meant to, and eventually to the place where Kest had fallen before the unknown man's knife. The recognition of that spot pulled me up short. I stood there in the darkness, reconstructing the crime, living over again the thrilling moments in which I had stared from the mill window, horror-struck, at the struggling men. That made me glance at the mill itself, standing black and gaunt against sky and stars, and as I glanced I saw, somewhere within it, a moving light.

There were cracks in the timbers of that mill; it was through them that I saw the light—a mere spark. But it moved. As I stood there, I saw it move from one side of the lower part of the structure to another; after it had wavered there awhile, it disappeared. But I caught it again, higher up. Evidently, whoever held it had climbed the stair to the upper chamber from which, through the hole in the floor, I had watched Kest eat his bread and meat, and sup at his gin-and-water, and examine his map. And after a time it went still higher, and I remembered then that from that upper chamber a ladder rose to the dome at the extreme top of the mill. Plainly this explorer was climbing it.

My first instinct was to go boldly forward, nearer, and to wait until whoever it was that was in the mill came out by the half-ruinous doorway—the only means of egress. But I suddenly realised that it would be a foolish, and probably a highly risky, thing to do. It was more than likely that the man inside would have a confederate outside, watching. If there was such a confederate, he might already be watching me. Still . . .

I dropped on hands and knees at last, curiosity getting the better of me, and, with infinite caution, began to wriggle my way across the intervening space, taking advantage of any available cover. And very soon I came to the conclusion that the man in the mill, whatever he was after, was doing his job alone, and had no confederate, either inside or outside. Once hearing the scream of a rabbit, chased, no doubt, by stoat or weasel, in some adjacent warren, I paused, wondering if it really was a rabbit's cry, or some skilful imitation of it by human lips, a signal to the light-carrier from a companion who had detected me. But it came again, once, sharply, and I knew it for what it was, and went on, crawling on my belly like a snake, and so I came up to where there was thick heather around the lower walls of the mill, and amongst that I lay still as a mouse when there are cats around, and waited, watching.

That spot was immediately in front of the ragged aperture in which the door had once been. I knew the man was still in the mill, for as I had wriggled along I had paused from time to time and watched the light. It was still in the slatted dome, high above, when I took up my position in the thick heather. And the holder of it must either have considered himself very safe from interruption or been prepared to take risks, for he was up there for a considerable time, fifteen or twenty minutes, I reckoned, before the light moved downwards. But—it moved at last, and presently, straining my ears, I heard steps, cautious but heavy, coming down the stair to the lower floor. I saw no more of the light, however. The next thing was a man, his figure silhouetted against the night and the stars, moving away from the mill in the direction of the woods.

The man was not Halkin: I knew that as soon as I clapped eyes on him. Nor was he Trawlerson: I knew that too. Halkin and Trawlerson were much alike in build and figure: men of medium height, and squarely built. But this—I saw his figure clearly enough, sharply outlined against the sky— was a tall man, of spare build; a fellow of long legs. Those legs carried him swiftly away. I had no sooner taken a good look at him than he was vanishing in the gloom; a second or two, and he was gone. And presently I heard the crackle of dry leaves, and the sound of a creaking branch as he set foot within the adjacent wood.

Presently, too, I sprang to my feet and raced down the hill-side, wondering and excited. But instead of bursting in on Trace and Macpherson with this latest news, I called again at Preece's cottage. All was dark there; Mrs. Preece put her head out of the bedroom window and told me that the sergeant had not returned. I went home then, and for the next ten minutes had Macpherson and Trace listening open-mouthed. Macpherson shook his head knowingly when I had done.

"Aye!" he said ruminatively. "All of a piece with the rest of it—mysteries to the end!—wherever that may be. Man about?—aye! Something'll have to be done, Captain, that's no been attempted so far!"

We did nothing that night—except talk a bit before going to bed. We were all disappointed, I think, that Preece didn't come knocking at the door, and I know that it was a long time before I went to sleep. I was awake before my time next morning too, and at half-past five I got up, and, going downstairs, lighted the kitchen fire and put on the kettle in preparation for an early cup of tea. And the kettle was just beginning to sing, and I was measuring the tea into its pot, when I heard a click of the garden gate, and, looking out of the window, saw Preece, half dressed, coming up the path.

# CHAPTER TWENTY-THREE

## THE REGISTERED PACKET

Preece dropped into a chair as soon as I had opened the door to him, and he cocked a longing eye at the kettle.

"Making tea, Tom?" he asked. "Give me a cup, my lad! I'm wanting something of that sort. Parkapple and me, we were with the chief and the inspector over yonder last night till I don't know what time, discussing things—it was past midnight when we got back here. You were enquiring for me, my missis says. And the Captain too?"

"We were both after you, Mr. Preece," I replied, handing him a cup of tea. "He was down there once, and I called twice. Did Mrs. Preece tell you what it was about?"

"She said—Halkin," he answered. "Now he's off, I understand! Nice game the way they sling their hook, some of 'em! First Trawlerson—now Halkin. But what did the Captain want? My missis, she says he had Mrs. Halkin with him."

Just then Trace himself came downstairs in his dressing-gown and slippers. He told Preece all about Mrs. Halkin's story of the money which she had seen in her husband's possession. Preece, sipping his tea, listened and nodded.

"May have something to do with all the rest of it," he observed. "I don't know! I'm sure my poor head got fairly thick with listening last night to the discussion between our bosses and Parkapple! It's like being in one of those mazes you read about—you don't know which turning to take. Parkapple—he jawed it all over last night at our headquarters from every standpoint you could think of!"

"Any good come of it?" asked Trace.

"None, so far!" replied Preece. "There's things going to be done, of course."

"Fewster?" suggested Trace.

"Fewster," said Preece, "satisfied Parkapple, before he let him go yesterday afternoon, as to his movements on the day of the murder of Chissick—never left his own house that day, and can prove it. All the same, our people at headquarters want to see Fewster, and that reminds me of one of the two things I came in for. One was to ask you, Captain, what you brought Mrs. Halkin to see me for; and the other was to ask Tom there if he'd go an errand for me—I'm hurried this morning, for I've got to shave and dress and be off with Parkapple as soon as we've had a bit of breakfast."

"What is it, Mr. Preece?" I asked.

"Nothing much," he answered. "Just slip along to Fewster's, and ask him if he'll meet me and Parkapple at our station at nine o'clock—say, to go with us into town by the 9.7. He'll know what it means."

He talked a few minutes longer about his and Parkapple's doings of the previous evening, and then went off, and soon after seven o'clock, when I thought I should be sure to find him up, I ran round to Fewster's house. Fewster, like Chissick, was a bachelor—a single man, anyhow—and, also like Chissick, he had a sort of charwoman-housekeeper, a Mrs. Singleton, who came at eight o'clock every morning and left after tea-time in the afternoon. I knew that Fewster was an earlyish riser. I had often seen him in his garden at seven o'clock of a morning. I expected to find him in it on this occasion. But when I got to his gate, the garden was empty, and all the blinds of the house were drawn. Clearly, Fewster was not up.

I knocked two or three times at the front door and got no answer. I went round to the back and knocked again, more loudly. Nobody came to that door either. And then it flashed upon me that now, most likely, there was another disappearance!—Fewster, once free of Preece and Parkapple the previous afternoon, had made his preparations and run away.

However, I began to prowl about the house, to see if I could find any crevice or loophole through which I could see into the interior. I poked up the slot of the letter-box in the front door and peered into the hall. I saw Fewster's hats and his overcoats, his umbrellas and his walking-sticks, but no sign of him. At the back door I found an old tub, and, mounting it, looked through the glass transom above the door into the kitchen. There was nothing to see there, except that on the table there was a supper laid out—cold beef, bread, butter, cheese, pickles, and a bottle of whisky and a syphon of mineral water by it. There was a knife and fork laid for one; on the plate between them lay a slice or two of beef, untouched. It looked to me as if Fewster had just carved beef for himself, and then, before picking up his knife and fork to eat it, had been interrupted by somebody or something. But—why had he never resumed his interrupted meal?

I was going away—hurriedly, for it occurred to me that I had better let Preece and Parkapple know of this as soon as possible—when, glancing again at the window of the front room as I passed it on my way through the garden, I noticed that one of the laths of the Venetian blind was out of place. At that I turned aside, and, stepping across the flower-bed under the window, looked into the room. And the morning was gloriously light and sunny, and the light flooded that room, in spite of the blind, and I could see everything in it, and the first thing I saw was Fewster himself—or what had been Fewster. He was sitting in a very big easychair, right opposite me. He lay back in it, his hands and arms dangling over the padded sides; his head drooped towards his left shoulder. And I knew that he was not asleep, but dead!—as dead as Chissick, as dead as Kest . . . dead!

The thing gave me a shock—but instead of running headlong away, I stood with my eyes glued to that window for a full minute, staring into the room. I think I was wondering if Fewster had died as the result of some attack on him. But the room was so tidy—as tidy as Chissick's. These men who lived all alone, I thought, must have a passion for neatness. No—there were no signs of any disorder there. It looked to me as if Fewster had just sat down in that chair and collapsed—suddenly.

The click of the garden gate made me start. Glancing round, I saw Mrs. Singleton entering. She carried a basket and a sweeping-brush; the difference between the evidence of her peaceful mission and my knowledge of what there was in that house struck me with strange force. At sight of me she opened her mouth and stared, speechlessly. I went towards her.

"Mrs. Singleton!" I whispered, as though we were already in the presence of the still figure in the parlour. "Don't be frightened, but—there's something wrong! I came here to see Mr. Fewster, and I couldn't get any answer at the door, so I looked through the window. He's sitting there in a chair, in the parlour—and I'm sure he's dead!"

Her mouth opened wider than ever, and it seemed quite a long time before her lips relaxed and let out something like a sigh.

"You don't say!" she exclaimed. "Well—he's been that bad with his heart this some time past that I can't say as I'm surprised, though, of course, coming so sudden, like . . . but we'll go in and make sure."

She fumbled in her pocket, found a latchkey, and made for the front door. But I drew her attention to the lath in the Venetian blind.

"Look through that first," I said. "See what I saw!"

She stepped up to the window, peered through, stepped back swiftly.

"I'm afraid it's what you say, Mr. Crowe," she said. "That peaceful and still, too! Yes, I'm afraid he's gone, poor thing!"

She opened the door and we went in, on tiptoe, and into the parlour. I laid a hand on Fewster's forehead—stone-cold!

The woman at my side was whispering; she too had laid her fingers on one of the dead man's hands.

"Mr. Crowe," she said, "we must get somebody here! He's been dead some time. And—there's the laying-out, you know. They—they get stiff, you see! If you'll run to fetch somebody——"

I left her there with all the stillness of the place about her and ran as fast as legs could carry me, first to Preece, then to our own house. Preece and Parkapple were at breakfast already, but as soon as they heard the news they threw down their knives and forks and hurried off; so, a few minutes later, did Trace and Macpherson, neither fully dressed. When we reached Fewster's house, the two policemen were already there, and Mrs. Singleton was telling them something.

"Anyway, that's how it is, gentlemen," she was saying. "The key of the back door isn't there, neither inside nor outside. It looks to me as if somebody had been in this house since—since that happened," she said, nodding towards the parlour, "and had gone out by the back door, locking it from outside, and had taken the key away. I've never known it to be missing before. Perhaps—perhaps somebody's done something to the poor man!—his heart, I know, was that bad that the least shock would give him the palpitations."

They all went into the parlour and looked at Fewster. Macpherson said something about a doctor.

"Sent for him as we came along," muttered Preece. "He'll not be long. No signs of any struggle here, I think—everything's in order."

He glanced at Parkapple, who, after a searching look at the dead man, had begun to inspect the room.

"No," said Parkapple, "I see no signs of anything. Judging from what we saw in the kitchen just now, I should say he was going to have his supper, came in here for something, had a seizure, sat down and died straight off. Well—I think he's probably taken secrets with him!" He paused a moment, and then glanced at Trace and Macpherson. "You saw that he and I recognised each other yesterday?" he continued. "Well—I'll tell you who he was—used to be, anyway. I told Preece last night. Last time I saw him was in the dock at the Central Criminal Court, a good many years ago now. He got five years."

"For what?" asked Macpherson.

"Receiving stolen goods," answered Parkapple. "I arrested him—I and another of our men. It was a second conviction. Of course, Fewster isn't his real name. Real name is Foester—came from Germany when he was a young man. I've often wondered where he'd got to. He was a cute, clever chap in those days. Well—that's over! And—just when we were wanting to get more news out of him! Unfortunate, this!"

The doctor came hurrying in. But we saw at once that Fewster's sudden death was in no way surprising to him. He said so, at once.

"His heart has been in such an absolutely rotten condition for some time that I've warned him over and over again against sudden exertion, excitement, anything of that kind," he said. "He was liable to go at any minute. And that's how he did go!"

"Quite suddenly?" asked Trace.

"With absolute suddenness!" asserted the doctor. "He probably felt himself turn faint, sat down where you see him, and died straight off. I suppose this'll have to be reported to the coroner. But there's really no necessity for an inquest. As I've attended him for months, I can give a certificate."

They carried Fewster away into another room, and left him to Mrs. Singleton and some women that she had fetched.

And then Parkapple began to look about the parlour, and suddenly drew our attention to certain matters which lay on an old blotting-pad on a side-table. There was some cotton-wool; some sealing-wax; some small sheets of brown paper; a length of string; a bedroom candlestick, on which wax, red wax, had been dropped.

"Making up a parcel, eh?" he muttered. "And—recently. Well——"

He hesitated a moment, then saying that he would be back presently, left the room; next minute we saw him walking quickly down the garden. The rest of us remained there, talking in low voices. Half an hour went by; then Parkapple came hurrying back. I saw by his expression that he had learned something.

"I've found out a bit of really important news," he said as he came into the parlour and carefully closed the door. "Early yesterday evening Fewster took a small, sealed parcel—evidently a cardboard box—to the post office here, and registered it. I've got the address it was sent to: 'Mr. J. Foster, Post Office, Brighton.' And now I want to find the receipt they gave him at this office when he handed it in!"

# CHAPTER TWENTY-FOUR

## THE UNCUT DIAMOND

It was easy to see that Parkapple attached some extraordinary importance to the finding of that receipt. Without any delay he went off to the room to which Fewster's dead body had been carried, and presently came back carrying the suit of clothes of which the woman had just divested him. Laying these garments on the table in the parlour, he began to go through them himself, examining every pocket in coat, waistcoat, and trousers with great care. First he removed and laid in order all the contents; then he literally turned the pockets inside out. There was nothing in the pockets but the things he took from them; he began, then, to examine those. A pocket-book—nothing; a purse—nothing; nothing, at any rate, in the shape of the thing he wanted, which, of course, was a mere scrap of flimsy paper. Parkapple began to look serious, and even perturbed.

"Likely he'd put it away in some drawer when he came home with it," suggested Macpherson. "He'd no doubt have a place for receipts, and would put it in there at once; he seems to have been a man of methodical and tidy habits. Ye'll be for considering the finding o' this bit paper an important thing, Mr. Parkapple?"

Parkapple replied, somewhat testily, that what he was doing showed that he did. Bidding us not to touch the things on the table, he turned to an old-fashioned writing-desk that stood in a corner of the room and began to examine that. In its top drawer he found a lot of papers, and a file of receipts—tradesmen's bills, and that sort of thing—but not what he wanted. Clearly, the next arrangement of things in that drawer proved Fewster's orderliness—but there was no receipt for the registered packet. Still, Parkapple went on looking for it; under his instructions we began to help. We examined every drawer and box in the place; we looked into every ornament on the chance that he might have popped the bit of paper aside in that way; we eventually ransacked every corner of the house, and I, personally, inspected every scrap of torn-up stuff in a waste-paper basket, while Preece even took the coals and wood out of the parlour grate to see if Fewster had thrown the receipt away in there. We were at the job for the better part of three hours, and at the end of that time we had found nothing. And at last

Parkapple gave up the search as a bad job, and turned to the rest of us with a shake of his head that had something enigmatical about it.

"Never expected to find it!" he exclaimed suddenly. "I only wanted to make sure. Of course, it's just what I expected. Stolen!"

We all looked at him in astonishment. He shook his head again, pointing towards the kitchen.

"You know what that woman drew our attention to, Preece, when we came in here this morning?" he said. "That the key of the back door is missing. Well, she's been coming here for years—ever since Fewster came to live here—and she's never known that key to be missing before. She's dead certain it was in the lock, inside, yesterday afternoon—it was her custom, she says, to lock the kitchen door from the inside when she went away, and to leave by the front door. Well, when she comes this morning, after finding her employer dead, she goes to the kitchen door, and finds it locked, but the key not in the lock. She goes outside—the key's not there. We've pretty well tooth-combed this house in searching for that receipt, and we haven't come across the key. What's the inference? That somebody came here last night, probably after Fewster's death, found the receipt for the registered packet lying about, took it, went out by the back door, locked it from outside, and took the key away."

"For what reason do you think, Mr. Parkapple?" asked Macpherson.

Parkapple shrugged his shoulders.

"Might be with the idea of returning," he said. "The front door, as you'll see if you go and look at it, is only secured by a latch-lock. Now, Mrs. Singleton says that there used to be two latch-keys, of which she'd one and Fewster the other. Fewster lost his, some time ago, and never replaced it: he used to go in and out by the back door. Whoever it was that came here last night—and I'm sure somebody did!—he may have had fears of being interrupted, and, noticing that he couldn't get in again at the front door, have taken the key of the back with him, intending to come back later on. Anyway, I feel sure that somebody was here, and that, whoever he was, he stole that receipt, and there's only one thing for me to do, and I must do it at once. I must get off to Brighton to see about the packet that Fewster sent there, to be called for. I only hope I'm not too late. How far is it, by road, Preece?"

"Twenty miles!" answered Preece. "And you can get a car here in the village—a good one."

"All right—that's the next thing," said Parkapple. "But first"—he turned to the drawer of the writing-desk and picked up a cheque-book which lay on top of a pile of papers—"I just want to look at this—an idea's struck me. Look at this!" he continued, after turning the book over. "Here's a somewhat significant entry! See this counterfoil—it refers to a cheque drawn in favour of self for five hundred pounds! What should Fewster want with cash to that extent—here?"

Preece pointed to the date on the counterfoil.

"That's the same date, the Monday that Chissick was found murdered!" he said. "Do you think there's any connection?"

"According to what Captain Trace there heard last night," observed Parkapple, with a dry smile, "I should say there was! It's my impression that the money which Fewster drew with the cheque of which this is the counterfoil found its way, there and then, into Halkin's pockets! That's about it! Well—I'm going off to Brighton, at once. You must see to everything here, Preece. Now, where do I find the car you spoke of just now?"

While he was putting on his coat, which he had taken off during the search, and Preece was telling him where the man lived who had a car for hire, Mrs. Singleton came into the room. She held out her right hand, in the palm of which lay something the exact like of which I had never seen—an object, about the size of a small bean, which looked, to me, like some sort of pebble, except that within it there seemed to be, deep down, a curious light or radiance. But Parkapple knew what it was, and he seized on it with a sharp exclamation.

"Good Lord!" he muttered. "Where did you get this?"

"It was lying on the floor of the bedroom, sir," said Mrs. Singleton. "Just in front of the cupboard by the bedside. Mrs. Pilch found it just now, tidying up the room."

Parkapple held the find out to the rest of us, turning it over with his finger.

"That's a diamond!" he said. "In the rough! I've seen plenty in my time. Unpolished, uncut, you know. You see, there's an interior radiance in it. That dull film over the outside is called, technically, the 'Nyf'—a sort of outer skin. Feel how intensely hard it is! And a good size too!—if all the rest of 'em are like that. . . ." He nodded significantly, and put the stone carefully away in his purse. "Well, that's another reason why I should be off. The rest of those things, my friends, are to be found at Brighton post office—unless I'm too late!"

Macpherson buttonholed him as he was leaving the room.

"Man!" he said solemnly. "Although you've no confessed it, you've come round to the theory that I put before you in the beginning of our acquaintance—that all this springs out of the black affair of two-and-forty years ago! Is it not so?"

"Something of that sort, Mr. Macpherson, something of that sort!" agreed Parkapple. "I'll give you all credit, and compliment you too, when we've got it over. But time's precious, so let me go."

Macpherson let him go, and soon after he had gone, he, Trace, and I left Fewster's body and house to Preece, and went homeward; my two elders suddenly remembering that, save for the cups of tea and dry biscuits I had taken to them early in the morning, they had not yet broken their fast. Macpherson was full of talk, and of self-appreciation; things were turning out as he had anticipated.

"There's little doubt in my mind how this affair has worked out," he said, as we sat over our late breakfast. "When yon young Dan Welgrave was murdered all those years ago, whoever murdered him, Flinch or Charlesworth, or both, placed the diamonds they found on him in yon old Cape Town tobacco-box under the tree on the hill-side up there below the mill. Through many a queer channel, through those channels—twisting and winding and black they were!—that we heard of from Pyker and Cushion, the news came along at last to Chissick. I think Chissick got it, somehow or other, when he was having his deal with Kest for the bit of land. I think Chissick murdered Kest. Tom here is a sound sleeper—it's me that's well acquaint with that fact, for hard work have I had to get him out of bed many's the time in the days when he wore an apron and sold currants and raisins—and I think he never heard Chissick and Kest in talk in that mill, nor saw the beginning of the fracas which ended in Chissick's sticking a knife in the other man's throat. Aye, I think Chissick murdered Kest—I do think that!"

"And who murdered Chissick, do you think, Macpherson?" asked Trace. "You'll have settled that in your mind, no doubt?"

"I'm no so sure about that as I am about the other," admitted Macpherson. "It may have been Trawlerson. It may have been Fewster. But certain I am of this—Chissick found those diamonds when he did his bit digging in yon new shed, and somebody knew that he'd found them. And I'm assured, too, of another thing—whoever murdered Chissick did it for the diamonds, and—dead sure!—the diamonds found their way, sharp and speedy, into Fewster's hands. Fewster?—aye, the man's dead, and, as yon detective said, it's likely he carried secrets with him—dark ones!"

"One of the queerest things about this business," remarked Trace, after a pause, "in its latest developments, anyway, is the almost simultaneous disappearance of Halkin and Trawlerson. I've wondered, Macpherson, if those two can have been in collusion over this affair?"

"There's the possibility," said Macpherson cautiously. "But my idea is that Halkin was in some way privy to these affairs—he may have been in collusion with Fewster; nay, would seem to ha' been because of the money evidence—and that Trawlerson got to know of it. I think Trawlerson's dogging Halkin! Halkin's off, and Trawlerson's on his track, thinking, no doubt, that Halkin had the diamonds. And, man!—from what I've observed o' the fellow, yon Trawlerson is the sort that would dog and dog and dog and dog a man till he ran him down! Look how he stuck to these parts like a leech after he first came here! Look how he haunted yon hill-side till the mere aspect o' the place seemed strange without the presence of his figure, perched on a rock, or stravagin' about under the trees. He's a sleuth-hound, yon man, and I ha' no doubt that he's after Halkin!"

"It may be," said Trace, "but there's this seems pretty certain. If Parkapple's theory is right, Macpherson, and some man entered Fewster's house yesterday evening and picked up the receipt for the registered packet, that man must be one of two—it's either been Halkin or it's been Trawlerson. For—we don't know of any other person that's ever come within range of suspicion. But what licks me is—how has Trawlerson, whose description has been very widely circulated, and who has now been missing since the day of Chissick's death, managed to evade arrest? Where is he? And—for the matter of that, though he hasn't been so long away—where's Halkin?"

But we were to hear something about Halkin before afternoon set in. About one o'clock Mrs. Halkin came to Trace's door; his housekeeper brought her into the parlour, where we were all three still engaged in interminable discussion. She had a dirty-looking envelope in her hand.

"Captain Trace!" she said, without preface. "I've had a letter from Halkin. And as there's talk going on in the village about him, and people are saying this, that, and the other, I've just let it be known that I have—he has faults, has Halkin, but he's not running away from justice, as some are saying. And he's sent money."

"Where did he write from?" asked Trace.

Mrs. Halkin drew a sheet of common-looking, very inferior notepaper from the envelope and, extracting something that was folded in it, passed it over.

"I have no objection to anybody seeing it," she said. "You can read it with pleasure. There's not much, but it explains."

Macpherson and I looked over Trace's shoulder. There was no address. The date was that of the previous day. The letter was short. It merely stated that Halkin was negotiating for a very good job as permanent gardener at a country-house near Chelmsford, and was going to see the place that afternoon: he would write again when he had made his arrangements. In the meantime he sent his wife a ten-pound note, to be going on with.

Trace handed this letter back to Mrs. Halkin, and asked if he might see the envelope. When he got that into his hand, he silently indicated the postmark to Macpherson and me as we leaned over his shoulders. I saw at once what he meant. The letter had been posted in London early the previous morning.

"Perhaps you'd like your ten-pound note changing, Mrs. Halkin?" suggested Trace as he gave her back the envelope. "I can do it for you—I've plenty of change in the house."

When the woman had gone away, Trace turned to us, fingering the ten-pound note. He gave Macpherson a significant glance.

"That's a damned clever dodge of Halkin's," he said, "but not clever enough! Halkin wrote that letter with the idea of being able to prove that he was in London yesterday. No doubt he was—in the morning! But he posted his letter before noon—and he'd plenty of time to come down here, to some wayside station, in the early evening, and to make his way to Fewster's, after dark. I believe, now, that Halkin and Trawlerson are in partnership in this affair. And now I'm going to find out something else—over the telephone."

He went out, in the direction of the post office, and was away a considerable time. When at last he came back he still had the ten-pound note in his hand, and he waved it at Macpherson.

"There!" he said triumphantly. "I've been on the 'phone with the manager of Fewster's bank in town. You see this note which I changed for Mrs. Halkin? Well—it's one of a series of ten-pound notes paid out to Fewster when he drew that £500!"

# CHAPTER TWENTY-FIVE

## THE PACKAGE OF COCOA

Macpherson showed his appreciation of Trace's cleverness in a series of approving grunts.

"Aye—aye—aye!" he said, becoming articulate. "Yon was a smart idea o' yours, Captain! I was wondering what made you so ready to change the woman's note for her. Aye—and ye'll ha' been 'phoning to the bank-people?"

"To be sure!" agreed Trace. "It struck me, you see, that the ten-pound note which Halkin had sent his wife was probably one of the notes she'd seen him handling that night in their cottage, when he didn't know she was watching him. Halkin's a deep, sly man, but the slyest and deepest make mistakes. He no doubt thought—if he ever thought at all!—that nobody would ever think of tracing that note; nobody about here, of course, knows anything of these money matters but ourselves and the police. But we know of Fewster's drawing £500 out of his bank—eh? And so I just rang up the manager and told him of what had happened here, and of our discovery of the counterfoil in Fewster's cheque-book—and there you are! This ten-pound note is one of several paid out to Fewster on the Monday on which Chissick's murder was discovered. Fewster drew the money himself, some of it in gold, most of it in notes, early that Monday afternoon. As far as I can make out—I've just seen Mrs. Halkin again—it was on that Monday night that she saw Halkin counting money and putting it in a belt. One thing with another, I think there's no doubt that Fewster drew that £500 to hand over to Halkin."

"None, I should say!" declared Macpherson. "And—the reason?"

"Ah! Now you're asking!" exclaimed Trace. "Reason? I've thought of two reasons why Fewster should have paid that money over to Halkin. One—that it was actually paid for those diamonds, in which case it looks as if Halkin murdered Chissick to gain possession of them. That's possible!—we know that Halkin was working in Fewster's garden on the Saturday on which Chissick was murdered. Now, from Fewster's garden to Chissick's garden—I'm talking about their back gardens and orchards—is only a hundred yards, and between them lies that thick coppice. Halkin, who may have been the man that Tom saw spying about Chissick's new shed the night before, could easily slip through that coppice to Chissick's house, perhaps with the original intention of blackmailing him, and, seeing his chance of finding Chissick alone, have murdered him, got the diamonds, and sold them to Fewster. Fewster, I think, wouldn't ask any inconvenient questions. That's one thing, anyway."

"And the other?" questioned Macpherson.

"The other is that what Fewster paid to Halkin was—hush-money!" said Trace. "And it's extremely likely. Fewster may have known more about Chissick and his doings than he ever confessed to knowing—he may have murdered Chissick, finding him alone, and Halkin, being about, may have known it, or guessed it, and bled him. I think that a very likely theory—very. But I also think something else may be put forward. I've an idea, vague enough, but still there, that somehow or other Halkin and Trawlerson are mixed up in all this. It's a significant fact that both disappeared about the same time. Now, they may both have known about Halkin—each may have got blood-money, hush-money, out of him. That £500 may have been shared between them."

"I doubt it!" exclaimed Macpherson. "Yon Trawlerson would no ha' been satisfied with the moiety o' £500! He'd have an idea o' the value of the diamonds. Halkin wouldn't. And there's the fact—important, if you're going on the collusion theory—that Halkin was quick to tell that he'd seen Trawlerson and heard his voice in Chissick's garden the evening o' the murder."

"I don't attach the slightest importance to that, Macpherson," declared Trace. "Halkin's as big a liar as ever walked, and he no doubt said that to distract attention from himself. But—if Trawlerson really was in Chissick's garden that night, and if he spoke to anybody, as Halkin says he did, then I think the man he spoke to was—Fewster!"

"Aye!" agreed Macpherson. "I should no be surprised at that!"

"However," concluded Trace, "it's all theorising, this. We shan't know anything definite until we hear something from Parkapple. I thought Preece would have had a message from him by now."

Preece did get a message from Parkapple about tea-time. He brought it up to us—a telegram from Brighton. Up to the time of its dispatch, four o'clock, nobody, said Parkapple, had called at the Brighton post office for the registered packet. But it was there—Parkapple and the Brighton police had seen it and were keeping a watch on it. If Preece had any news his end, he was to wire it. Preece had none; nothing had happened since morning. All we could do, as Trace had said, was to wait.

I had a job of my own, of a vastly different sort, to carry out that evening. I have already said that Captain Trace in his retirement devoted a good deal of his time to the keeping of bees and breeding of prize fowls. As regards the fowls, he made it a business speculation as well as a hobby. And on this particular evening, tea being over, he sent me on an errand across the hills at the back of the village, to see a farmer at an outlying hamlet who had some fine Leghorns for sale. With money in my pocket and a commission to buy, I set off about six o'clock on an hour's walk.

The place to which I went was a lonely farmstead lying in one of the narrow valleys to the northward, behind the deep woods in which I had wandered so much at my first coming to these parts. I had difficulty in finding it, and when I got to it, the man I wanted to see was out on the hillsides. Altogether, what with waiting for him and bargaining with him, it was past eight o'clock when I set out on my return journey. My thoughts had been concentrated all the time on the recent events, and I was eager to get home and hear the latest news—in my absence, no doubt, Preece would have heard again from Parkapple. And so, instead of sticking to the route by which I had come, I determined on a short cut through the woods. I knew the exact point of the compass at which our village lay, and I decided to make a bee-line for it. But I knew nothing of these particular woods, and before I had been in them half an hour I got hopelessly mixed and bewildered, and began to wander about, searching for any sign of a southward path. Taking other short cuts in this endeavour, I got more mixed up than before, and it was as I stood in a bit of clearing wondering which was east and which west—for the trees and undergrowth were so thick that I could not make out where the fading sunlight came from—that I suddenly caught sight of something, the discovery of which led there and then to revelation which I had certainly never anticipated.

This something was a small, square packet of the sort that you can see by the score in any grocer's shop. I had handled thousands of such packets in my time. I picked it out of the clump of green stuff into which it had been dropped, and saw at once what it was, a packet of a certain brand of prepared cocoa. The wrapping was damp; the thing had evidently lain there for many nights and days. But the lettering on the green and gilt band around it was legible enough, and these words at the foot of the band immediately caught my attention—*Scale, Grocer, Barlaton.*

It needed no more than the sight of those words to convince me that I had made a discovery which might be of immense importance. Scale!— that was the man who had told Preece and Trace and me of the visit to his grocer's shop at Barlaton of a mysterious man who had bought an unusually large supply of provisions from him, and afterwards calling at the village inn, had purchased some bottles of rum. He had said, that man, that he was working a steam-roller somewhere up in the hills, was camping out, and wanted to provide himself. Scale had told us that his neighbours knew of no steam-roller at work in the district, and that he had wondered if the man was Trawlerson. But from his description of the man—a tall, spare-built, elderly man—we knew this was not Trawlerson. So much for what I recalled of Scale's talk. What was really important now was that this packet of cocoa was undoubtedly part of the purchase made by the unknown man at Scale's shop and dropped by him out of his sack as he made his way through the woods to—where?

I began to look about me in the dusk, and after a close examination of the little clearing, I found a path going off it from one corner—or, rather, not a path at all, but signs, evidence that somebody, heavy-footed, had gone that way through the undergrowth. And being always keen for any adventure, I went that way myself, there and then, looking about me, and scarcely knowing what I expected to find. What I did find, having pushed my way through the trees for fifty yards or so, was a narrow, defined track, which I unhesitatingly followed. I could see that it was little used; last year's leaves were thick on its surface. It went deeper and deeper into the heart of the woods. Very soon it descended, and presently I found myself in a sort of ravine, with dark limestone cliffs overhanging the trees and bushes on either side. A black, eerie place, that!—and the silence, when at last I pulled up and stood, looking and listening, was profound.

I was thinking of turning, of going back, and I suddenly realised that, if I did, I should run! There was something about the place that was frightening. I was conscious of fear then, and I had a queer feeling that if I once turned to retreat I should be far more frightened. And, just to brace myself up, instead of retreating, I dared myself, as lads will, to go a bit farther. I went—deeper into the narrowing ravine. The rocks rose more steeply on either side; there was a general atmosphere of decay and damp. I saw that this was one of the places you find in woods like those thick, neglected woods into which the sun scarcely penetrates. The trees, all ancient, were black and impenetrable, and amongst their boughs I heard strange flutterings—birds, doubtless, startled by my presence.

Still, sheer solitude though the spot seemed to be, the bit of a path was there, and I kept following it until it narrowed between two high rocks. And in the face of one of these, that on my left hand, I saw what was evidently the mouth of a cave. After all I was little more than a boy, and I suppose there was never a boy in the world who, seeing a cave, was not tempted to explore it. Indeed, the sight of that black, yawning mouth revived my spirits at the same time that it excited my curiosity, and without more ado I stepped off the path and advanced boldly to the foot of the rock. There was still enough light for me to see into the cave for two or three yards, and I went close up and peered in. The next instant I started back, heart leaping and pulses throbbing. There, just within the cavity, doubled up a queer way, which, somehow, did not convey the impression that he was asleep, lay a man!

I stood where I was for a good minute—motionless. I had made no effort at silence as I approached the cave. If the man was awake, he could not have failed to hear me. But I did not think he was awake—and I did not think he was asleep. I scarcely knew what I thought. His back was towards me, and I could not see his face. The attitude in which he lay was peculiar: he was all bunched together, as it were; knees drawn up, arms in a queer position. And all this time my eyes were growing more accustomed to the light, and I began to feel a vague conviction that the suit of blue serge— which, even in my perturbation, I noticed pretty observantly—was familiar to me, stained with earth and clay though it was, and as if its wearer had been rolling on the damp ground. I knew somebody who always wore such a suit. Who was it, now? But I had not answered that question when, nerv- ing myself to the effort, I suddenly moved into the cave, and to the man's side, and bent down to his face—to recognise him at the first glance. Trawl- erson!

Trawlerson was dead. I knew that before even I put a finger on him. And he was the second dead man I had found that day. But I think I scarcely thought of that, at the moment. I stood staring at him. There was a terrible lump on his left temple—a great, ugly swelling, suffused with blood. But there was more than that. Round his throat was knotted a striped handker- chief, such as sailors wear, only, instead of being all black, it was of gay colours. It was tied so tightly about his throat, and knotted at the back of his neck with such fiendish purpose, that I could not thrust even the top of my little finger between its folds and the skin. And I realised then how Trawler- son had come to his end. He had been lured to this place by somebody, and first stunned by a blow on the temple, and then—strangled. The blow on the temple was an awful one: perhaps that had killed him. But the murderer had left nothing to chance.

If I had been nearer the village, I should have rushed off, there and then, for help. But the village, to my reckoning—for I had certainly got astray in these woods—was some distance off, probably from two to three miles, and I thought it best, my first sensations of fright and horror over, to make some examination of the dead man's clothing. It looked to me as if he had been dragged into that cave, but I did not go out then to see if I could find any signs of that near by. Instead, I felt in his pockets. And I soon came to the conclusion that he had been robbed. I remembered a few facts about Trawlerson. The landlord of the village inn had spoken of him more than once in my presence as a man who carried plenty of ready money about him. Besides, hadn't he come to me at Trace's and offered me a hun- dred sovereigns for the map, giving me to understand that he had them on him? Well, there was no money on Trawlerson now—except a few coppers, which, to be sure, were not on him at all, but lying on the ground near, as if the murderer and robber had thrown them aside, contemptuous of them. Then, again, I knew that Trawlerson carried a good gold watch and a gold chain, of the heavy cable pattern; there was no watch and no chain there now. Murder and robbery, this. . . .

I had ascertained all these facts within a few minutes of my recognition of the dead man, and as soon as I realised all that had happened, I left him and made for the open. But as I was about to step out of the cave I heard two sounds. Heavy footsteps were coming down the wood, close by, and a man's voice was singing—some country-side ditty which seemed strangely incongruous. I drew back into the shelter of the cavity, waiting and watching. In another minute the man came in sight.

# CHAPTER TWENTY-SIX

## THE SILK NECKERCHIEF

I took a good and careful look at this man as he went slowly by, and I saw that there was nothing to fear from him. He was a tall, long-legged, elderly man, very alert of movement; a man who, after his day's work, had cleaned himself up for the evening and changed his working clothes for a decent suit. He had a stout stick under one arm, and an empty sack flung over the other shoulder. Evidently he was going somewhere to fetch something. And he was still singing cheerily:

> *"As I was going to Derby*
> *All on a market day!"*

I slipped out of the cave and stopped his melody with a call. No doubt my voice sounded excited, for he turned sharply and, looking at me with wonder in his eyes, came towards me.

"Eh?" he said. "Something wrong, young fellow? You seem——"

I motioned him to the mouth of the cave.

"Look!" I whispered. "There's a man in there! Dead!"

He made a startled exclamation, dropped the sack from his shoulder, and, walking into the cave, stared at Trawlerson's dead body.

"Lord ha' mercy!" he muttered. He stooped, and looked closer; then started and stared at me with a quick catching of his breath. "Why—why!" he exclaimed. "That's the man as used to wander about!"

"You know him, then?" I asked.

"By sight, young master, yes!" he said. "Seen him a time or two, on the downs and in these woods. Always at a bit of a distance—never close to. But I know him! Never had speech of him, to be sure. Did—did you find him?"

"Just now!" I answered. "I got lost in the woods and wandered down here. And I looked in at this cave and—saw him, just as you see."

"Do you know him?" he asked.

"I do! He's a man named Trawlerson, that's been missing some time—several days, anyhow," I replied. "The police have been looking for him—everywhere!"

He made no remark on that, but stooped closer and again looked at the dead man.

"Appears to me as if he'd been dead some time," he observed musingly. "Can't say, of course, but—I should say so. Well—I never heard anything of any fight, or struggling, and my hut's not so far off: only just back of the wood there. Of course, it may ha' taken place in the night, whatever it was, and I'm a good sleeper. However, there 'tis. Dead—right enough! And murdered, too—look at that lump on his forehead—and he's been strangled as well. Murder!—and close by one! I've been up there—oh, two or three weeks. And never heard—nothing!"

I had been sizing him up as he talked, and now I asked a direct question.

"Are you the man that bought a lot of stuff from Scale, the grocer, of Barlaton, a bit since?" I enquired. "Groceries?"

"That's me, young fellow!" he answered. "Working a steam-roller, I am, up in these hills, and have a hut not a quarter of a mile from this. I'm on my way to Scale's now," he went on, indicating the sack. "Stores run out, d'ye see?—or nearly so, and wants replenishing. But this, now—as I say, I've seen this here man a time or two. And once I saw him with another man, one night towards dark, near that old mill on the downs."

"Another man?" I exclaimed. "What was he like?"

"Rather a thick-set chap—about his build," he replied, indicating the still figure at our feet. "They were talking together, as I say, near that old mill."

A sudden notion struck me, and I put it into words.

"Was it you that was in the mill last night?" I asked. "With a light?"

He nodded, immediately; it was easy to see that he had nothing to keep back.

"That was me!" he assented. "I often take a walk of an evening round these parts, and I thought I'd like to see what there was in that old place, so I slipped a lantern into my pocket when I came out. Queer old spot, that!—and by what bit I've heard, there's been a good deal of mystery about it of late."

"Haven't you heard much, then?" I asked, surprised that anyone in the neighbourhood should be in any way ignorant of the recent happenings. "There's been plenty of talk, and plenty in the newspapers!"

"Aye, no doubt!" he remarked. "But up there where I've been working, I'm not in the way of hearing much talk; and as to newspapers, well, I haven't set eyes on one for a fortnight."

"This man was mixed up in it," I said, "and, as I told you, the police have been searching for him—for him and that other man you mentioned just now. I shall have to hurry down and tell them what I've found here. I wish you'd come with me—they'll want to see you, you know, after what I tell them."

He nodded and glanced at his sack.

"Aye, that'll be so," he agreed. "But—is there a shop, a good shop, in your village, for I want provisions?"

I answered him that there was a shop where he could buy anything he wanted, and he picked up his sack and his stick. But the next instant he put them down again, turning to me with a knowing look.

"This is an out-of-the-way spot!" he said. "But you found it, and others might find it, before the police can get up here. Have—have you looked to see if there's anything on him?"

He pointed significantly to Trawlerson's pockets, and I knew what he meant.

"I have!" said I. "There's nothing! I know for a fact that he carried a fine gold watch and chain, and always had plenty of cash. Well, there isn't a penny left in his pockets, and the watch and chain are gone!"

"Robbed, as well as murdered, then!" he remarked. "All right!—I'll go down with you to the police. But first" he paused, pointing to the neckerchief twisted so tightly about the dead man's throat—"first," he went on, dropping on his hands and knees at Trawlerson's side, "we'll have that off! To take with us!"

"Why?" I demanded.

"Evidence!" he replied. "Evidence! We've both seen it—here!—and we can both swear to it. And the police had better have it, at once."

But it was no easy work to disengage that neckerchief from the dead man's throat; it had been knotted and double knotted. He worked it loose at last, however, and, putting it in his pocket, signed to me to follow him.

"So you were lost in here?" he remarked as we went away. "Aye, well, I've been about here long enough to know that it's not a difficult matter to get out of your bearings in these woods. You've no idea whereabouts we are, then?"

"No very clear idea," I replied.

"You'll ha' been twisting and turning about," he surmised. "As a matter of fact, we're within half a mile of that old mill we were talking about—on its west side. But I'll show you."

He went ahead, and, presently turning off the narrow path, forced a way through the undergrowth for fifty yards or so, emerging from it on a grass track that I knew well enough as one that cut clean through the woods to a bridle-gate near the mill. In ten minutes we were passing the mill;

ten minutes more, and I burst in on Trace and Macpherson with the news. Macpherson hurried away for Preece. The steam-roller man, who gave his name as Kilham, and I, told our story. Kilham produced the neckerchief. Preece took possession of that, and when he had heard all we had to say, he made some remark to Trace and left the house. He was away for half an hour, and we were still discussing the details of my discovery when he returned.

"I've soon settled that point!" he said, with an air of triumphant satis-faction. "I'd an idea that it would prove to be his, as soon as I saw it! That silk neckerchief is Halkin's!"

"You've made sure?" asked Trace, almost incredulously.

"Certain!" replied Preece, with a grin. "Mrs. Halkin's still down in the village, stopping at her mother's. I took it to her—told her it had been picked up in the woods. She identified it as Halkin's immediately. Bought it for him herself, she says, at Portsmouth, not so very long ago, and he was wearing it round his neck last time she saw him. So——"

He paused, looking from one to the other of us, either for applause for his cleverness, or for some suggestion as to what was next to be done. But nobody spoke, not even Macpherson, who seemed stricken dumb by the crowding together of these doings, and Preece went on.

"We'd best get to work," he said. "There's three of our men in the vil-lage now; they're coming along here as soon as they've finished a mouthful of supper. Kilham, you'll have to show them the way to this cave where you've left Trawlerson's body—they'll see to everything after that. As for me"—he glanced significantly at Trace and Macpherson—"I'm off to Brighton! We've heard no more from Parkapple, but he must know of this at once. There's just nice time to catch the last train—just time, and no more."

Within the moment, Trace and Macpherson determined to go with him. They made no objection when I begged not to be left behind—I wanted to be in at the crisis which I felt was coming. And five minutes later Kilham was leading the other three policemen and a couple of labourers with a hand-cart away to the woods, and Preece, Trace, Macpherson, and I were hurrying to the station. It seemed to me as if there was a certain fitness about that hurrying. I had, I suppose, some intuition that everything was tending to a crucial point, and that we, actors in this drama, had just got to move rapidly—were, indeed, being moved rapidly. Of late I had watched Trace and Macpherson playing chess of an evening—something led me to compare that with the game we were now hard at work on. I fancied we were all pawns, being moved by some hand invisible to us. I, for instance, had had no idea when I woke that morning that I was going to find Fewster dead in his parlour, and Trawlerson brutally murdered in that cave; yet I had made both discoveries, and now I was on my way to . . . I scarcely knew what, but I had no doubt it would be no less startling.

It was just half-past ten when we reached Brighton. Preece bundled us all into a cab and told its driver to haste to the police-station. He hurried inside there as soon as the cab pulled up, and presently emerged again with an official with whom he talked for a while before motioning us to get out.

"Parkapple's at an hotel close by," he said as the official turned inside again. "I've got the name of it—we'll go round there. Nobody had called for that packet at the post office up to closing-time," he went on as we all moved off. "The police here know all about it, of course—Parkapple's posted them up. Odd—if the receipt really was stolen from Fewster! But we'll hear more from Parkapple."

We found Parkapple in a quiet corner of the smoking-room of an hotel on the sea-front, evidently meditating over his pipe. He looked as if all business cares had left him for that day, but he sprang sharply to his feet as he caught sight of us entering the room.

"Something fresh?" he asked quickly. "More news! But you wouldn't be here——"

"Come back to that corner," said Preece. "Yes, we've news," he answered as we all seated ourselves round the detective. "That's why we hurried here. You'd better hear it from the fountain-head," he continued, nodding at me. "Tell Mr. Parkapple all about it, Tom!"

I told Parkapple the story I had already told the other three. He listened closely, without interrupting me. At the end he only asked a question or two about minor details. Then Preece got in.

"The neckerchief they brought has been identified," he said triumphantly. "I managed that!—within a few minutes. It's—Halkin's!"

Parkapple showed no surprise.

"You're sure of that?" he asked.

"Positive!" declared Preece. "His wife identified it." He felt in an inner pocket and drew out the neckerchief. "This is it!" he said. "Mrs. Halkin bought it in Portsmouth—shop in Commercial Road—not so long ago." Then, as Parkapple took the thing from him, he rubbed his hands, chuckling. "I reckon that'll hang Halkin!" he went on, nodding at the rest of us. "A settler, that!"

"Ye've got to catch him first, man!" muttered Macpherson. "And, so far, Mr. Parkapple there has had no luck, I understand?"

Parkapple handed the neckerchief back to Preece. The news I had given him had evidently roused some new train of thought in him.

"Tell you anything at the police-station?" he asked, glancing at Preece.

"Only that nobody'd called for that registered packet at the post office here up to closing-time," answered Preece.

"That's so! There's been a strict watch ever since I got here," said Parkapple. "I kept out of the way myself, having been seen at your end, you know. No—no application had been made up to the hour the post office closed. But—an inspector and I have examined the packet."

"Aye—and what's inside it, man?" exclaimed Macpherson. "Is it—diamonds?"

"Diamonds, sure enough!" assented Parkapple. "Some cut and polished; most in the rough, like the one picked up this morning. There are seventy-four of them, some a good size. And we did more than examine the packet—when we found what it contained, we got an expert to come round to the postmaster's private office and look the diamonds over—just to give us a rough idea of what the lot might be worth. A well-known man, you understand—one whose opinion can be trusted. Of course, he only named an approximate figure. But—he said that he'd give it himself."

"Aye, aye!" said Macpherson eagerly. "And what did he say they were worth, now? A deal o' money, no doubt?"

"Twenty-five thousand pounds!" replied Parkapple. "At least!"

# CHAPTER TWENTY-SEVEN

## THE BILLIARD-ROOM

Macpherson threw up his hands—in dismay, or in admiration, or in sheer surprise; perhaps in a mixture of all three.

"Man, that's a powerful sight of money!" he exclaimed in awestruck accents. "But maybe I didn't hear you aright? Did you say——"

"I said twenty-five thousand pounds!" repeated Parkapple. "At least! And, as the gentleman said he'd give that for them just then, cash down, if they were for sale, I reckon they're worth more—probably considerably more. For—as most of those chaps who deal in that sort of thing are—the gentleman was of the Jewish persuasion, and, accordingly, sure to know a bargain when he saw one."

"Aye, no doubt!" agreed Macpherson. "But twenty-five thousand pounds! To think of all that amount of wealth lying there in the ground doing nothing for two-and-forty years! If it had been realised and put out at five per cent., it would ha' brought in—aye, now, what would it ha' brought in? I'm no so quick at the mental arithmetic as I was when I was a mere callant back there at Jedburgh——"

"It would have brought in £52,500, Mr. Macpherson," said I. "Just that!"

"Good lad!" said he. "Aye!—I ga'ed ye a good schooling, Tom, and I'm thankful to see ye can still cast figures in your headpiece wi'out the vain adjuncts o' pencil and paper! But that's neither here nor there—what did you do with these valuables, Mr. Parkapple, if one may be so bold?"

"Put them all back in the original package, Mr. Macpherson, which had been very skilfully opened and was just at skilfully closed up again," answered Parkapple. "And there it is, all safe at the post office, till called for. I'm a bit puzzled," he went on, "that nobody's called for it to-day. For I haven't changed my opinion one whit—somebody stole that receipt from Fewster last night! And I think that somebody would have a pretty good idea what the receipt referred to."

"That's arguing that whoever stole it knew that Fewster was in possession of the diamonds," remarked Trace.

"Oh, undoubtedly!" agreed the detective. "I think Halkin certainly knew, and it may be that Trawlerson knew. I think that, all unsuspected by you people on the spot, there's been a certain amount of collusion between Halkin and Trawlerson for some time. Possibly Trawlerson, during his wanderings and excursions, nocturnal and otherwise, came across Halkin and got to know so much of his doings that Halkin had to take him into his confidence."

"Well, there's no doubt that Halkin settled Trawlerson in the end," said Preece. "This neckerchief's a proof of that!"

"Aye, well, it's a certain amount of evidence," said Parkapple. "Only a certain amount, though. Halkin, for instance, can easily say that it was stolen from him; his wife, if she finds that it's being used against him, can easily swear that somebody filched it from her clothes-line on washing-day. However," he added, seeing Preece's countenance fall at these throwings of cold water, "it is evidence, and if we catch Halkin, we'll make the most of it. But what I'd like to know at present—how long had this man Trawlerson been dead when Tom there found him this evening?"

"Kilham said some time, Mr. Parkapple," I told him. "He thought, from what he saw, several days."

"And Halkin posted a letter in London yesterday morning, did he?" continued Parkapple musingly. "You made sure about the postmark, Captain Trace?"

"Quite sure!" replied Trace. "There was no address beyond the word 'London' in the letter itself—a mere scrawl of a few lines in pencil on a sheet of unusually poor quality paper—the sort of stuff you'd pick up in a poor shop in a poor district. The postmark was 'London 8 a.m.'; the date, yesterday."

"Posted at the head office, then, if there were no qualifying district letters," remarked Parkapple. "Well, Halkin could have been in London yesterday morning before eight o'clock, aye, and right well into the afternoon for that matter, and still have been at Fewster's last night! It's only two hours' run from either London Bridge or Victoria to your district. I think Halkin is the man we want—now that Trawlerson's out of it. I'm going on the supposition that Halkin called on Fewster last night for some purpose of his own, not clear to me, found him dead, saw that receipt lying around, guessed what it referred to, appropriated it, and cleared out with the intention of calling at Brighton post office to collect any correspondence awaiting demand in the name of J. Foster. I think Halkin would come on to Brighton last night—probably by the last train—and I'm a bit uneasy and surprised that he's not called at the post office. But according to your accounts of him, Halkin's a sly sort of man, eh?"

"Sly!" exclaimed Preece. "Deep as they make 'em! He'd circumvent the devil! I should think he is sly! Cunning!—that's what Halkin is."

"Then he'll be cunning to the last," said Parkapple. "He's no doubt working on some plan of his own, cleverly conceived. And——" He paused, and then, shaking his head, left his sentence unfinished. Macpherson spoke.

"You said just now—if we catch him?" he suggested anxiously. "Surely you've no fear o' that—if your theory's right? He'll be bound to call at yon post office, sooner or later! You'll ha' made arrangements?"

"Oh, we've made arrangements, Mr. Macpherson!" assented Parkapple, smiling. "Good and thorough ones, I can assure you! From just before eight to-morrow morning, when the post office opens until it closes at night, there'll never be a moment that would be a safe one for Halkin if he turns up there. And that reminds me—as he knows the whole lot of you, and would have his suspicions aroused if he saw you here in Brighton, what about you? Going to stay here the night, and see what comes of to-morrow?"

Trace replied that we should have to; there were no more trains our way at that late hour of the evening.

"Very good—you may be useful, one way or another," said Parkapple. "But—you'll have to lie low in the morning until you get the word from me. Halkin will never suspect the Brighton police, and he'll have no chance of seeing me here, even if he ever saw me over there. But if he saw as much as the nose-end of any one of you four—all up! So mind that! Doggo!—that's your game till I give you the office."

We soon arranged all that. There was plenty of room in the hotel in which we were talking. Trace presently booked accommodation for all four of us, and presently I, at any rate, went to bed. I had gone through some exciting adventures that day and seen things that I could never forget, however long I lived, but I hadn't a single dream about them. I was asleep within a minute of putting my head on the pillow, and still asleep when Macpherson came into my room, which adjoined his own, and shook my shoulder.

"Past eight o'clock, Tom, my man!" he said. "And the table-doty breakfast is at the half-hour. I'd ha' wakened you before, but you were sleeping that sound. It's a braw morning, Tom—losh! I wonder what we'll see or hear before it's night again!"

"Halkin!—with the handcuffs on, Mr. Macpherson!" said I, bloodthirstily. "That's what I want to see. Did you say 'twas past eight?—they may have got him! Likely he'd go to the post office first thing this morning."

"Aweel, I canna say!" he answered. "Parkapple's been gone about his business a good hour—he took his breakfast at seven o'clock, by arrangement wi' the hotel folk. But as for us—we must just bide till we hear from him."

It was my idea—due, no doubt, to the impatience of youth—that we should hear from Parkapple, if not immediately after breakfast, at least before noon. But the morning wore on, and we heard nothing. It began to seem dull work. We could not go out, lest Halkin should catch sight of us. For the same reason Preece warned me not to stand at the hall door nor look out of the windows. I got bored with the whole thing; so too, I think, did Macpherson. And it had passed noon and nothing had happened when Parkapple came in and found us, the three elder men reading newspapers, myself with my hands in my pockets, loafing around.

"It's odd!" he said, when we had gathered round him. "Deuced odd!—but up to twelve o'clock nobody's called about that packet! And yet—somebody's got the receipt!"

"Are ye so sure o' that, now?" asked Macpherson. "Ye jumped to that conclusion, Mr. Parkapple, but if ye'll just cast your mind back to day before yesterday, which, owing to the remarkable nature of intervening events, seems a long way off, ye'll remember that I said then that you might be mistaken. Fewster may have destroyed that receipt."

"Why should he destroy it?" demanded Parkapple. "A receipt for a packet containing twenty-five thousand pounds' worth of diamonds! Come!"

"I'll grant ye that in the ordinary way o' business it would ha' been a foolish thing to do," said Macpherson, "and one that no business man would ha' done. But you'll admit that the circumstances were peculiar. Although you and Preece professed yourselves satisfied with Fewster's explanations at Chissick's garden gate, and left him to go his ways to his own home, he may ha' felt, probably did feel, that he was by no means safe from another visit from you that afternoon or evening; he didn't know, indeed, that you mightn't come and search, not only himself, but his house. I think that what we know he did proves that I'm correct, Mr. Parkapple. For he makes up those diamonds into a package, and he goes to the post office and gets rid of it. He'd never think that you'd go making enquiries at the post office, and maybe you wouldn't if you hadn't found those wrappings and the sealing-wax on Fewster's side-table. But, having sent away his package by registered post, Fewster had the office receipt on him! Now, still thinking that you might yet come, and that you might search him and his belongings, and knowing that if you found a receipt for something, evidently valuable, posted that afternoon, you'd certainly want to know what that something was, what in the name of common sense d'ye suppose Fewster would do with his receipt? Man!—as a whole day and half a day has passed without anybody, Halkin or another, calling at yon post office, I think I know what Fewster did wi' his receipt. He put it in his fire!"

Somebody—Preece, I think—made a grunt of acquiescence in this view of the case.

But Parkapple shook his head.

"I don't think so, Mr. Macpherson, with all respect to you, I don't think so!" he declared stoutly. "You put the matter very clearly, Mr. Macpherson, as clearly as a lawyer could, I'm sure. But I still think somebody stole that receipt—nay, I'm as sure of it as a man can be without being able to put forward absolute proof. A—a feeling, sir!"

"Aye!" assented Macpherson. "Ye'll not be devoid o' the intuitive faculty, no doubt, Mr. Parkapple. And so you'll be for continuing your watch?"

"This day out, anyhow," replied Parkapple. "And, of course, the post office authorities are aware of the nature of the contents of that packet, and whoever calls for it at any time will be detained till the police are communicated with. No!—I've not given up hope yet, Mr. Macpherson!"

Then, saying that he trusted to have some news for us before long, he bustled off again, and we prepared ourselves for more waiting. But hours went by and no news came, and it had got to close on eight o'clock at night, and Trace and Macpherson were talking of taking the train home, when suddenly a young man who was clearly a constable in plain clothes entered the hotel, and, having ascertained that we were the people he wanted, asked us if we'd step round to the police-station to see Detective-Sergeant Parkapple at once.

The police-station was not three minutes' walk from the hotel, but I think we were there in two minutes; even Macpherson hurried. Our guide led us through various passages to a private office, where we found Parkapple, two or three men who, I presumed, were detectives, and an official or two of evident high standing, grouped around—not Halkin, but a young man who sat in a chair in their midst and who was evidently surprised, puzzled, and—I fancied—just a little amused at finding himself where he was. He was certainly not the sort of person I should have expected to see there in that affair, with its background of murder and robbery. A more ordinary individual you could not have met in the street outside. He looked to me like a clerk of some sort, well and respectably dressed in conventional attire; he had a top-hat on his knee, and a neatly rolled umbrella at his side. And though there were so many pairs of interrogating eyes turned on him, he was by no means abashed, but looked frankly and fearlessly from one man to another—and from them to a small, red-sealed package that lay prominently displayed on the table before which he sat.

"Willing to answer any questions you like, of course!" I heard him saying as we filed in. "Why not? Nothing to do with me!"

Parkapple turned to one of the officials as we entered, and whispered something to him; then he turned to the young man of the top-hat and umbrella.

"What we want to know is—how did you come to ask for this package at Brighton post office this evening, and to be in possession of the receipt for its posting?" he asked. "Tell us in your own way—everything! We've already told you that this package contains stolen property. Now—your account!"

"As I said before—why not?" responded the interrogated one. "I've nothing to do with the thing! Just what might happen to anybody—anybody who's good-natured, that is. My name's James Wellings. I'm a bank-clerk; been nine years in the South-Coast Bank here in the town—best of characters too, if you want to know! I live at Rottingdean, three miles along the coast, with my mother and sisters. Well, sometimes of an evening I go along to the hotel, or to one of the hotels, just for a modest drink and a smoke, sometimes for a game of billiards. Last night I was out that way—in the billiard-room of an hotel. There was an elderly man there, well-spoken chap, respectable and all that; I got talking to him while I was waiting for a game. He told me he'd just come there for a week or two for his health—got run down after an illness, or something. Affable chap!—knew a lot about gardening. That was really what made me talk to him; gardening came up somehow, and we have a garden that I put in some of my spare time at. After I'd played a hundred at billiards, I'd another talk to him—he told me all about growing roses. We walked up the street together—he was lodging near where I live. I'd told him what I was, and before parting he asked me, when I came into Brighton to-day, if I'd call at the general post office and collect any letters for him—name of J. Foster. He said there'd be a registered one, a packet, and, so that I shouldn't forget the name, he'd give me the receipt for it—which he did—you have it there now. I told him I'd do the errand with pleasure, but it would be unusually late when I got home to-night, because we should be balancing at the bank. He said it didn't matter—he was in no hurry about his letters; they were of no importance; the registered one only contained some article that had just been registered for safety. And—that's all there's in it, as far as I'm concerned! I don't know the man—know nothing but what I've told you."

"Didn't you think it rather a curious thing that a man who was expecting a registered letter should be in possession of the receipt issued to the sender?" asked Parkapple. "Didn't that strike you? As a bank-clerk, you must have sent off hundreds of registered letters in your time to customers. You don't send the receipts you get at the receiving office to customers!"

"To tell you the truth, I never even thought about it!" answered Wellings frankly. "As it was, I nearly forgot to call at the post office. I'd got half-way to my bus, going home, when I suddenly remembered and went back. Then—but you know."

"Where were you to meet this man?" asked Parkapple.

"In the billiard-room where I met him last night," said Wellings. "Nine o'clock."

Parkapple glanced at a clock on the mantelpiece—twenty past eight. He turned to the official to whom he had previously spoken; together they walked away to a corner of the room and engaged in a whispered conversation; eventually they came back to Wellings. The official took him in hand.

"How do you go back to Rottingdean?" he asked.

"By bus, always," replied Wellings. "You know the Rottingdean buses."

"And your next is—what?"

"Twenty to nine."

"And you are to meet this man on your arrival?"

"We arranged to meet where we met last night—in the billiard-room."

"That billiard-room's separate from the hotel, isn't it?" said the official. "You go up steps to it, don't you—a building somewhat detached from the hotel itself? Just so!—very well, now listen carefully. You'll go along by the twenty to nine bus, and you'll take this package in your pocket. From the instant you step out of this room you'll be followed shadowed!—by two of my men, plain-clothes men, of course. They'll go in the same bus with you, but they won't know you, you know, and you won't know them, and they'll take good care to show no interest in you. But—they'll be there! As soon as the bus gets to Rottingdean—it stops at the hotel, of course— you'll go straight up to the billiard-room, and if the man's there, you'll hand him the packet. You'll also ask him to have a drink, and send the marker for what you order. His appearance at the foot of the stairs on his way to the bar will be the signal for my men to enter. Do you understand all that? Is it quite clear?"

Wellings made a wry face.

"It's clear enough!" he said unwillingly. "But—I don't like it! Supposing this chap's armed? He'll see there's been a trap laid for him, and he'll turn on me! And, you know, when all's said and done, it's no business of mine! Can't you manage it amongst yourselves?"

The man addressed looked at Parkapple. Parkapple, after hesitating a moment, turned to Wellings.

"We want to take this man with that packet actually in his possession," he said. "We've reasons! There'll be no danger to you—we shall be on him, if you do what you've been asked to do, before he realises anything! See?"

"No, I don't see!" retorted Wellings doggedly. "I don't like it at all! If he's got a revolver, or the like of that, on him, it wouldn't take him the fraction of a second to draw it, and he'd be quick to see I'd given him away. I won't do it—so there! But I'll tell you what I will do. I'll go up to the billiard-room, give him the packet, stay a minute or so with him to have a drink, as you suggest, and as soon as we've had it come away. But—mind!—you're not to go up, any of you, till I come down! I won't do it otherwise—not for you nor anybody. I've got a mother and two sisters partly dependent——"

"That would do!" said Parkapple. "Your coming down from the billiard-room is to be the signal for our entrance? Very good. Now let's get to work!"

He handed the packet to Wellings, who, still muttering that he didn't at all like the job and was only doing it to oblige, put it in his inside pocket and went away, followed at once by two very ordinary-looking individuals in plain clothes who had carefully listened to all that had passed. And within a few minutes the rest of us were on our way too, judiciously instructed by Parkapple and the Brighton official, and disposed of in two taxi-cabs, the drivers of which were ordered to convey us to Rottingdean in such wise that each set his load of humanity down at different parts of the village and at about the same time that the bus was due to arrive at the hotel. No detail was left unattended to; it seemed as if we already held Halkin in a halter, and had nothing to do but tighten it at our pleasure. But that, as Macpherson grimly remarked, would come later.

It was dark, quite dark, when stealing upon it from various directions, we gathered in front of the hotel. There were a great many people about— Rottingdean is a favourite resort of Brighton people. We mingled with them; Macpherson and I got a good place opposite the hotel where a crowd awaited an outgoing bus. Behind us, deep down at the foot of the cliffs, I heard the tide roaring as it surged up the shingly beach; in front of us, across the space filled with motor-cars, men, women, children, we saw the lighted windows of the billiard-room. I pictured Halkin sitting there, awaiting the arrival of his cat's-paw with the packet of diamonds.

The bus came in—a few minutes late. We saw Wellings dismount and go straight up the stairs to the billiard-room. We saw the two plain-clothes men dismount too, and play their parts very well by affecting to lounge and stare about them, close to the foot of the stairs. And near by I saw Parkapple, amongst a group of excursionists, and Trace, and Preece, all carefully disposed.

A boy, carrying a tray, came running down the stairs from the billiard-room and went into the adjacent bar. That, I could see, was crowded with customers; it was five minutes, at least, before he went back again with two glasses of beer on his tray. More minutes elapsed. Wellings ought to have come down at any second. And then . . .

But Wellings did not come. Nobody came. And at the end of ten minutes Parkapple moved towards the two plain-clothes men, so did Preece and Trace; Macpherson and I followed. Before we reached them Parkapple had sent one of the Brighton men upstairs; the next instant the man was calling loudly on all of us to follow him.

The peaceful appearance of that billiard-room was in violent contrast to the emotions which raged in the hearts of us who presently rushed in there. There was not a soul in the place except the boy, who, having nothing else to do, was calmly practising shots on the table; on a stand close by rested his tray with the two glasses of beer on it, untouched. But for any sign of Wellings and Halkin . . .

"Where are those two men who were here just now?" demanded Parkapple. "Quick!"

The boy, without laying down his cue, turned lazily.

"I dunno!" he said. "They sent me for two bottles o' Bass, and when I come back they was gone! There's the drinks, a-waiting for 'em."

"Gone?" snarled Parkapple. "Which—when—how could they go?"

The boy pointed the tip of his cue to a door in the corner of the room.

"There's a way out through there," he said unconcernedly. "Down at the back of the bar, and through a yard into the other street. I expect . . ."

* * * *

As far as it concerned Captain Trace, and Andrew Macpherson, and myself, that was the end of this business. True, we had an exciting time for the rest of that evening, trying to find things out. Nobody knew anything of any bank-clerk in Rottingdean named Wellings; the widowed mother and two dependent sisters did not materialise. Nor had the boy in the billiard-room any recollection whatever of having seen the young man and the elderly one in conversation in that room the night before; he had never seen either, he swore, until a quarter before nine that night, when the elderly man came in and loafed about, evidently waiting, and the younger one came some twenty minutes later. But we learned certain facts. The two men—the elder being Halkin, without the shadow of a doubt, and the younger (as the police subsequently ascertained) a nephew of his who had no very good record in London, where he had been employed as a clerk—arrived in Rottingdean by bus from Newhaven during the afternoon of the critical day, and had tea together at the hotel, and were later seen in its smoking-room. Subsequently the younger was seen boarding a bus for Brighton . . . the rest we knew. But nobody knew which way the pair fled when they cleared out of the billiard-room after sending the boy for beer. It was dusk, past mere dusk—and behind Rottingdean lies the solitude of the South Downs.

www.ingramcontent.com/pod-product-compliance
Lightning Source LLC
Chambersburg PA
CBHW011445170626
46816CB00008B/2534

* 9 7 8 1 4 7 9 4 7 6 6 7 1 *